China Hand

China Hand

BRUNO SKOGGARD

DODD, MEAD & COMPANY · NEW YORK

1 2 3 4 5 6 7 8 9 10

Library of Congress Cataloging in Publication Data

Skoggard, Bruno.
China hand.

I. Title.
PZ4.S619725Ch   [PS3569.K6]   813'.5'4   79-522
ISBN 0-396-07662-9

China Hand

one

PERHAPS it all stems from my amah's birthday gift to me when I turned seven in 1928. She took me to see a beheading. In my innocence, I found the occasion as festive as did the Chinese, until that startling jet of blood arced from the severed neck. But after a few more festivals, which always had an execution as the *pièce de résistance,* the nightmare disappeared. I even saw humour in an event other Occidentals might find grotesque.

When my mother took my older teenage sisters home to Canada in 1933, I gained the freedom of Huck Finn. My father, preoccupied with his work at West China Union University and his Chinese studies, assumed I was safe with one of our many relatives in Chengtu. With cousins covering for me, my friend Ta-ko and I often disappeared for weeks to wander happily through the countryside, either on our horses or hitching rides on the river.

One day we reached Kuang Han, a small walled city to the north, during a festival. Instead of only one or two, six river pirates were to be executed. They arrived so jolly in a tumbrel drawn by a water buffalo, I thought them a troupe of actors unsteady with wine. Not even their fetters and placards could convince me they had but a brief moment left to strut upon the stage. They shouted greetings to friends in the crowd, and joked and laughed foolishly when bumped off balance. A boy sat against a corner post giggling at his toes. They had been humanely stoned on opium.

With hands tied behind their backs, they knelt in a row and were encircled by the now hushed spectators. The executioner, the best the relatives of the condemned could afford to hire, strode majestically back and forth, flexing his muscles and taking practice swings with his heavy scimitar. Then, with merciful speed, he addressed his first victim. On his up-swing, he tapped the man on the nape of his neck with the blunt edge of the sword. Startled, the pirate lifted his head as the blade returned, and, for a moment before his eyes glazed, he stared up in amazement at his own thighs. The swordsman stepped nimbly around the toppling corpse, took the second, third, and in a matter of seconds, seven bodies were bent over their heads as if in deep devotion.

Seven!

The executioner was outraged. He had only been paid for six. Who had slipped in a ringer?

When the cause was discovered, the crowd roared at the joke. A dull-witted country boy had crawled too far forward and, by kneeling at the end of the line for a better view of the fun, had fallen victim to the headsman's zeal for rhythmic showmanship. And I, aged twelve, laughed as heartily as the Chinese.

Ta-ko, whose name was Chen Yi, grew up with me in Chengtu, a prosperous walled city in Szechwan, whose irrigated basin was the only one in China that had never known famine. Though the envious claimed that Chengtu dogs barked at the sun because they saw it so rarely, we could often look across a hundred miles of fertile land to the southwest and see the Minya Konka, a magnificent 25,000 foot cone.

Chen Yi was an aristocrat, heir to the House of Chen, yet we were so inseparable the Chinese called us "the brothers." He was Ta-ko: elder brother, and I was Hsiung-ti: younger brother. Our parents called us the bane of West China.

Ta-ko's brilliance was as dazzling as the wealth of the Chens. After reading Voltaire in English, he learned French to read all the French philosophers in the original. Marx, Schopenhauer and Nietzsche inspired him to study German—all this before he was fifteen. Regarding languages, Ta-ko was like Arthur Waley, the great English translator of Chinese and Japanese classics. In other respects, I sometimes thought Ta-ko was mad.

One day while riding our horses along the canal to school, Ta-ko reined up to watch the body of an unwanted baby girl float by. It was so common a sight, I grew impatient and shouted at him to come on. "We're late now."

When he swung off his saddle and started down the canal bank, I wheeled my horse around and galloped back. "What are you doing? Let's go. We're in enough trouble with the teacher." As he fished for the tiny corpse with a stick, I became frightened. "What do you want that thing for?"

He came up the bank, carrying the body by its foot.

"Throw it back! Ta-ko, please."

He emptied his saddle bag—"Take my books"—and stuffed in his grisly prize.

The punishments for tampering with the dead terrified me. "What are you going to do with it?"

"We're going to dissect it," he said matter-of-factly.

"Ta-ko, you can't!"

"We dissect frogs in school, don't we?"

3

"But—but frogs are animals."

"So is this."

No matter how I tried, he would not excuse me from the autopsy, not even when I threw up all over his makeshift operating table in an abandoned hut. To my relief, the body was gone the next day, probably stolen by dogs.

We used to act out the books we read. The Chinese folk tale, Monkey King (which Arthur Waley later translated) was our classic game. But Ta-ko always took the role of Monkey, a saucy demi-god who gave himself the title "Great Sage Equal to Heaven" and then proceeded to give Heaven and everyone in it a bad time. I was always the naive priest sent to India to get the holy Buddha scriptures.

The summer he was fifteen and I thirteen, we read *The Adventures of Tom Sawyer* and *Huckleberry Finn*. Ta-ko proposed we float down the Min River on a raft. Our parents consented if we took Pei, Ta-ko's slave. It was perfect. Pei would be Jim, I would be Tom, and Ta-ko Huck Finn.

Our raft was a miniature copy of the huge bamboo rafts that carried yak wool down to Chungking. The deck was on stilts above the lashed-together bamboo logs. On it was a bamboo-mat cabin, and a mast gay with flags and pennants.

A claque of cousins came to see us off. After a chicken had been killed and the bow smeared with its blood and feathers, and evil spirits kept ashore by a barrage of fire-crackers, we cast off. While Huck and I lounged on pillows like a pair of pashas nibbling sweets, Pei manned the long scull oar.

Pei was a stocky, broadshouldered farm boy about eighteen years old. He had been bought at Ta-ko's birth to be his playmate and servant. Like a faithful dog, he always had his eyes on Ta-ko, watching for the slightest gesture to obey. Whenever Ta-ko glanced at him, Pei grinned with pleasure.

4

We tied up to a ma-t'ou, village wharf, for the night, and Pei went ashore to buy a chicken or duck, and vegetables. While he chopped up the food with a huge cleaver, and cooked rice in a wok on a small clay stove, Huck and I sipped bowls of wine from the jar he had stolen from the House of Chen.

During the day, we acted out parts of *Huckleberry Finn*, and tried to teach Pei to talk with a Negro accent like Jim. But after a few words, he would start giggling and collapse. Now and then we passed a junk being towed upstream by a gang of naked coolies. We rounded every bend anticipating pirates or adventure, but the Min was peaceful, and soon monotonous.

For excitement, we began to steal our food. We studied the villages and farms as we drifted past. When Ta-ko saw a likely victim, we would anchor, and he returned on foot or in our towed sampan to reconnoiter. He planned each foray like a battle and drilled us for every contingency. To silence watchdogs, we captured a bitch in heat and soaked a wad with her odor, which we tied in the opening of a wire snare at the end of a bamboo pole. Each plan was different, all but the simplest unnecessary. Chickens and ducks wandered free, and the dogs always barked at nothing or at each other, and were ignored by their masters.

As our stealth and skill improved, Ta-ko became bolder. To distract the sleeping inhabitants on a farm, one of us attacked from the opposite direction with firecrackers. We drew another family away by firing an outbuilding.

Then one morning, we saw a man standing on the river bank. He was idle, not even fishing. "I think they're on to us," I whispered.

Ta-ko grinned. "All the more fun."

Later a sampan with three men overtook us and slowed as they passed. We were being watched! I begged Ta-ko to abandon the raids but he agreed only to caution. At the three-river junction, he insisted we land at Kiating. I wanted us to escape across the Mon to the 300 foot Buddha carved in the cliff.

"There's too large a crowd on the ma-t'ou," I cried with fright.

He was contemptuous. "They would not dare harm us. I am of the House of Chen."

"But we're not in Chengtu!"

He ordered Pei to scull us to the wharf. We disembarked and the surly crowd parted as we advanced, then closed in behind, and suddenly attacked us with sticks. Two police-men ran to our rescue and took us to the Yamen, where an angry official recited our crimes. I grandly admitted to pranks and was ignored. Ta-ko's status did not impress the official, who threatened to serve him up to the headsman at the next festival. Ta-ko finally calmed him with a pouch of coins and promise of more if he would summon the most prominent Chen in the city.

While waiting for Mr. Chen, the official turned on me. I would be reported to the British Consul in Chunking. The local missionaries would be forced to pay a hundred-fold for my thefts. I would be returned to Chengtu fettered behind a drum-beating escort, who would announce my crimes in every village. Oh, how he relished the prospect of embarrassing the foreigners, and he had already tasted his gain of face.

Mr. Chen was a distant cousin under obligation to the House of Chen. Unfortunately, he was out of favour with the official, who renewed his harangue with sadistic de-light. Mr. Chen countered with horrible threats if the heir to the House of Chen were harmed. After long and loud bargaining, they arrived at a price, and Mr. Chen put his chop to a guaranty.

6

But the official was not satisfied. "The people know you were taken. I must give them one to pay for the crimes."

With a single glance, Ta-ko, Mr. Chen and the official condemned Pei to death.

Returning home on horses supplied by the cousin, I rode ahead or behind Ta-ko to avoid him. At stops, he ignored my sullen silence, and tried to act as if nothing had happened. But one night in a small inn, he turned on me savagely. "There was nothing I could do!"

"You did not try. You did not lift a finger."

"It would have done no good."

Insight choked me. Pei was a disposable. He had no one to protect him or revenge his death. He was one of the meek multitude harassed and slaughtered by the hunters, who were determined to inherit the earth.

"Go back and buy his life," I shouted. "Give it back to him. It is all he has!"

"He was my slave," Ta-ko snarled. "Mine to do with as I please."

"Then his death pleases you!"

He slapped my face and we both burst into tears.

From then on we saw less and less of each other. Perhaps it was Pei, or simply the new interests of adolescence. Ta-ko buried himself in books by Marx, Engels and Lenin, and took up with a group of Chinese students rumoured to be dangerous radicals. When we did meet, he bored me with lectures about the decadence of capitalism and the coming world revolution. He preached as fervently about a man called Mao Tse-tung as my relatives did about Jesus. But he disturbed me most when his diatribes against foreigners included me. Refusing to believe he rejected me as his brother, I shrugged off his polemics as cant, something he would outgrow as I would my acne.

two

THE Chinese say that the moon is no sooner full than it wanes. In 1938, I had no sooner arrived in Canada to attend the University of Toronto, when Ta-ko died. I had explored west China and parts of Tibet, yet Toronto frightened me. When I was fourteen, my amah recommended I be assigned a girl, whom my dear, naive father assumed was for linguistic reasons, and yet I was shy with the college girls. By the age of fifteen, I had cornered the northwest China supply of musk, yet in the Rosedale homes of Bay Street barons, I felt very much the country bumpkin.

Yin and Yang.

The saddest portent that my life in China had ended was Ta-ko's death. He had left China two years before me to enroll at the Sorbonne. While he was there, a homeward-bound Chinese ambassador was assassinated in Paris, and Ta-ko—known for his communist activities—was sought for questioning. When a dead Chinese, who seemed to fit his description, was fished from the Seine, the Paris police closed the case. The Chen family claimed the body and had it shipped to Chengtu. I mourned for my brother, yet I believed he was still alive in the underground.

I was in Montreal the summer war began and enlisted in the Royal Canadian Air Force. My second new life started in the Lachine Manning Depot, followed by ground school in Victoriaville. After a course in Quebec City to improve my math, I arrived at #11 Elementary Flying Training School, Cap de la Madeleine, Quebec, where we learned to fly the Fleet Finch on skis off an open, snow-packed field. Eight hours after my familiarization flight and first breathtaking spin, I soloed the small biplane. Then came the freedom to explore a world I had climbed mountains to reach.

At #13 Service Flying Training School, St. Hubert, Quebec, I drew a double bunk with an American, who pumped my arm while almost shouting, "Tex Burke from Floresville, Texas." He eyed my six foot three frame.

"Where you from, Highpockets?"

"China."

"No kidding! Hey, is it true their cunts are sideways?"

Before I could answer, he yelled, "Hey gang, we got ourselves a Chinaman who don't even look Jewish." And he fell back on the lower bunk braying with laughter.

The lower bunk became his. Flipping for it, Tex spun up a twenty dollar gold piece. Though in China I once had a candy box full of ten tael gold bars concealed as Hershey bars, I felt very much the poor missionary kid and was impressed. I won the toss, yet I let him draw me into two out of three and lost.

Like all new boys, I was wary, content to let the group sort itself out gradually. But not Tex. While we unpacked our gear, he strode through the barracks pushing his hand at everyone. "Name's Tex Burke from Floresville, Texas. What's yours?"

Another American shouted, "Hey, Tex! Stop running

9

for dog catcher, for Christ's sake."

But the Texan's affable brashness touched our loneliness. His fractured French drew grins from the French Canadians. "That not right?" he asked, feigning surprise. "But that's what she used to say to me, this Cajun girl I used to *couche avec* down New Orleans."

Four of the class had gone to St. Andrew's and Trinity. They had come from Cap de la Madeleine with me so Tex had never met them before, yet he instantly recognized them as private school boys and verbally flashed his old school tie. "Choate. We always wanted to play you chaps in cricket."

While Tex was equally close-mouthed about his background, he casually hinted at a fortune from oil. But unlike the Toronto Establishment lads, who would lend you a fiver and remember the loan only when you repaid it, Tex would lend you four for five back next pay parade. Perhaps he was *nouveau riche,* or maybe it was just an American custom, one reason the country was so wealthy.

To Tex the class was a gang, and it soon became his gang. Instead of remaining terrified of our sergeant, Tex quickly became his unofficial corporal. "Okay guys, if we're going to win cleanest barracks award this week, Ole Sarge says we gotta use better wax than we get from supply. So ante up two bits each you guys, and Sarge will get us wax we can play hockey on." While the new wax did not look any different, it was very expensive, because we had to kick in to buy more a week later. Tex also became Ole Sarge's purchasing agent. Anyone with a pass would be drawn aside by Tex and asked to pick up this or that in Montreal for Ole Sarge.

When Sarge kept forgetting to repay us, we realized that the wax and shopping favours were graft. Tex listened to our outrage with a grin. "Sure took you long enough to wise up. I spotted him as a horse thief the minute I saw him."

"That makes you his accomplice!"

He laughed at us. "You dumb hicks. I'm the oil on the gears. Without it, he would have slapped 'em to us."

And he made us feel the smallness of our farm or mining town pasts, like Flinflon, Medicine Hat, Moosejaw, Kapuskasing, Chicoutimi, Stellarton and Come By Chance. I felt more provincial than the others because I had grown up where corruption was an art and until then believed it existed only in China. At the same time, it gave the Air Force a human face and we lost some of our awe. Tex was rewarded with new admiration.

On the eve of our first C.O.'s parade, Tex spit and polished the high-heeled cowboy boots he always wore instead of the regulation: "Boots, black, Airman for the use of." The two St. Andreans sauntered over to admire them and asked if he planned to wear them on parade.

"You betcha."

"Aren't you afraid the C.O. will gate you?" Big Mac Macdonald asked.

"Look, Son, I been wearing high-heeled boots since I first toddled. My legs ain't built to walk in those sidewalk city shoes. Why, I'll just take the Old Man aside and explain carefully how we do things down home. He'll understand."

"I'm sure he will," they said.

On parade, the commanding officer and his entourage walked briskly up and down the blue ranks of airmen, ramrod and correct form—

Great Scot! Brown, hand-tooled, high-heeled cowboy boots?

The warrant officer drew his pad like a gunslinger and glared at the tittering ranks. But the C.O., instead of roaring "Put that man on charge," listened and walked on with the understanding Tex had predicted.

We were stunned until a week later when Tex was paraded in front of Group Captain J. E. G. MacDonald, who handed him a pair of black airman's boots, regulation except for triple heels. In them, Tex clomped along like a strange cripple whose short leg alternated with each step. To his credit, he also laughed at himself; in fact, he enjoyed the notoriety.

Tex began to fill the void left in me by Ta-ko. Often a quip stemming from the American's audacity and affable scorn would spark a *déjà vu* that snapped my head in a double take. Once it was a tale.

After lights out one night, he was telling the bottom of my mattress about Texas until I bolted upright. "What did you say?"

"I said there was nothing I could do."

"About what?"

"About this nigger kid. Goddammit, Highpockets, it ain't polite to sleep when people talk to you. This nigger kid, Jim, who grew up alongside me. The family worked on our farm. He was maybe eighteen and I was a couple of years younger. We played together as kids. Nothing wrong when you're a kid. Anyway, he rapes this little white trash whore, leastwise she hollers rape after he fucked her 'til she sizzled. Jim swore she pestered and wiggled her ass at him 'till he had no choice, and I believe him. He had a dong like a horse, and that Betsy Ann was cock crazy. Anyway, they strung him up. There was nothing I could do."

I lay back and stared at a vision of Pei in the darkness.

"Poor bastard," Tex murmured. "He shit himself."

The smell of execution.

Tex became a superb pilot, and topped the class in ground school. But he only studied the curriculum. My reading Tolstoy's *War and Peace* puzzled him. "Why?"

"It's one of the great novels," I answered.

"But what'll it do for you? Does it tell you how to make a buck?"

"No."

"I feel sorry for you, Highpockets."

But barrack life was minor. Paramount was our advanced trainer, the North American Harvard, whose size terrified us at first. How that yellow, two-seat, all metal monoplane worried us in the beginning. Suppose you forgot to lower the undercarriage? She's a killer. They say the torque on takeoff is murder. Ground loop. She's a ground looping fool. And we spent every free minute of our first days out on the tarmac watching the old boys on circuits-and-bumps. Not an accident, but we were not assuaged.

"You must handle an aircraft as gently as a woman," an instructor said, and as we learned to fly the Harvard, I think we loved her more.

We were taught navigation, gunnery, aircraft recognition, mechanics, a dozen different courses, but strangely, no politics, no history, no *raison d'être* for the war. I doubt if they assumed we knew. Things simply had not changed since Kipling's time, and ours was not to reason why. Nor did we. Few worried beyond winning the coveted wings. Oh, we solemnly discussed the rumoured short life of a fighter pilot on operations, but the statistic impressed the girls more than it did us. Even the three empty, inspection-tight bunks in our barracks tolled no bells for us. I became more intimate than most with every death on the station because my height made me an ideal pallbearer. I accepted it as a joe-job, even for the student with whom I was almost killed.

Before taking off on a solo cross-country flight, I had checked my compass against the runway heading and found it to be thirty degrees off. Rather than cancel the exercise, I set the directional indicator to the runway heading and took off. A few minutes out, the gyroscopic DI spun. Instead of returning, I formated on another Harvard flying the same route, and while he did all the navigation, I played alongside, irritating him with aerobatics and mock attacks. On the homeward leg, a low overcast blotted out the ground. About twenty miles from the airfield, my friend began to let down through the clouds. Without thinking about the two gumdrop mountains in the vicinity, I banked away to increase our separation, and followed him down. The flash of light in the mist puzzled me until I broke through alongside a wooded slope that rose like a wall.

He was a French Canadian from a nearby village to which the funeral party was taken by truck. We waited outside by the baroque hearse drawn by four black horses and attended by gaunt men in black. When we pallbearers were sent up to the tiny apartment to retrieve the coffin, we panicked at the narrow stairs with its sharp turn at the top. The undertakers ascended, closed the coffin, and took it from the mourners. On the landing, they stood it on end to make the turn.

"My God," I thought. "He'll be all in a heap at his feet."

All the way to the cemetery, I worried about his condition when they opened the lid for a last look over the grave. But he was stretched out peacefully, not a hair out of place. To all appearances, he had survived the crash remarkably well.

Because it was easy to lose track of time, a 48 hour pass came as an unexpected gift. There were great shouts and showering, buttons were polished twice as hard as for parade, money counted, pooled, or borrowed, and "Who's got a clean shirt?" Kit bags packed, we passed through the guardhouse, signed out, drew our ration of condoms and prophylactic kits, and ran for a waiting taxi.

Montreal!

Tex was heavy-lidded with anticipation. "First, I'm going to get laid."

But first we checked into the Mount Royal Hotel, then went over to the bar in the Barclay Hotel for Planter's Punches as we studied the girls and waited for better ones to arrive. Then the four of us, Big Mac, Little Frasier, Tex and myself, our great coats buttoned to white silk scarves, the high collars up over our ears, all slightly drunk, would hail two sleighs and bundle in with our girls. With roars and shouts and giggling, we would egg our drivers to race down St. Catherine Street. Snug under the heavy robes, we would test our dates with kisses and little feels, and before we reached our destination, each knew his prospects.

At Christmas we were given a 96 hour pass, and I phoned Maggie to accept her invitation to spend the holiday with her family in Toronto.

"Who's Maggie?" Tex asked, looking glum.

"Maggie is Margaret Roxanne Rutherford-Jones." I grinned, expecting some ribald exclamation, but Tex was depressed because he had no place to spend Christmas. When he learned that Maggie was the daughter of Lord and Lady Rutherford-Jones, he grew so pathetic, I phoned Maggie to ask if I could bring a friend. "He's from Texas and has no place to go."

"Of course you can bring the poor lamb."

But it was a wolf I brought into the fold.

three

THE Chinese say that he who steals a hoe is executed, while he who steals a province is made a prince. Sir John Rutherford-Jones was knighted after the First World War, despite rumors that he had supplied the Canadian Army with watered pork to increase his profits and already vast fortune. Before the turn of the century, he had built a huge castle in Toronto. The barns on his farm were made of brick and stone, and resembled armories. But few fortunes could withstand the gargantuan extravagances of Sir John, who once took a two thousand man regiment, at his own expense, to England for a coronation. In 1920, his empire collapsed, and the Central Bank of Canada called a meeting of his creditors. Drowsy after his usual luncheon repast of one roast chicken, a bottle and a half of claret, plum pudding and two brandies, Sir John snored peacefully while the bankers discussed his debts. Finally the chairman nudged him. "Sir John."

"Eh?"

"I say, wake up. What have you to say about this wretched business?"

Sir John grunted thoughtfully. "Where did I make all the money I lost?"

Though he was into them for a million, the bankers were so distrubed by the thought of Lady Rutherford-Jones living in penury on Sir John's demise, they settled a handsome trust fund on her. Then damned if she didn't up and die, and Sir John got all the money.

The bankers put their wise heads together to find Sir John a suitable new wife. Since she had to have a fortune sufficient to pay off his debts, and still keep him in his accustomed style of Henry the Eighth, it was not easy. But find her they did in Surrey, and the tiny spinster, Lady Ann, was enticed to visit the Colony, where she became the second Lady Rutherford-Jones. In due course, to everyone's astonishment, she also became the mother of Margaret Roxanne Rutherford-Jones.

Maggie and I had been students together, and when the war began, she also enlisted. Because of her family, who had kept her in pinafores until she was eighteen, Margaret Roxanne was made the officer commanding two hundred eager girls billeted amongst two thousand horny men. It shook her faiths.

Margaret Roxanne had inherited her mother's pretty face and figure. Sir John had supplied the genes that scaled her up to a statuesque six feet, plus his capacity for alcohol. In the Officer's Mess, transient pilots gawked, rubbed their hands, and fought to buy her drinks. One by one the Lotharios would stagger out, leaving her to a quiet nightcap and an innocent saunter home.

When Tex and I arrived by cab in front of Sir John's home, Tex thought it was a hotel. "You mean this is their private home?"

"Don't let it fool you. They're really quite poor."

Tex guffawed.

The grandeur, servants and eccentricities in that palatial home so awed Tex, he became shy and charming. Her Ladyship adored him, and Maggie thought him cute. But they were really quite daft, Maggie included.

Lady Rutherford-Jones had a compulsion to entertain. The table was never set for less than twelve, twice as many on weekends. It kept Her Ladyship as busy as Philippe of the Waldorf-Astoria. Over her breakfast tray, she planned the dinner for a week next. Except for arranging the flowers, that evening's party was finished, the guest list so forgotten that she was surprised by the people who arrived.

During the dinner, Lady Rutherford-Jones sat at her end of the long table lost in reverie or the menu for some future party. The one at the moment she ignored. Like a true artist, she did not waste time on a finished painting. She covered her preoccupation with two words, and was renowned as a brilliant conversationalist.

"I say, your Ladyship, but this Chateau Lafite is superb."

"Oh, really?"

"Now you take the Americans. As I was saying just yesterday to the Leftenant Governor, if we don't stop those bounders soon, they'll own the whole country."

"Oh, really?"

"Madame, the kitchen stove is on fire!"

"Oh, really?"

"Mother! Father has fallen off his chair!"

"Oh, really?"

Usually it was only the chair collapsing because he bounced as he pounded the table. Close to eighty, six foot three, and weighing over three hundred pounds, Sir John believed any foreigner could understand English if one simply shouted and beat a tattoo. Failing in sight and memory, he assumed that all but a few cronies were foreigners.

18

Thus dinner was bounded by Sir John's bellow and pounding at one end, and on the other her Ladyship chirping, "Oh, really," as she stared into next week. In between, guests cleaned up the gourmet dishes and vintage wines.

Maggie, while not as fey as her mother, remained a few veils from reality, and our romance was Yin and Yang. She wanted to, but wouldn't. She had come out in college—almost literally the way her figure strained her dress seams. To save her RCAF uniform, I tried my best, whenever I could, to take it off her. The closest I came was one night in a rowboat when I talked her into a skinny dip. I skinned, but she refused to part with her underpants. Anyway, I think it would have been impossible while treading water. Just as well, because I often had the feeling that Maggie was really a fecund goddess of fertility within whom all contraceptives would fail; and once started, she would produce a staircase of children.

Poor Maggie. She despised her approved suitors. If young, they had more Adam's apple than chin. If older, they were twice her age and their jaded eyes only glistened when they appraised the *objets d'art*. They courted her by fawning over her Ladyship, and flattering Sir John. Maggie said, "I feel they're wearing a jeweller's loupe when they kiss my hand."

Hands were as far as she would go, and while she moaned, "No," and I groaned, "Please," we did each other. We even had fun talking, but not when she brought up marriage by saying she wanted to be a virgin on her wedding night.

"Marriage is a long way off for me," I would say sadly. "First I have to survive the war, and then I have to get back to China."

"Can't you go back married?"

"No."

"Why?"

"A fortune teller told me." One must have, so I wasn't really lying. "I must remain a virgin also."

"Are you?" She seemed concerned. "I mean after I—" she blushed.

"Aren't you?"

"But is it the same?"

"Only a deflowering deflowers."

"Oh."

Maggie had a lot to learn about sex, and was eager to become a pupil. The tragedy was her belief that she needed a certificate first.

After Christmas dinner, the ladies left the men to their cigars and brandy. Tex began dropping names of Texas oil tycoons, and made no more impression than if they had been the names of Bay Street barons. The assembled expected everyone who crossed Sir John's threshold to know the same people they did.

However, one gentleman, after mouthing the name "Burke" as if trying to identify the taste, asked, "Your father T. C. Burke of Dallas?"

"Do you know him, sir?" Tex asked eagerly.

"Only by reputation and some money I made investing in one of his companies. Oil, I think."

"I understand he's into aircraft now," Tex said proudly.

"Yes, yes," another grunted, "good move these days. But this war is all wrong. Wouldn't you say, Sir John?"

Sir John twirled his cigar between gross lips. "I told Winston only last year. 'Team up with the Germans. Finish Russia. They're the ones. Finish what you started after the first war.' He wouldn't hear of it. Wouldn't hear of it. Winnie worries me at times. 'If we don't do it now, we'll only have to do it later,' I said. He wouldn't hear of it."

"It's world Jewry, of course."

"Hear, hear."

"Why?" Tex asked.

They chuckled and marked him as a wit.

One of them turned to me. "MacCloud. What about this Chinaman, Ching, or whatever his name. Can he hold the Japs?"

"Chiang Kai-shek?"

"That's the fellow. I remember back in twenty-seven when he lead the revolution to unite China and throw the foreigners out. Gave our consortium a bad time, I don't mind telling you. But for once we got together, all of us, and we talked some sterling sense into him." He smiled at his pun. " 'Throw us out, and you're a rice country again,' we told him. 'Who'll run your factories, eh? Your trade? Throw us out and no one will trade with you.' Oh, yes, we were all together on that one. Had to, you know. Even the greedy American buggers. Well, it didn't take Chiang long to see which side of his rice bowl was up, I'll tell you. Oh, it cost us all a pretty penny, and many of us think it was what this fellow had in mind all along. You know, the Chinese are worse than the Jews. They really are. Well, he came around just before his army reached Shanghai. The amusing thing is that the communists, who were in this with him, rose up and took Shanghai before he got there. When he arrived, they expected thanks, I suppose. Instead, he got rid of the whole kit and caboodle. Shot the whole lot of 'em." His cheeks chuffed with laughter. "Wish I could have seen the look on their faces."

I thought I heard a laugh behind me, and looked back, but it was my memory of Ta-ko. We had always fought over Chiang Kai-shek. Ta-ko insisted Chiang was a lackey of foreign interests, while I believed Chiang was the saviour of China. I had been brought up to include Chiang in my prayers. The missionaries loved him. He had not only united China, and allowed the foreigners to stay, but he was a *Christian!* They could scarcely believe their good fortune. God was rewarding them for their life of sacrifice and hardship in a heathen land.

Ta-ko, with all the fierce scorn he could muster, would say, "You support Chiang because he lets you stay and patronize us. Who asked you to come? We have many Gods, all of them far more sophisticated than your stupid one, who only knows two things: good and bad. And I spit on your 'love for China.' You love only the good life here and the cheap servants."

The next morning, I found Tex and Maggie talking earnestly in the sunny breakfast room. As I helped myself to kippers and scrambled eggs from the silver platters on the sideboard, I overheard Tex saying, "This room reminds me so much of the one we have at home. In the house at the ranch, that is, not the one outside Dallas."

It was his voice that had caught my attention. Overnight, he had lost his Texas drawl and now spoke with a faint English accent. I kept listening. His brash, "Tex Burke from Floresville, Texas," had been replaced by a subtle imitation of the voices heard in the Rutherford-Jones house.

Chameleon skittered into my mind and I chased it out as being ridiculous.

If not chance, perhaps it was preordained. After our wings parade, I was sent to Arnprior to become an elementary flying instructor, and Tex was posted to Maggie's bomber and gunnery school. Just before I graduated, Maggie wrote that she and Tex were married.

four

THE Chinese say that the whole of life is the interaction of the opposing forces of Yin—female, darkness, death—and Yang—male, light, life, etc. One can also attribute to Yin and Yang the incongruities in life.

Despite my knowledge of China, my fluency in Mandarin and Szechwanese, and my pleas to be posted to the CBI Theater, I was sent to England in early 1943 to become a fighter pilot. They should have known it was a mistake from my inability to hit even one clay pigeon. Yet for six months, I was kept roaring around over the low countries in a Spitfire, even though I could barely hit the broad side of a barn with eight machine guns. Except for routing a field-full of German soldiers doing calesthenics, and scaring the shit out of cows, I only damaged the Third Reich by making their Messerschmit 109's waste precious fuel and ammunition chasing me.

Then in the fall of '43, I was mysteriously taken off operations, given a course on Dakotas, and sent to New Delhi. My new job was to be pilot/interpreter (number two backup) for Lord Louis Mountbatten, Supreme Allied Commander of the China Burma India Theater of War. But first they assigned me to the U.S. Army Air Transport Command in Dinjan, Assam, to learn the ropes. "Sticky wicket that Hump," the group captain said.

In ATC operations, I was surprised to see Captain Burke's name on the flight schedule board. "Is that Tex Burke?" I asked the operations officer.

He removed his cigar, and without losing his thick Southern accent, tried to speak Cockney. "Y'all mean Grup Cap'n Burke, late h'of the Royal Hair Fohce, Spitfeya h'ace o'the Battle of Britain and dufaindah o'the faith?"

It was the wrong Burke, I thought, because Tex had never been more than a staff pilot at a bomber and gunnery school before he transferred to the U.S. Army Air Corps after Pearl Harbor. Then maybe the operations officer was only kidding. "Tell him Highpockets was here."

"Right you are, Lootenant. Now, we gonna let you fly right seat with Major Fulton, and don't let him rattle your marbles none. He may fly like his grandpappy drove that steamboat, but he ain't killed nobody, leastwise not yet. Pay no never mind to his Fulton Controlled Approach. You stick to GCA."

Luckily the weather was CAVU, and I was only nervous of Major Fulton's cigar among the fumes of gasoline from our cargo of aviation fuel in drums. But the view of the Himalayas made me tremble with excitement. I was going home.

We landed at Paishihi, the new airfield a mountain range west of Chungking. Flying the Hump—one of the most treacherous air routes in the world—was a piece of cake to being driven from Paishihi to Chungking by the Chinese. They were convinced you avoided an accident by beating it to the scene. They raced to cross intersections, and approached hairpin turns as if to reach flying speed before the edge. Skidding around a road doubling back from a thou-

24

sand foot drop, they talked over their shoulder about Wong who didn't make that one last week.

The route was dotted with the huge, manpowered stone rollers used to construct the twisting road. Every ridge was terraced to its top, every rice paddy bank planted with vegetables. The ancient road, a footpath of steps, was still used by coolies, who carried passengers sitting backwards in a chair strapped to their backs.

Safe at last beside the Kialing Ho as it curved east to flow into the Yangtze, we drove by the caves dug into the high bluffs. These were the homes of thousands of refugees from the East and, where the Japanese bombs had scored hits, their mass tombs.

Chungking, with every radio on full volume, was a cacaphony. The fat red columns along the curbs were as alive with Chinese writings as the arcades were with people milling along the frontless shops. At every corner, the jam of mancarts, barrows, rickshas, trucks and jeeps ignored the frantic semaphore of the white-sleeved gendarme on his concrete stanchion and honked or shouted their way past and around each other. They gave way only for two men wearing black vests decorated with white characters, who came hup-hupping along the main street, carrying below their bamboo pole two stiff corpses lashed head to the other's dirty feet.

That evening, I invited Major Fulton to a Szechwan restaurant that used to be excellent. When he hesitated, then said, "Guess I should try some of this slopey food at least once," I almost withdrew the invitation.

On the sidewalk outside our billet we were surrounded by ricksha pullers offering their services. As I stepped into one, I saw a ricksha man with a red vest standing idly between his shafts. Shouting, "Next time, Major," I ran to the ricksha and got in. My heart pounded. If he asked my destination, I was wrong. If he didn't, Ta-ko wanted me. It was a method we had often used to summon each other to a secret rendezvous.

Without a word, he trotted off with me.

Ta-ko was alive!

Nearing the black mouth of a hutung, he barked, "Pu chan 'rh."

I felt around, and under my seat cushion found a long Chinese cotton gown. Inside the dark alley, I slipped it over my uniform, and hid my Air Force hat. Emerging from the hutung, I saw my puller had shed his red vest. We merged into the main street traffic, he naked to the waist as the other ricksha men, and I a hunched Chinese passenger. Again, we went through hutungs, narrow streets between high compound walls. He swerved through an open gate in a wall, and we stopped deep inside a compound.

When I climbed down, he said, "Chau-chu-pa!"

I stood still as ordered, and he frisked me. Walking behind me, he directed me to a pavilion in a garden. I turned to ask for orders, but he had vanished. Trembling, I wondered if it could be true, and hesitated to enter in fear it would not be Ta-ko. Slowly, I opened the door onto a small room lit only by an oil lamp on a low table in the center. At first I thought the room empty, then I made out a seated figure in a gray gown.

"Ta-ko?"

"Welcome Hsiung-ti."

I wanted to rush in and embrace him, but when he did not move, I approached with decorum, hands up my sleeves, and facing him, bowed.

He looked different. As a boy, he had been fat from too many sweets indulged him by his adoring grandmother and maids; as a youth fleshy from debauchery. He was thin now, his face long, and his nose, always large for a Chinese, was aquiline. His once shaggy black hair wore a military crew-cut. But even if his face had been altered by plastic surgery, there was no escaping his eyes. To look into Ta-ko's eyes was like staring down a well in which you saw the stars and your own reflection. Then, as if the surface rippled, a phantasmagoria forced you to withdraw in awe, often fear.

He motioned me to sit, and his finger invited me to pour myself a drink from the bottle of Johnny Walker Black Label, his favourite Scotch. I lifted my glass to him and he returned the silent toast, then said in Szechwanese, "You must leave China."

I was shocked, more by his rudeness than his order. We were brothers. No word of friendship. No explanations.

"Go back to hell, Ta-ko!" I shivered at my words. Was I meeting with a ghost? Or was he, as I had often imagined, an Immortal? His life so resembled the hero, Chia Pao-yu, that I used to daydream over the Chinese novel that Ta-ko was also a god visiting the Red Dust.

"I'm sorry, but you must leave," he said.

"Stop ordering me about. You have always ordered me about."

"The privilege of an elder brother."

"You do not act like a brother."

"Forgive me, Hsiung-ti. How is your honorable father?"

"He is well. They are still in Chengtu. And your father?"

"I hear only that he lives."

"My family writes that your father, for his years, enjoys good health. He has recovered from his grief over your death. Does he know?"

"No one must know. Thus you must leave China."

"Do you think I will betray you?"

"Not intentionally."

"Then why did you summon me? You should have left

me thinking you were dead."

"Your presence opens old wounds."

"How?"

"When an agent reported that you, of all people, had arrived in New Delhi to become Mountbatten's interpreter, I read your dossier. If you stay, others will read it."

"I have nothing to fear."

"I do. Your dossier documents your association with Chen Yi. You know Chen Yi's scent, and they will try to make you point me."

"But everyone believes Chen Yi is dead."

"They have not closed my dossier. They were not fooled by the waiter fished from the Seine."

"Did you kill him?"

"The waiter? No."

"The ambassador?"

"It matters not. They think so, therefore I did. He was of the Soong family, and the Soongs resent being proved mortal."

"I still don't see."

"Then open your eyes, Hsiung-ti. I could have ignored you, let you think me dead. But they would have watched you, hoping we would meet accidentally. One sign of recognition and I would be dead within the hour."

"How could we meet?"

"Perhaps in your line of work."

"Who are you now?"

"Ta-ko," he said.

"I mean really."

"I will tell you when China is a People's Republic."

"By then you will be Chen Yi again."

He smiled. "With luck."

"Do they suspect you?"

"Generalissimo Chiang suspects everyone. His lackeys

trust no one. The Kuomintang spies spy on the Kuomintang. You would become their best lead in years. Not that they lack intrigue. Chungking boils with it and corruption. No, you are too dangerous; my work too important. We have spent too many years creating my cover. You must leave China and not return while this war lasts. If you do, you will be killed."

"I won't go!"

"You will."

Forgetting myself, I stamped my foot as I had many times as a boy, enraged because he was always right. Even when I wanted to obey him, I resisted and tried to prove him wrong. If only once he had let me decide something. But he was always ahead of me. He had answers to problems I did not even anticipate.

"I can't leave. I just got here. China is my home. It is as much my country as it is yours."

"You fight the invaders. Japan. Germany. Our war is with the Kuomintang. When you have finished yours, we will begin ours."

Ta-ko's politics had always bored me. Though I knew I invited a dialectic harangue, I said, "Destroy the old. Build the new. All for the people. Admit you will be as heavy on the peasant's back as Chiang. Admit it is all nonsense. Admit you only want the power."

Instead of a communist sermon, he smiled. "Perhaps. But the peasant's load will be lighter. You high noses will not be on his back with us. His back will grow strong. You are a poor man, Hsiung-ti. You live in constant twilight. You do not know the land covering your ancestors. You have no ancestors covered by the land you know. In thy father's house are many mansions, and you are prepared to dwell in the one most comfortable. You love China, yet you will leave it. You do not love Canada, yet you will be content in it. The Master said, 'To prefer it is better than only to know it. To delight in it is better than merely to prefer it.' I suspect you do not hate the Germans even in battle."

"Not really."

"You are a spectator, Hsiung-ti."

"Better than a murderer."

"More lives are lost to neglect than to the bullets that follow."

"Bullshit," I cried in English.

He laughed. "You have not changed. You always preferred excretion to assimilation."

"I'm here on orders," I shouted, my temper rising. "What am I supposed to do? Tell Lord Louis Mountbatten to shove my job right up his royal arse?"

"It would do the trick," he said, laughing. "Come. Let us eat."

My petition to remain in China had been dismissed.

In a dining room, we sat at a small round table, waited on by my ricksha puller. We toasted each other with little bowls of hot wine, as I talked about the war in Europe. When I asked him about the war in China, Ta-ko leapt to his feet, and striding back and forth, burlesqued the characters in his recitation.

"President Roosevelt." He flicked ashes from an imaginary cigarette in a long holder, and mimicked the American president. "My friends, we have nothing to fear in China but Confucian itself. Good American know-how logic tells us China is simple. Eleanor and I love China. Our missionaries love the heathen in China. Standard Oil loves the lamps of China. Pearl Buck loves the good earth of China. Chiang Kai-shek loves Christ. Christians love democrats, thus China is a democracy. We are dedicated to save the world for democracy. Give Chiang half the fifty million he demands this week. On one condition. He must keep

30

Madame Chiang at home. Talk about Madame Pompadour!

"General Stilwell." He drew in his cheeks to appear gaunt, and hunched his shoulders. In a flat American accent, he said, "Now look here, Peanuts. The only way to lick the Japs in China is to lick the Japs in Burma. The Limeys don't give a damn about Burma. You don't give a damn about Burma. But I give a damn about Burma. The Japs beat my ass off in Burma. Just beginner's luck, and I aim to prove it. Now Burma ain't worth a pinch of coon shit to nobody, all mountains, swamps, malaria, no roads, the most Godforsaken country in the world. But I want Burma. You give me your armies, and I'll give you Burma.

"Generalissimo Chiang Kai-shek." He perched himself as if on a throne, slipped his hands up his sleeves, and spoke pidgin English. "Burma? No want Burma! Want more Lend Lease. Want more supplies over Hump. Want more money. No money, no fightee. Sell China to Japanese. Japan offer much money. You tell Plesident Rosyfelt, he no buy China, I sell to Japan. Okay? Hey, T.V. Soong, you got offer from Stalin and Hitler yet? This year China in big demand. Missey say no sell whole piece. We subdivide. Smart cookie, Missey. Hey, General Vinegar, you want nice little province? Got running water. Velly nice. Big steal for little money. What you say? I sell you cheap 'cause you first customer today. Okay?

"Lord Louis Mountbatten." He pretended to groom his hair, adjust his tie and preen himself in front of a mirror. "Mirror, mirror, old chap, tell me again. I know I am the very fairest Supreme Allied Commander in all of the CBI but it does delight me to hear an outside, unbiased opinion. What's that, Brittlebottom? General Stilwell is doing *what?* Fighting? Did I hear you say *fighting?* Dear me, what will this bloody war come to. What gets into these Americans? Rowdies. That's all they are. Rowdies. Fighting where?

Burma? Burma? I say, Frignewton, do we have a place called Burma? We do, eh? Worth anything? Isn't eh? But you say it does keep the others out of India. How does it do that? No roads east and west through mountains running north and south. How very clever. Tell Stilwell to stop his fighting this very instant. This instant! Tell him to meet me for tea. No, make it tiffin. He probably drinks coffee. Dear me.

"Comrade Chou En-lai." He drew himself up to look suave and with a charming smile, moved a graceful hand. "Ah, General Stilwell, I hear the Generalissimo will not allow you to train his army. What a pity. If I may offer a suggestion, why not train *our* army? Just a little something to keep your hand in. We will even fight the Japanese. Just for practice, you understand.

"Chairman Mao Tse-tung." He stuffed a walnut in each cheek, and grinning broadly, rubbed his hands with glee. "That Chiang Kai-shek. With one like him in Moscow, we'd own the Kremlin by next year. The mandate from Heaven must be mine. Why else would the Gods have favoured me with such a perfect agent as Chiang Kai-shek?"

He bowed and took his seat, while I applauded and wiped my eyes of tears from laughter. "You should be on the stage."

"I am," he said, wryly.

The food began to arrive; hot, spicy Szechwan dishes. The highlight was Szechwan duck; mallards marinated in spices, steamed, then deep fried in peanut oil. They fell apart at the touch of our chopsticks.

"Delicious," I said. "Were they stolen?"

I had meant it as a joke, but Ta-ko was not amused. "Pei still bothers you, doesn't he?" There was contempt and a touch of anger in his voice.

"Not really. Does he you?"

"No."

But we both lied, for the meal was no longer festive. Reverie led me to pick absently at the food, and Ta-ko sat in silence, as if following my memory with his.

"Did Pei make you a communist?" I asked.

He looked annoyed. "You are being a romantic Christian capitalist. You believe communism is so evil, only some trauma can convert a man."

"It is evil. Just as evil, anyway. Perhaps your communism will value a man's life more than a few ducks, but you'll kill him just as quickly for some other petty reason."

"All systems have values higher than life," he said wearily. "Life is too cheap. If man was scarce and expensive to reproduce, it might be different."

"He will be at the rate we're going. Why do you bother fighting? You won't make life any better in China."

"We will. Not what you consider better with cars and junk. You Westerners assume a chance to live is your birthright, and the tinseled trappings your reward. In Asia, a chance to live is the reward." He shrugged, and poured me wine from a new pewter pot. "Gampei."

I tossed down the bowl of wine, and almost immediately the room began to spin. "Ta-ko!"

From a great distance, I heard him say, "Pu p'a, Hsiung-ti."

Fear not.

five

IN New Delhi, I braced myself to have a stripe torn off by the group captain. Instead, I was paraded in front of a Lt. Colonel Fitzgerald, British Army Intelligence. Despite his uniform, the colonel looked like a shaggy Oxford don. He returned my salute by waving me into a chair and leaning toward me conspiratorially. "Do you smoke?"

"Yes sir," I said, prepared to accept whatever he had to offer.

"Good. Give me a fag, will you? I've given them up."

For the first few drags, he was lost in ecstasy, then he eyed me with amusement. "Now what's a nice missionary kid like you doing getting caught in an opium den?"

"Just bad luck, sir."

"We can dispense with the sir shit." He tapped the file on his desk. "You have a good record, MacCloud. No pattern of this sort of thing. You requested duty in the CBI, and yet you blow it the first day." He pursed his lips as if to keep from smiling. "Why?"

I shrugged.

"It doesn't figure." In excellent Mandarin, he said, "Did

you run into some old warlord you had once cuckolded? Or did you refuse to make a deal? Why did they turf you out of China?"

"No one did," I answered in Chinese.

His eyes twinkled. "Have you any idea why the American military police should have been tipped off that you were stone cold in a den of iniquity?"

"I didn't know they had been."

He nodded, and became serious. "Look, MacCloud, I'll be honest with you, so try to reciprocate. Aside from entrusting His Lordship's precious arse to your piloting, we were also going to entrust him to your interpreting on the days I had the squits, clap, or whatever. Being a new boy for such an exalted position, we naturally kept our eyes on you. We know you left your billet at nineteen hundred hours, got into a ricksha and disappeared. It must have been the fastest goddamn ricksha in the world, because your tail said you made two turns and vanished. Where did you go?"

"To the opium den."

"You were picked up at oh two hundred. Seven hours of pipe dreaming?" He shook his head.

"I don't remember."

"About as original as drugging someone and dumping them in an opium den. MacCloud, I can square this frame-up. Up at Oxford, we are all familiar with your father's work. When your name came up for this job, I rather looked forward to having you on my staff. Tell me what happened, and we'll forget the whole incident."

"I've told you all I know, sir."

He sighed. "So they told you not to come back."

"No one told me anything."

"That's too bad. You would have enjoyed Colonel Chia Pao-yu."

I started. "Who, sir?"

"Chia Pao-yu." His smile escaped. "Do you know him?"

"Only from the Red Chamber. But who is *Colonel* Chia Pao-yu?"

"Generalissimo Chiang Kai-shek's interpreter."

I almost laughed out loud. Ta-ko! Only Ta-ko would have the audacity to work for his number one enemy and assume the name of the hero of an old Chinese novel.

"He would have been your counterpart at the meetings I could not attend," the colonel said.

No wonder Ta-ko had forced me to leave China.

"To avoid any scandal, which might embarrass His Lordship, there will be nothing about this on your record. After the war, if you happen to be around Oxford, knock me up."

And so I was sent back to roar around over the low countries and curdle the milk in cows. But during this part of my tour, the war struck me twice. Each time I was able to reach the Channel before bailing out.

Then suddenly the war was over, and we were still alive, frightened by a future returned to us. What were we going to do? We did not know what existed in the civilian world. One fellow went out to look and returned to sell us life insurance. We were shocked.

Back in Canada, I retreated into the University of Toronto and tried to pick up my life where I had left it five years earlier. Ottawa had promised me a government job in Shanghai when I had my degree. Return to China became the focus of my life.

It was a lonely year. I did not revel in reminiscing about the war. The men with whom I'd had camaraderie were dead or in some other part of the world. With other veterans, I refused to compete with tales of heroism and horror, or lies. With my family and relatives in Chengtu, I was alone. There were Sunday dinners in Rosedale and Forest

Hill, but the incentive was gone on both sides, and the silences were embarrassing. There were too many tables with empty chairs, and the quiet sorrow of those women, young and old, made their excellent food stick in my throat. I refused all hospitality after a party where the elegant, charming people were a postwar tableau. I worried them by saying their clock had stopped. The women tutted me, "poor dear," and the men became annoyed at my littering their path to new and greater profits.

Then one day I met Maggie coming out of Eaton's. She shrieked "David!" and almost knocked me over with her embrace. "When did you arrive in town?"

"About a year ago."

She looked hurt. "Why didn't you call?"

Seeing her classic beauty, I regretted my poor manners. The lines of her face, pastel-soft as a girl, were now bold strokes tracing high cheekbones and a strong chin. Her thinner face so enlarged her wide-set brown eyes, she could have modelled for the bust of Queen Nefertiti. "I thought you were in the States with Tex. Or didn't he make it?"

"Oh, yes," she said vaguely. "He's in China flying for some commercial airline. At least that was the last I heard. He rarely writes."

"I was sorry to read that Sir John died."

"Poor father," she said, with a faint smile. "When the wretched doctors cut off his whisky, he simply lost interest and turned up his toes. Will you come to dinner?"

"Thank you. When?"

"Why not this evening."

Lady Rutherford-Jones had become a barely life-sized porcelain, so fragile I hesitated to take her hand. She peered up at me for so long I thought she had forgotten me and gave my name.

"Oh, I know who you are, David. I'm not senile. I was

just wishing Margaret had married you instead of that appalling American. You're not married, are you?"

"Now, Mother," Maggie said.

"Shush. You'll have a whisky, David?"

"Thank you."

She rang for a maid, saying, "I do so miss the men in here drinking their whisky and smoking—do you smoke cigars, David?"

I started to shake my head, then nodded.

"The humidor is on the desk," she said.

I lit a long Havana, and Lady Rutherford-Jones sniffed with pleasure. Agnes appeared with a whisky tray, and whispered, "Delighted I am you're back safe, Mr. David."

I thanked her, and asked Maggie's mother if I might pour her a drink.

"No, no," she said quickly, "but perhaps I will have a sherry."

"A *small* sherry," Maggie said, which surprised me.

With our drinks in large crystal glasses, Maggie and I sat back to study each other. Though still wide-eyed, her younger look of wonder was gone, as was her pout, which had begged kisses. Instead, her mouth smiled within faint brackets of cynicism. Her castles had been washed away and she stood on higher ground, confident, but without direction or purpose, other than that of all women. Men have the urge to rush toward the death they fear, while women, knowing they will reproduce themselves, feel immortal and are more content. This was Maggie's goal.

With the passing of guests, the long dining room table had shrunk to an intimate oval for the survivors. Lady Rutherford-Jones, no longer lost in future dinners, rewarded my tales of wartime lunacies with bright laughter. I even told them about my meeting Ta-ko in Chungking.

"What is opium like?" Lady Rutherford-Jones asked.

38

Reluctant to admit Ta-ko and I had tried it as boys, I lied. "I don't know. I never smoked any."

"What a pity," she said.

A delicate fillet of sole and chilled bottle of Chateau Haut-Brion Blanc was followed by a saddle of pink lamb with a decanted Chateau Margaux. A bottle of Chateau d'Yquem came with dessert, and I wondered what other treasures lay in Sir John's cellar.

Then out of the corner of my eye, I saw Lady Rutherford-Jones slowly sink until only her chin was above the table. I looked with alarm at Maggie, who tightened her lips. "Mother, the bell is *not* under the center of the table. Why do you want Agnes?"

With her eyes following her invisible feet as they searched for the elusive bell button under the rug, Lady Rutherford-Jones surfaced as slowly as she had submerged. With a look of triumph, she drew herself up regally. "I want Agnes to serve the rest of the wine."

"David can do it. Just a drop for mother. It upsets her tummy."

"Nonsense!" she cried with indignation. "I have the stomach of a horse. Fill it up, David. That's a good boy. Upsets my tummy, indeed."

Maggie and I were talking about mutual friends when Lady Rutherford-Jones said, "And the trumpets sounded on the other side."

I looked quickly at her. "Pardon?"

"And the trumpets sounded on the other side."

Maggie sighed. "Mother swears she heard the trumpets sound the night Father died."

When Maggie and I were alone with our coffee in front of the fire, I said, "That was the first time I've seen your mother take more than one glass of wine." I grinned. "I think she went to bed a little tiddly."

Maggie rolled her eyes. "More than a little, and not from just two glasses of wine."

"You're joking?"

"You didn't know? David, how unobservant can you be? Mother has been a closet tippler for as long as I can remember."

"I knew your father was rarely sober, but I never suspected your mother. Is that why she only said, 'Oh, really?' "

"Of course. By dinner time, she was looped from all the little nips she took to steady her nerves so she could face her guests."

"I thought she loved having dinner parties?"

"She hated them. She only gave them for the excuse to drink."

I burst out laughing and she joined me for a moment, then grew serious. "I wish I could find it as amusing. You have no idea how difficult my life has been."

"How about Alcoholics Anonymous?"

"If I could endure the scandal, it would be a disaster. Mother would invite them all home to dinner, and that would be the end of that AA chapter."

I laughed again, and apologized.

"I'm sorry, too," she said. "Even if I wanted to join Tex in China, I couldn't leave mother."

"What's with you and Tex?"

"We were separated even before he went back to the States. I haven't seen him since. I keep writing for a divorce, and he answers, begging me to join him in China. It's just a ploy. He knows I won't and can't. He's convinced I'm going to inherit a fortune. My lawyers say that as long as he wants me to join him, and sends me a pittance now and then, I can't sue him for desertion. It's all very sordid."

"Was it just another wartime marriage that didn't work?"

She shrugged, hesitated, then her mouth hardened. "He was a phony! A congenital liar. Oil wells, thousand acre ranch, Choate—" She laughed scornfully. "He came off a dirt farm. He was poor white trash!"

The barb stung me. I was surprised by the news, also the insight that within Maggie was Margaret Roxanne Rutherford-Jones—snob. I waited uncomfortably for the blame to be pinned on me.

Though glowering, she tried to reassure me. "Don't look so guilty. It wasn't your fault. I fell in love with him. He took us all in. When we decided to marry on the station rather than have a large Toronto wedding, mother was certain the Burkes would have us struck from the social register. "And father," she gave a bitter snort, "was so anxious to assure T.C. Burke that we were quite proper, he sent some minions down to call on him in Dallas. Only *that* Mr. Burke had no son, so they went to Floresville and found the right one. The nasty man ran them off with a shotgun."

"Well I'm sorry he wasn't up to your pedigree," I muttered, then winced as I realized I had stupidly lit the short fuse on a bomb not three feet away.

And she blew—up, across the room and back, shrieking how dare I call her a snob? "I didn't marry him for money! *He* married *me* for *my* money! He didn't give a damn about me." She took an angry swipe at her tears. "He was unfaithful a week after our honeymoon," she sobbed. " 'What's so damn sacred about sex anyway,' he'd say when I'd have hysterics over his philandering. He—he was straight out of Tobacco Road. He was an amoral animal!"

When she collapsed wailing into a chair, I escaped to the

41

pantry for drinks. On my return her face was dry, but the glass chattered against her teeth. Ashamed to meet her swollen eyes, I studied the Persian rug while she gasped for breath.

"I threatened to take a lover—"

"I'm sorry, Maggie."

"—and he encouraged me. He—"

"I'm sorry, Maggie."

"He was so sincere, I wanted to kill him. *Stop saying you're sorry!*"

"Sorry, I mean—"

"If I hadn't been brought up in this mad household, I would have had the sense to simply go to bed with you or anybody. But no—it was marriage first since I was a child. Nor was it marriage first, then fun. Mother always hinted that wifely duty was rather disagreeable. You made me doubt that and I guess I was just too eager to find out what it was really like." She sighed deeply. "Well, there's no use going on about it."

Mumbling an excuse, I rose to leave, but she said, "Stay," and I sat nervously waiting for the next round. But Maggie was so deep in thought, I felt I could have walked out without her noticing. Finally she came out of her trance wearing a smile that made "oh" echo in my head.

"David, if I can get Aunt Maud to spend the weekend with Mother, I'm going up to close the cottage. Aunt Maud is as mad as Mother, but on the side of temperance. Will you come with me? I could use your help."

All week I was trapped in a rotating debate and each night lofted a conflicting prayer, until I half expected a celestial rebuke: "Make up your mind!" If the old WCTU veteran refused to lush sit her sister, I remained lonely, celibate, but free. If she said yes, I was in; the fantasy replaced sleep. But once in could I ever get out?

I sensed that Maggie was formidable in her need of a husband and children. I foresaw the affair bounded fore and aft by ecstasy and agony. Yin and Yang. By Thursday, cowardice had won and I was rehearsing my excuse when Maggie phoned to say that Aunt Maud was a trooper, and my pragmatist joined the hedonist in cheering.

On Friday afternoon, Maggie picked me up in front of Burwash Hall. Nipple-breasted in a tight sweater, and with her skirt riding up her long thighs as she drove, she talked excitedly, and tossed her loose brown hair when laughing. She sped the big Buick up Yonge Street and, clear of the city, told me there was a flask of cognac in the glove compartment. By the time we reached Honey Harbour, I was singing obscene RAF songs, and Maggie had the hiccups from giggling.

The green taxi boat took us north for almost twenty miles, its wake shattering the reflections of Pre-Cambrian shield islands and their twisted pines. The shuttered cottages stood lonely, and seemed to be listening for the north wind and snow. The Rutherford-Jones cottage had weathered into the landscape. The dock sagged like a nag's back, and winters of ice had left it with a drunken tilt. We stepped gingerly over rotten planks, and in two trips had our supplies in the darkening kitchen, which smelled of the mice who had moved in.

I lit the small wood stove, opened a bottle of Chateau Brane-Cantenac to breathe, and bartended while Maggie gaily made dinner. We ate by candlelight on the screened verandah. The steady southeast wind was warm, and over coffee we listened to the loons calling, and watched the glow in the east bubble up into a harvest moon.

"Let's go for a swim," Maggie said abruptly.

"Skinny?"

She laughed. "Why not. There's no one around to see us."

We followed a flashlight's spot over the warm rock, through the perfume of pines, to a tiny cove at the end of the moon's shaft across the water. We stood a dozen feet apart and, back to back, undressed; Maggie saying, "Don't look." I did when she entered the water: *September Morn* in moonlight.

She shouted, "Come on, it's lovely and warm."

Aware suddenly of the moon aiming a spotlight on my erection, I became too embarrassed to wade in toward her. Afraid of running aground if I dove, I turned and fell in backwards. In the shallow water, I floated with periscope up. Before I could execute the brilliant idea of swimming side stroke, I bumped into Maggie. With great splashings, we groped for footing and each other, and tried to become lovers standing navel-deep in the Georgian Bay. Finally, I took her hand, waded ashore, and hurried her to a bed of moss.

six

I BECAME a regular weekend guest at the Rutherford-Jones. Since they had stopped all entertaining after Sir John died, I was the only man in that enormous house, which had catered for so many decades to men. If Michelin had sent an inspector, the kitchen and cellar would have won two stars, three for Maggie.

In contrast to her nature naked, Maggie was prim when clothed. She thought it improper for us to be seen together in public, which made me a prisoner. At first I filled the days with stratagems to lure her into some secluded room, and overcome her whispered protests by arousing her until we undressed each other with frantic haste. Sometimes, by not wearing underpants, Maggie would seduce me to drag her into a closet for a knee-trembler. At night she was willing and eager for anything.

While Maggie flung off her clothes with one wanton hand, her Presbyterian hand struggled to keep her decent. She resolved the conflict by believing herself the victim of helpless love. When overtaken by guilt, she wanted verbal proof, like Elizabeth Barrett Browning's tedious list of how did I love her.

Instead of leaving our affair as it had begun, a therapeutic toss on the moss, Maggie transmuted it into a classic love. When she did not see us as Tristram and Isolde, we were Antony and Cleopatra or Romeo and Juliet. Her talk of those tragic lovers gave me goose pimples when I became convinced she would one day stretch us both out with a slug of something quick.

Left alone when she shopped or had to attend a tea, I read until bored, paced until exasperated. I studied the Henner, Gainsborough, and doubtful Rembrandt; held long conversations with Bonnie Prince Charles in the aquatint etchings. I made the rounds of silver-framed photographs of Sir John shaking hands with the Prince of Wales, Churchill, and other greats. I snooped into cupboards, opened books, undisturbed except by dusters for half a century. I prowled the cellars, passing the locked wine cave with the obeisance of a priest, and finally talked Agnes into lending me the key. "I won't touch anything," I promised, and she laughed. "Why not?" The key helped until I overdid it one afternoon, and Maggie, with one glance, guessed my prize and demanded it back.

I rarely saw Lady Rutherford-Jones before lunch, usually not until tea, and she always greeted me as if delighted I had just come to call. I wondered how she could avoid knowing I was a satyr chasing her daughter through her halls, and concluded she was innocent. The mind of Lady Rutherford-Jones may have lacked the vastness of Saint Peter's dome, but her convictions were as stoutly supported, and she had no niche for hanky-panky.

Maggie and I talked as lovers do, but only of the past, since we had no foreseeable future together. I told my life story, but refused to listen to Maggie's when it involved Tex. Her account of his betrayals did not put my teeth on edge so much as the vision of them in bed. Had she been as passionate with Tex as she was with me?

"He had a compulsion to philander. As if he could only enjoy sex if it was a conquest. He—"

"Don't tell me about it."

But she had to. "You can imagine the state I was in. First as a bride betrayed, then as the commanding officer of a girl he got into trouble. I was the laughingstock of the Air Force."

"Forget the bastard!"

"I wish I could," she said sadly.

The greatest strain was her notion that if we were not seen out together, she was not being unfaithful. In desperation one Saturday, I said, "Let's go to the football game. We're playing Western."

"You know I can't, Darling. You go."

"Come on Maggie, we're not fooling anybody. I'll bet we're common gossip around town."

"I won't give him that reason for divorce."

"But you want a divorce, dammit! What the hell difference does it make?"

"He would throw everything I called him right back into my face. I won't be put in that position. I won't be put into his class."

One rainy Sunday, she watched me pacing restlessly and cried with startling anger, "Go! Go away! I know you're bored to death with me. *Get out!*"

I hurried to her and she pushed me away, screaming, "Don't touch me!" With sudden tears, she ran from the room. Unable to coax her from her locked bedroom, I waited in misery, then walked dejectedly through the rain back to Vic, where a note on the board said to phone her immediately. She answered sobbing, and begged me to hurry back.

One weekend I arrived to find her strangely agitated. I

47

thought I had annoyed her, but she absolved me. She remained aloof, switching around like an angry cat, and I assumed it was menstrual. Settling down to wait for her to feel better, I told her about some idiocy at school, when she interrupted.

"I had a letter from Tex. He says I don't stand a chance in hell of suing him for desertion. He has copies of all his letters to me."

"Have you no other grounds? How about his adulteries?"

"I have no proof."

"How about yours?"

She was furious. "Don't call me an adulterer!"

"You are, goddammit, whether you like it or not. So am I. Tell him about it and let him sue you for divorce."

"He still wouldn't. Besides, the scandal would kill Mother."

"Maggie, for Christ's sake, do you honestly believe your mother doesn't know we sleep together?"

"Perhaps, but I know she doesn't think there's anything carnal about it. Even if she caught us in the act, she would only think I was trying to keep you warm."

I burst out laughing, and Maggie was forced to smile, then she grew sulky. "I don't know why I worry about a divorce, anyway. You've never promised to marry me if I were free. Have you?"

I was taken aback. "Of course I want to marry you."

"Don't lie. Why should you? This way you have all the fun and games, plus your freedom."

We argued about whether I would or would not, until I became angry, because she was right. I had not thought of marrying her. It was impossible until she got her unlikely divorce. Also, there was my old fear. I was convinced I would never get back to China if I was married.

Still, our love flourished, even though I came to dread

being left alone in that huge house. Some Sundays when I left, I would walk slowly until out of sight, then run happily to the street car on Yonge Street. All week I went contentedly about my school work, missing her more each day, and ran to be with her on Friday night.

Her obsession about our not being seen together made me stubborn about the Senior Ball, and I willfully insisted she go with me. We argued for hours, with Maggie saying, "Take some coed."

I did, and as I steered my lovely young partner through the shuffling throng, I could only think of Maggie. Muttering a lame excuse, I took my date home instead of to a post-dance party, and ran back to the waiting cab. I let myself in with Maggie's key and, finding my bed empty, went to her room. She was reading in bed, and greeted me without a smile, her eyes smoldering. She turned her face away from my kiss, then stopped me as I began to undress. "Go to your own room."

"Will you come?"

"Not tonight. I'm tired."

I pleaded, but she shook her head, until I shrugged and said goodnight. "I'll come if you take a shower," she said.

"What?"

"I can smell her."

I waited so long, I was afraid she had changed her mind, then she entered with a bottle of sherry and two stemmed glasses. She got into bed without removing her tightly belted robe, and sat stiffly as far from me as she could. We sipped the sherry in silence. I had learned not to tempt the storms within her by foolish or facetious remarks.

"Was she pretty?"

"Couldn't compare to you."

She sniffed. "Liar."

After a silence, she asked, "Did you?"

"Did I what?"

"You know what I mean."

"Maggie, I didn't even kiss the girl."

"You still didn't answer my question."

"How could I if I never kissed her?"

"It's been done. There's no connection."

I laughed, and she faced me with great tears splashing from her eyes. "Stop laughing at me! What right have you to come from another woman, and expect me to jump into your bed like a whore? That's what you think of me, isn't it? I'm just a whore! What do you want me to do? Tell me! Suck you off? The price is the same."

Her face wet with tears, she debased herself. The more she ranted, the viler her language. "And you're no better than Tex!" Racked with sobs, she told how Tex would come to her smelling of his musk and of perfume, and force her to submit, laughing at her accusations. "Then one of my girls reported she was pregnant by my own husband, who shrugged and said, 'Pack her off.'"

Gradually, she stopped fighting off my attempts to hold her, and sobbed into my neck until calm. I tucked her in, and stroking her cheek until she fell into a troubled sleep, I became awed by the love and tenderness I felt for her. We were as committed to each other as if our union had been blessed by the Pope.

I spent the summer with them at their cottage as boat boy. While it was common practice to hire a student to look after boats and chores, I doubt if the fiction fooled anyone. Not that it mattered. Their cottage was the only one on a large island, and we rarely saw the neighbours.

It was halcyon. We fished, swam naked in secluded coves, made love on moss, sailed to picnics on deserted islands, canoed up the moon's highway, digested Agnes's meals and Sir John's wines while Lady Rutherford-Jones murmured about her family and England. At night, Maggie would come to my cabin, even when she couldn't, because both of us slept badly when our bodies were not touching in bed.

One day while sunning ourselves on the rock, Maggie suddenly shivered, though no cloud darkened the sun. When I asked what was wrong, her gaze left the horizon and stabbed me with sadness. "Next year you will be in China, and I will be here alone."

Those large brown eyes brimming with despair made me leap up and rush around as if the answer lay under the moss, or behind a crooked pine. What could I do? I could not marry her. I could not take her as my mistress to a country where her husband lived. Not as a lowly civil servant.

Forget China!

I was being forced to choose between my two loves.

"Maggie!"

She absolved me of decision. "Forgive me, Darling. I have no right."

seven

THE approach of Christmas 1947 depressed me. The cheerful letters from my family in Chengtu made me more homesick. China, now only six months away, seemed to recede. I was filled with foreboding, convinced my love for Maggie would prevent my return. I wanted to be with her when we were apart, yet after a few hours together, I grew restless. Love needs a life beyond passion. Codes and mores had made us shut-ins. Adding to my frustration was lack of money. I had five dollars to buy her a Christmas present.

Maggie, with her frightening intuition, brightly suggested we spend a week in New York before Christmas. "We can't stay at the Waldorf, because everyone I know stays there. But if we stay at the—. Oh, there *must* be another hotel. Think of one, David."

I had never been to New York.

"The Ritz-Carlton," she cried happily. "Father used to go there after he had some kind of tiff with the manger of the Waldorf. No one I know stays at the Ritz. We'll fly down. I'll make all the arrangements, send you a ticket, and we'll meet as strangers on the airplane."

"I'll wear a false mustache, dark glasses, and speak with an accent."

She giggled. "You can be Count—"

"Basie."

"In black face?"

"That and a small piano."

"But seriously, Darling, when we get there you'll have to be John Burke."

"Negative."

"I know it's a bore, but all my luggage, identification, checkbook, everything is in my married name. I simply can't change it all."

"And since you'll be paying the tab, I will be a good gigolo and trot along behind as your estranged husband."

"Now please don't get grumpy. It'll be such fun. I have all sorts of shopping to do and we can have breakfast in bed and do anything we like. It'll be like a honeymoon."

"Never thought I'd be a stand-in, or would it be lie-in?"

She ignored my bitterness and burbled with plans. I did appear on the Trans Canada DC-4 Northstar with a mustache, and when I sat next to her, she said quickly, "I'm sorry, but that seat is—" and her gloved hand stifled a shriek of laughter.

It was my first flight since I had left the Air Force, and the memories evoked made me want to fly again. When flying, problems became as remote as the earth, even in war. Attacks were so sudden, so engrossing, there was no time for fear. Then they were gone, and life was again serene.

Most of my operational flights had been low-level sweeps and I came to enjoy hedge-hopping. My wingmen worried I would fly them into the ground, the way I did the ME 109 who got on my tail. While I was free to concentrate on barely missing trees and farm houses, he was distracted by the need to frame me in the circle of his gunsight. Leading him into a pylon turn around an oak, his wingtip caught the ground, and cartwheeled him into a ball of flame. Without gun camera evidence, and with my wingman too busy with the other 109 to be a witness, my claim was denied. The senior officers found it all very amusing, and in the mess would introduce me to transients as "Our fox hunter. Says he's the fox, and ran a Jerry hunter to ground. He wants us to stick a gun camera up the arse of his Spit."

Maggie pressed my hand, and asked the reason for my smile. "Just reminiscing about flying," I said.

"Do you miss it?"

"Not until now."

We checked into the hotel as Mr. and Mrs. John Burke, and settled into a sumptuous suite. Room Service brought a tray of drinks, while Maggie studied a copy of *Cue*, circling the plays we should see. At dusk, we walked to Radio City, admired the huge Christmas tree, and watched the ice skaters. Maggie window shopped on Fifth Avenue and we went to the Press Box for dinner. Back at the hotel, we showered and bathed, and made ourselves cozy in one of the twin beds with a night cap and *The New York Times*.

The next day, I followed Maggie through Saks Fifth Avenue, Bergdorf Goodman, Macy's, Gimbel's, others, and tried to show interest in the endless parade of dresses, hats, slips, suits, and sweaters. Unable to steer her away from the men's departments, I was forced to try on cashmere sweaters and sports jackets.

"Maggie, I have a sweater," I protested.

"*A* sweater. Darling, it looks lovely on you."

"But I don't need two sweaters."

"That's ridiculous," she said and called the clerk.

I became testy about the jacket. "I don't want another.

I have a good Harris Tweed I bought in Scotland during the war."

She sighed and let it go, but I suspected she would return without me the next day and buy the damn thing. "Maggie, please don't buy me stuff. I wouldn't mind if I could afford to buy you presents, but I can't. So don't. Please."

She thought me unreasonable and apologized for dragging me through all the shops. "Let's stop off someplace for a drink."

By lunch, I was so exasperated with shopping that Maggie suggested I return to the hotel for a nap or something. "But do stay in the hotel so I can find you when I get back."

"Don't worry," I grumbled, "I can't afford to go anywhere I can't sign your name."

Maggie blushed and slipped me some money, which only increased my pique. After lunch we were both glad to part, and I walked back to the hotel, cursing the parcels and my lot. Dumping the bags on our bed, I hurried down to the bar and had just ordered a drink when a voice shouted, *"High-pockets!"*

I peered around and, after a second shout, made out a man waving wildly from a dim corner. As he struggled to get out from behind the table and past his woman companion—who refused to move—I walked over.

Tex Burke.

"Highpockets!" He pumped my hand, spilling part of my drink. "You old sonofabitch! Sit down. Sit down. Christ, it's good to see you. Pull up a chair. Dawn, move your ass, and give my old buddy here some room."

When my eyes adjusted, I saw he was fleshier, almost plump, but his tan face was still handsome. He wore an expensively tailored silk gabardine suit, and a large diamond sparkled on his ring finger.

"I heard you were in China," I said.

"I am. I am. I'm just home on three months leave. Just brought Dawn here up from Dallas to do a little Christmas shopping. How the hell are you? You're looking great. What are you doing?"

I told him and said, "I hear you're flying over there."

"That's affirmative. After the war, I took my discharge in a place called Calcutta, in India, and went up to a place called Shanghai, in China, and got me a flying job with an airline called China Air Transport. Know what they pay? A thousand bucks a month base pay for sixty hours and ten bucks an hour overtime. And guess what we log a month? Hundred and fifty hours, and then some. What with night bonus and extra hazard pay, I'm knocking down over two grand a month, all tax free. And let me tell you, it costs almost nothing to live in this place called Shanghai. You should see the apartment I got with three servants who'd do anything for me. Hell, they'd wipe my ass if I wanted. What a country!"

"Tex," I said, seething with envy, "I grew up in China."

"Honey," Dawn moaned.

"So you did. How come you never went back?"

"Honey?"

I waited for him to answer her, and when he ignored her, I said, "I am as soon as I get my degree. I have a job waiting for me. I'll be trade commissioner in Shanghai. Well, assistant trade commissioner."

"Honey, when're we going to eat? Ah'm hungry."

"Hey, that's great," Tex cried. "We'll see each other. Soon as—"

"Honey, Ah'm right starving."

"What?"

"Ah'm hungry. You promised we'd eat right away."

"Okay, okay." He snapped his fingers at a waiter. "Hey,

boy." He winked at me. "That's what we call all the slopey servants over there in China."

"Yes sir?"

"Bring a menu. The little lady here's a mite hungry."

"I'm sorry, sir, but we don't serve meals in the bar. The dining room upstairs is still open."

"I'm busy here with my friend. Bring a menu."

"I'm sorry sir."

"Get the manager."

The waiter left and Tex went on. "Soon as I finish my leave, I'm going back via a place called Karachi, Pakistan. I'm going to ferry a DC-three over." He bounced with sudden inspiration. "Hey, when's your college finished?"

"May or early June."

"Shit. I'm going the end of January. I need a copilot, and—"

The manager bowed toward Tex. "Is there something you wanted, sir?"

Tex removed his cigar. "Yeah, I want a menu."

As the manager repeated what the waiter had said, Tex dug a roll of bills from his pocket, peeled off a twenty, and handed it to him. "Now how about a menu?"

"I think it can be arranged."

Stuffing the cigar into a triumphant smile, Tex winked at me. "Never fails. Listen, the hell with that government job. Come back with me as copilot. I can get you a job flying with any of the airlines in China. There's three of 'em, and they're all crying for good drivers. And let me tell you something, Highpockets. The money you make flying is nothing. Nothing to the real dough you can make out there. China is as fucked up as Hogan's goat. A package here, a parcel there, and oh, how the money rolls in." Snapping his fingers, he sang off key, "Oh, everybody's doing it, doing it, doing it."

57

The waiter dealt out menus, and Tex asked, "Want some chow, Highpockets?"

"I've had lunch, thanks."

Dawn, a baby-faced doll with platinum hair, handed Tex her menu without looking at it. "Ah just want a big steak, Honey, with fries and trimmings, and something to drink."

"Wine?"

She nodded as if too famished to speak.

"The little lady here will have the thickest steak you got, and you heard her. Bring her a bottle of the best red wine you got, and bring my friend here and me another drink. What're you drinking, Highpockets? Hey, where you going?" he said to the waiter.

"To get you a wine list, sir."

"Never mind, just bring what I ordered. Whisky, Highpockets?"

I nodded.

"And two whiskies. That's Scotch to you," he said to the waiter.

He grinned happily at me. "Wait'll you see when he brings the wine, Highpockets. You'd be surprised how many people don't know you're supposed to sample the wine first to see if it's okay. Did you know that? Bet you didn't."

"I'd heard about it."

"What do you say, Highpockets? Just you and me in a plush DC-three sashaying half way around the world as first class as the Aga Khan himself. Just think of the you-know-what we'll get. It'll be like old times. Come on, what do you say?"

Yin and Yang.

I stared at him as if seeing an unexpected rescuer. Home to China, and not as a dull trades commissioner. To fly again. To sit in a cockpit instead of an office. To travel all over China instead of staying in Shangai. And the money. Three times what the government would pay me. The freedom. The fun. As Tex said, 'Like old times.' To be as young and foolish as we had been early in the war.

"Are you serious?" I asked.

"Would I shit you?"

"Yes."

He laughed. "Okay, but not this time."

"You're on."

He yahooed.

The waiter showed him a ten year old bottle of Chateau Margaux, and suggested we not drink it for a half hour. But Tex was too excited about my going with him, and tasted it absently. He ordered more drinks, and while Dawn sawed into her huge steak, he told anecdotes about China.

"Honey, can Ah have some of that there wine?"

Without interrupting his tale, he filled her glass. She sipped it and wrinkled her nose. "Sour."

I asked to taste it. "It's not sour." It was exquisite.

"Well, it ain't sweet. Honey, can I have a Coke instead?"

The waiter rolled his eyes in horror, and removed the bottle when Tex insisted he change it for a Coke.

"Hey, Highpockets? Remember Maggie?"

"Oh, Christ," I whispered.

Tex looked concerned. "What's the matter?"

How could I tell Maggie? Leaving her was bad enough, but to leave with the man she hated. Oh, Jesus.

"You're not sore at me for marrying her, are you? I mean, she was your girl."

"What? Oh, no. No. I was in no position to marry her."

"Good. I thought you might be sore. You ever see her up there in Toronto?"

"I ran into her once or twice."

"She's a great broad, but—well, it didn't work out. We

59

busted up before I transferred to the U.S. of A. Haven't seen her since. She writes for a divorce, but being married to a broad who keeps out of your hair stops you from making the same mistake a second time." He jabbed a thumb at Dawn. "If you know what I mean."

As if Maggie had overheard us, a page boy entered carrying a telephone. "Call for Mister John Burke."

Before I could move, Tex shouted, "Over here, boy."

The page boy plugged in the phone, and accepted Tex's dime tip with contempt. Tex answered, "Captain Burke speaking," and became pale. "You got the wrong Burke, Lady." He hung up with a nervous laugh. "Speak of the devil. That broad on the phone said, 'I'm back, Darling.' You know, I could have sworn it was Maggie."

He was scared of her! Then, so was I. Before the page, I had decided how to deceive her, how to get to China without telling her about Tex. I had phrased the promise I hoped would placate her.

"Back to business," Tex said, and told me how to get a commercial pilot's license by presenting my Air Force log book. We traded addresses, and he said he would confirm the job in a week. "The copilot gets eight hundred bucks for the ferry flight. You finished, Baby?"

I noticed we were both watching the entrance.

"We got to go back to Dallas tonight," Tex said.

Dawn wailed, "Tonight? But, Honey, ah ain't hardly bought a thing yet."

"You can get all you need in Dallas. I got to get back and square Highpockets away with the ferry people."

We parted in the bar, and in our room I found Maggie sitting quietly, staring at the wall.

"Hey, what's the matter?"

"The strangest thing just happened. I had you paged, and the man who answered said I had the wrong Burke. But it was Tex. David, I swear it was Tex."

A few days later, I told Maggie I had a business appointment. I spent the afternoon in a movie and when I returned she wanted to hear all about it. When I refused to say, her eyes began to smoulder. She came to me, for a kiss, I thought, and sniffed my neck.

"What the hell are you doing?"

"Have you been with a girl?"

I pushed her away indignantly.

"Where were you?"

"Okay. I might as well tell you now. I had heard about an office down here that recruits pilots for an airline in China. The other day, while you were shopping, I dropped in, more out of curiosity than anything else. When they heard I spoke Chinese, they asked me to fill out an application. Today, I had an interview. That's all."

"You're going to fly in China? David, what about your degree? Your civil service job?"

"The hell with my civil service job. Maggie, this airline job would pay three times as much."

"But it's dangerous!"

"Nonsense. Now sit down and listen. If Tex won't divorce you, and I go to Shanghai as a civil servant, there is no way you can join me. Civil servants are not allowed to live in sin. But if I go over as an airline pilot, I'll probably run into Tex. If I can't talk him into divorcing you, the hell with him. I'll send for you and we'll simply live together."

It worked.

eight

ON my way to Fort Worth, Texas, I could not keep from smiling, while at the same time guilt made me clench my fists. I *did* love Maggie, yet how glad I was to be free. If not for Tex, I would probably be commuting between some job on Bay Street and a pregnant Maggie, instead of on a flight to adventure and home.

Ta-ko always claimed China was not my home; that I had only lived a more Chinese life than most foreigners. "You have no ancestors covered by the land you know," he had said in Chungking. "You do not know the land covering your ancestors."

China *was* home. Every other place was a way station. I had not seen my parents for nine years, and not too often for years before, yet I was drawn to them by the same atavistic warmth that makes a lover nuzzle his mistress' breast. We were strangers, my parents and I, but they knew me as the child who might have the clue to help me understand the man he became. I was being nostalgic, but certainly China in turmoil would be my crucible and test whatever I thought myself to be.

Which was what? The honest, God-fearing, upright,

hard working stereotype desired by parents? No. But neither was I dishonest. I respected their God, if kept at a distance. Upright? Any attractive woman could tilt me, in which position I probably worked hardest. I was neither/-nor. Ta-ko was right. I did live in a twilight zone. My love for Maggie was the strongest commitment of my life, yet I was able to leave her. My excuse was China, which Ta-ko said I would leave. "In thy father's house are many mansions," he had said, "and you will live in the one most comfortable." If true, I was a dilettante in the art of life. But if so, would I have such strong feelings for China? It filled my dreams, aimed my plans.

Aside from China and Maggie, I had no list of hates and loves. In the war, I did not want to kill, yet I had, and I mourned the death of comrades with a flip toast instead of tears. Nor did I fear my own death. If it came, it came. But I was not totally indifferent. I wanted to find Ta-ko, feeling he had my key. He could unlock my clockworks and rewind the springs by admitting I was his brother and China my home.

Tex met me at the airport. He was dapper in gray flannels and a gaudy silk sports shirt; jaunty, delighted to have me in his country, and proud of Fort Worth. "This was some boom town during the war."

Fort Worth looked as if it had been nailed up in a hurry by weekend carpenters and was now held together only by its cat's cradle canopy of power lines. Our motel was on the strip, near the desolate, almost deserted, aircraft plants. Most of the bars, finance offices, and used car lots were closed. At night their dead neon signs were like missing teeth in a weary whore's smile.

The bar we went to that evening was like a dusty relic preserved in some pathetic war museum. The missing squares of acoustic tile made the ceiling look like a huge crossword puzzle begun and never finished. The cheap plywood walls were splintered and peeling, and the bar stools creaked. The only substantial object, still oiled and polished, was the cash register. The bartender, a grizzled veteran of the years when the place was jammed full every night, kept muttering, "You should have been here then."

Peace seemed to have left the people of Fort Worth with a bitter taste. Their eyes were as empty as their wallets, and the only glimmer was resentment for having lost their Camelot.

"Don't you worry none," said the older of the only other two men in the bar. "We gonna fight them fucking Russians soon and these here plants'll be hopping agin."

The younger, his meaty shoulders hunched sullenly over his beer, slid me a mean look. "Sheet, by the time them fuckin' Yanks in New Yawk wise up to what's gotta git done, Ah'll be too old to enjoy all the fuckin' we used to git."

But the older man was wiser and optimistic. "It'll come. It's gotta come. We can't afford not to."

The one in the dirty T-shirt kept his angry eyes on me. "Was you in the war, Yank?"

Tex sized him up with one glance, and drawled, "We was all in the war."

"Wasn't talkin' to you, Cracker. Was you, Yank?"

"He's no Yank," Tex said softly. "He's a Canuck. Canada. Ever hear of it?"

"I heered of it, Cracker. Don't make no fuckin' difference. He's a fuckin' nawthanah."

Tex measured the red neck, calculated the strength of the older man, then eyed the bartender, whose sinister leer tipped the scales. He picked up his change, and slid off the stool. "Night, Gents."

64

"Motha fuckin' Yank!"

Outside, Tex grinned. "Too bad there was three of 'em. One less and we'd have had some exercise."

On our way back to the motel, Tex said, "Let's hunt up some ass."

"Not tonight." After my last night with Maggie, I felt I would never desire a woman again.

Tex had put in a supply of bourbon, and as we sat drinking and talking, I snapped my fingers. "Just remembered. I think I fell into a deal for us."

His eyes became hooded. "Yeah?"

"One of the guys at school told his father about my going to China, and it seems his father had a friend who is president of a company in Buffalo."

"So?"

"It seems this company has bought the engineering rights for the C-forty-six from Curtiss, and they own an airfield full of surplus forty-sixes."

When I went to refill my glass, he shouted, "Go on, for Christ's sake."

But I had seen the greed in his eyes and wanted to torment him for the pain he had caused Maggie. I made the drink slowly, returned to my chair, and after a careful sip, grimaced with doubt. "Ah, hell, it's no good."

He became alarmed. "What's no good?"

"That deal."

"You're not cutting me in." He squinted with suspicion.

"It's no good."

"Let me decide." He had always had a low opinion of my affinity for money. "Stop fucking around, Highpockets. Copilots are a dime a dozen. Cut me in, or you'll only see China as a trade commissioner."

"Well, this aircraft company in a place called Buffalo,

that's in New York State," I grinned, but he was too intent for the jibe. "This aircraft company in Buffalo has acquired the—"

"You said that, goddammit! Go on. What's the deal?"

"This aircraft company has a lot of surplus Curtiss Commandos, you know, the aircraft you flew on the Hump. Now this particular aircraft is used extensively in the Orient, and—"

He glared with amazement. "What are you pulling? I just came from there, for Christ's sake. Don't tell me what they're flying in China."

"That's right. I forgot. Now where was I?"

"You son of a bitch," he hissed, still uncertain of my motive.

"Well, to cut a long story short, I spoke on the phone to this aircraft company. I think they're called American Air Products. Anyway, they wanted to know if I would entertain the offer of acting as sales agent for C-forty-sixes and spare parts in China."

"Good God!" he whispered, then demanded, "What did you say?"

"I'd think about it."

He screamed, *"Think about it!* Jesus everloving Christ. Three airlines in China all flying forty-sixes, all looking for more, all desperate for spare parts, and you'll *think* about it? God Almighty. CNAC! I know CNAC plans to buy ten surplus old crates in California. How much do they want?"

"Who?"

"I'll kill you one day."

"Forty thousand a copy."

"Jesus! Our cut?"

"Five percent."

"Holy Mother. I know I can switch CNAC. Ten planes at forty per. Maybe a hundred thou in spare parts. One half of that big one. Twenty-five thousand bucks commission! And that's only CNAC. Where can we reach this guy?"

"I think I have his name and phone number somewhere."

"Don't lose it," he said coldly.

"Just a minute," I said, unable to resist a final needle. "Who said anything about we? They asked *me* to be their sales representative."

He was beyond fooling. "No split, no China."

"Who needs you? With this deal, I can take myself to China."

He nodded gravely. "But can you take yourself out of Texas?"

Recalling the bully boy in the T-shirt, I knew he meant it.

Our Orient Airways DC-3, which Temco had converted to a plush airliner from a surplus C-47, had been promised for the next day. When Tex phoned the chief engineer early in the morning, he was told they had engine trouble, and to stand by. After three days of delays, Tex was in a rage, sulking in bed, and worrying about American Air Products, who were waiting for us to come to Buffalo to sign a sales contract.

"Call 'em and tell 'em—"

"I did."

"Did you tell 'em I was your partner?"

"Relax."

He tossed angrily on the bed. "Jesus. But let me tell you something, Highpockets. On this trip now, we're not going to rush, y'hear? I don't care how many days we got to sweat out the weather, we ain't flying unless it's Ceiling and Visibility Unlimited. CAVU. Got that?"

After drumming that refrain of caution into me, Temco released the aircraft, and without a flight test we took off at dusk into a three hundred foot ceiling with forecast thunderstorms between us and St. Louis. What a ride.

The next day's flight to Washington was not much better, where we stayed overnight because of a snow storm in New York. In the morning, I was surprised when Tex filed a flight plan for Roosevelt Field, Long Island, instead of Buffalo.

"How come?" I asked. "Buffalo is as close. They've been waiting four days for us."

"We have to go to New York first."

Since he was the captain and responsible for the aircraft, I dropped it. Besides, I was too excited to argue because Tex had said I could fly the leg from the left seat. Handling the controls again after over two years was a thrill, and my landing at Roosevelt Field was so smooth I blushed from pride and Tex's compliment.

A cab took us to the Garden City Hotel, a huge brick pile with large, old fashioned rooms, where all afternoon Tex was quiet, disturbed by something.

"This route is crazy!" he finally blurted. "Flying the North Atlantic, over Greenland to Iceland in February is crazy! They should have routed us via the Azores. With those extra cabin tanks, we've got more than enough fuel."

After an almost silent dinner, he said, "Okay, I've made up my mind. I'm going back to Washington tomorrow. I'll take the shuttle out of LaGuardia, and go down there to see if I can clear us via the Azores. I'm not about to cross that North Atlantic this time of the year."

"Why didn't you think of that yesterday when we were in Washington?"

"I can't think of everything!"

"Why don't we go back in our own bird?"

"Because tomorrow you got to go to New York, down to the surplus joints, down on Canal Street, I think, and buy us some cold weather Arctic clothes, just in case I don't get us cleared to the Azores. Because if we gotta go the northern route and that Rube Goldberg hot water heating system craps out, all we can do with our balls is sell 'em cheap to Birdseye as prairie oysters."

The next morning, we took the Long Island Rail Road and Tex left at Jamaica to catch a bus to LaGuardia, while I went in to Penn Station. After missing a subway change and landing in Brooklyn, I arrived at Canal Street, where a bitter wind blew from river to river. I browsed through the surplus stores, fascinated by all the junk. One sold clothing and I bought us each a heavy parka, knee-high fur-lined Arctic boots, and thick mittens.

Back in the hotel by three, I put in a person-to-person call to Maggie, and heard Agnes tell the operator that she was not at home. I left word for her to call back and lay down to wait. A knocking woke me and when I opened the door Tex burst in as if escaping a storm. He flung his coat angrily into a corner. "Where's the booze?"

It was eight o'clock, and he was as wound up as any traveller after a long day. When he had his drink, he asked if I had bought the winter gear.

"Yeah. You mean it's over the pole?"

"That shithead running the ferry service! You'd of thought I was asking for the moon. 'We've sent all our flights via Greenland and Iceland,' he says. 'At this time of year?' I ask. 'Well, no,' he says. 'You're fucking right,' I says. 'Don't you think the Azores are better?' Sure. But do you think I could get him off his ass to change the papers? Hell, no. 'Impossible,' he screams. 'It would take weeks.' And you should have heard him when I said we had to detour to Buffalo. 'You're only cleared from Presque Isle to Goose Bay. You can't fly across Canada.' "

"He's full of shit."

"That's what I told him. Then he screams there isn't time. Orient Airways is desperate for the airplane. We can't waste the time. We have no right to deviate from the flight plan for personal reasons. We have no right to put ten extra minutes on those engines. You should have heard him. He went on and on."

"But what about the contracts? Those guys are still waiting up there for us. I'd better phone. Hell, it's too late now."

"It's okay. I sent 'em a wire saying we couldn't get there."

"Guess we blew that one," I said.

"Negative. I said we'd write 'em from Shanghai."

"What the hell good will that do?"

"Plenty. We just won't send them an order until they send us the contracts or a letter spelling out our commission. Hell, a letter is as good as any contract."

When I did not answer, he became agitated. "Well, don't you agree, goddammit?"

I shrugged. "Sounds reasonable. Hey, want to see the stuff I bought?"

With a slow smile, Tex dropped into a chair. "Yeah. Show me the stuff you bought, Highpockets."

nine

ONE of Tex's lectures was on our need for early starts, so we would not be caught flying at night. When the alarm rang at six, he yelled, "Shut it off!"

"You told me to set it for six."

"Shut it off!"

He refused to get up until ten. By the time we bought food, and loaded the DC-3, it was mid-afternoon before we took off from Roosevelt Field, and dark when we landed at Presque Isle, Maine, on a U.S. Air Force base, closed to civilian aircraft.

"But we were cleared for here," Tex told the angry operations officer.

"I know you were," the captain raged, "and you're the sixth goddamn Orient DC-three that's landed here, and we've had to boot them off just like I'm booting you off. Can't that goddamn outfit that handles these ferry flights read? We've raised hell with them after every one of you guys land here and still you come. You're supposed to land at Houlton."

"Where the hell's Houlton?"

"You flying from here to India without maps?"

"How come you didn't stay with Bob Hope?" Tex sneered, and we returned to our aircraft. Houlton was easier to find on the chart than it was from the air at night in a snow storm. Without an instrument letdown chart for Houlton, we had to fly under an overcast barely higher than the low hills. After a nerve-racking search, we picked up the rotating beacon, then had trouble seeing the runway lights. The tower was closed and we had to guess the wind direction. Tex made a tight circuit and brought her in like a fighter. The high snow-banked runway was slippery, and we almost ran off the end. Before taxiing back, we sat quietly at the controls.

Mimicking Tex, I said, "Now let me tell you something. We're gonna git up early every morning. Y'hear? There's one thing we're not going to do on this here flight and that is take off late and git caught having to fly at night. Got that?"

"Shut your fucking mouth!"

Convinced the flight had brought him religion, I believed his bedtime ranting about an early start. But he slept in again, and by the time he got up and we cleared customs it was another mid-afternoon takeoff. We picked up Sept Iles on the north shore of the St. Lawrence River by its lights. The night, however, was clear and the moon full.

A cockpit at night—lit only by the glow of instruments —is a cozy platform. Over the empty snow, bluish in the moonlight, we seemed suspended within an inverted bowl of stars with aurora borealis flickering along the northern rim.

"We got stars like this down in Texas," he said.

And suddenly I saw my dilemma. If Tex was still acting the scion and I let slip I knew the truth, he would know that Maggie had told me and suspect I had seen her more than casually. Husbands I had cuckolded always made me nervous, especially when cooped up in a cockpit with one. My only hope was to make him admit to the charade.

"Is your father still in aircraft?" I asked.

"He got laid off like everyone else."

"I thought he owned the aircraft plants."

"*Who?*"

"Your father, T. C. Burke."

He looked at me as if I had gone crazy, then guffawed. "I'd forgotten. Choate, you know. Pip, pip and all that." He laughed, shaking his head. "What suckers you were. It was all down home brag where everybody knows you're full of shit. But you saps fell for it. I couldn't believe it. At Christmas in Toronto I just wanted to see how far I could con all those smug bastards. I never thought I'd see 'em again. Then where do I end up but at Mountain View Bomber and Gunnery School and there's Maggie hotter than a herd of heifers in heat. When it's no go without wedding bells and they all think I'm rich enough for her, I find the bullshit has dealt me a royal flush."

"I don't understand," I lied.

He studied the instruments, steady under the control of the automatic pilot. "Then let me tell you what I come from," he said grimly. "I got back to the States just after my older brother, Louie, got killed in Italy, so I went on down home."

He lapsed into silence, common while flying, and you know the hours to fill. I admired the stars, wondering who and what was out there.

"My old man," he said.

We watched borealis raise a rippling curtain.

"You should have heard him. The new refrigerator. Hell, the first one they'd ever had. Louie had paid for it. His new secondhand pickup truck. Louie had paid for it."

I switched fuel tanks.

73

"Louie this. Louie that. One night, I slam down my beer. 'What's the matter?' I say to him. 'You sore I didn't get killed, so you'd get another lousy ten grand?' He looked at me as if wishing some of my brothers was home. When we were kids, he'd get two of the bigger boys to hold the one he aimed to punish. If he'd hit you once, or twice, and let it go at that, I wouldn't have minded so much. But he was a mean bastard. He'd slap your face, gentle like, one side, then the other, all the time talking about how you thought you was better'n he was, and you never knew when that beef-knuckle fist of his would almost tear your head off."

He tuned in the Goose Bay radio beacon, and we watched the ADF needle swing slowly up to almost zero. Right on course.

"I almost killed him once. I was rabbit hunting and came on him fixing a fence. For I don't know how long I lay there in the bushes holding a bead on his head. Still don't know why I didn't pull the trigger."

There were no lights on the ground.

"He died just before Christmas."

A meteor slit the sky, and the night healed.

"I was in Dallas, but I never went down for the funeral."

He caged and recaged the artificial horizon. "Still acting up. Reckon we'd better get us a new one this stop. I sent my mother some money, though."

I thought about Maggie, wondering why she had never phoned me back in New York. I had called her from Houlton, but she was out again.

"Did you ever see much of Maggie up there in Toronto?" Tex asked.

"I told you. I ran into her a couple of times on the street."

After a long silence, he said, "That's too bad."

I did not answer.

Lights winked faintly on the horizon. Goose Bay.

74

"You missed out on a good piece of ass," he said.

"That's a hell of a way to talk about your wife."

"In name only. Somebody is getting a piece of her. Never knew a woman to save it. Could have been you."

At Goose Bay, we were given bunks in the transient crew barracks, and the batman woke us at ten instead of six as requested. Tex was furious.

"Look outside," the batman said. "It's snowing to beat hell."

"Look, Buster," Tex shouted. "I say if we fly or don't fly. Not you."

"Captain, the field is closed. Nobody is getting off today." He walked away, muttering, "And here I thought I was doing them a favour."

Tex stayed angry all day, and lay on his bunk cursing the weather, Canada, and Labrador for being the frozen asshole of the world. "Call weather."

"I did ten minutes ago."

"Call 'em again."

I returned to report, "Same as before. Goose Bay is five hundred feet with a half mile visibility, drifting snow on runways, field closed."

"What about Greenland?"

"The same. Zero, zero. That big front hasn't moved."

"Keflavik?"

I shrugged. "Why worry about Iceland weather when we can't get out of here?"

"Because as soon as this crap lifts, we're going. The hell with Greenland. We'll go on to Keflavik. It'll mean a ten, eleven hour drive, but with those fuselage tanks, we got more than enough range."

"Now let me tell you something," I said, mimicking him. "We ain't gonna rush. Y'hear? If there's one cloud in that old sky, we're gonna sit tight."

"Don't get smartassed, Highpockets," he said sullenly. "You want to get to China? Then let me do the flying. I been at it a bit longer than you. If we don't figure all angles, and move at the first break, hell, we could be here until summer, not that there'd be much improvement."

"But you said—"

"Fuck what I said!"

He was a paradox. He lived Yin and spoke Yang, and there was no connection. He had no faith in words. Perhaps where he had grown up words were used mostly for abuse and bragging. Promises proved to be lies. Words must never have saved him from a beating. The rhetoric in church was a droning heard by no one, because it bore no relationship to their harsh life in a dry land stretching from horizon to horizon.

Unable to put a call through to Maggie, I wrote her a letter of love and loneliness. I tried to nap, but Tex remained a wakeful martinet who kept ordering me to check the weather or the new artificial horizon they were installing. By evening I was tired of him.

At 2100 hours, the field opened. It was still snowing, but the wind had dropped, and the runways stayed plowed. When they forecast Greenland to be clear by 0600, we prepared to leave at two in the morning. While Tex did the preflight check, I filled the water tank for the steam heating system, which we had to drain at each stop. The tank was up in the starboard wheel nacelle and the quantity was a mystery. Temco had neglected to brief us on the strange heating system, and every airline mechanic we asked enroute either said we were crazy, there was no such system, or told us a different number of quarts. Hurried by the danger of the water freezing before we could get the engine started, I swore at all the advice. Instead of quarts, the damn tank held two gallons.

We were airborne at 0310 and as the gear thumped up, the pipes suddenly burst, filling the cockpit with steam. I had overfilled the tank and left no room in the system for expansion. With every window frosted over, we were forced to fly instruments by hand, because the automatic pilot quit when the inside air temperature matched the forty below outside. The cold soaked through our Arctic clothing and stole the heat from the galley stove. Soup remained cylinders in the pot, and we had to eat deep frozen chocolate bars.

We scraped the windshield clear, but there was nothing to see. Clouds covered the stars and below was the black Labrador Sea. We reached Greenland at dawn and crossed the tip of the desolate five thousand foot thick icecap with mountain peak islands. Tex had decided to continue to Iceland, despite the cold and my chattered protests. "Look, Highpockets, there won't be anybody down there who can fix this lousy heating system. Let's get it over with."

"How lu-long do you figure?"

"Four, maybe five hours."

"I'll nu-never make it."

At *Point of No Return*, Tex switched on the long-range fuel tanks installed in place of the first four seats on either side of the cabin. The cross-valves, lying on the cockpit floor with its branching lines, leaked. Tex chewed angrily on his cigar, while I tried to tighten the hoseclamps with a knife since we had no screwdriver.

"No good," I said. "We'd better shut it off."

"Negative. We can't make it on the regular tanks."

"Then how about shutting off your cigar? With these fumes, this crate is a bomb."

Grumbling, he ground it out and chewed on the stub. We took half-hour turns at the controls and, when not flying, jogged up and down the cabin.

The sky and water were the same leaden colour, and the icebergs and cumulus clouds began to look alike. They became faces. There was Maggie, her smile changing into a look of hatred. A giant lay on his side. And over there, a beggar; a Chinese beggar with a crippled leg. I looked for Ta-ko.

"Hey!" Tex yelled, running into the cockpit. "Where the hell are you going?"

We were in a spiral dive, heading back to Greenland. The cold and fumes had given me vertigo.

For two hours we flew by dead reckoning. Our tail bearing had faded and we were beyond the range of Keflavik. Our compass, off by a thirty degree variation, was erratic. If our gyroscopic directional indicators froze, we were lost —dead. We put on our headsets and listened intently for the Keflavik signal, but the radio only crackled.

"Shouldn't we p-pick it up soon?" I was chattering from the cold and anxiety.

"By and by. Sure you can't crank up that stove and cook some soup?"

I shook my head.

Tex, squatting on his heels in his seat, remained impassive, disturbed only by my not letting him light the cigar he chewed. "You know, we could be thirty, forty degrees off course, and never know it. We could miss Iceland, go right past it, and never see it. Wonder if we have enough fuel to get to Norway or Scotland. Hand me my calculator." He worked his circular slide rule and looked up with a grin. "You know, we might just make it if we had to."

"Nu-never," I said, shivering violently.

"Sure. Here, look."

I could only shake my trembling head. "I-I don't mean the bucket won't mu-make it, I m-m-mean me."

He took the controls. "Run."

I trotted up and down the cabin aisle on numb feet. When they tingled, I returned to my seat. "Anything yet?"

"Negative."

According to our ETA, we were an hour and a half out.

"Do you really think we could be that far off course?" I asked.

"You bet." He was so cheerful I wondered if he had a death wish, but it was simply confidence. He knew we would reach some shore eventually. In contrast to his irritable, often sullen nature on the ground, in the air Tex was relaxed, calm in emergencies, and happy. He talked about Maggie and admitted he had treated her badly. "But, shit, it wasn't near as bad as she made out. Sure, I had the odd piece of nooky on the side, but this damn little WD that got knocked up blamed me. Hell, half the station had laid her but she told Maggie I had done it. The bitch."

"What was wrong with Maggie?"

"You mean in the sack? Nothing."

"Then why did you chase the others?"

He grinned. "You gotta keep your hand in. But that was only part of it. All them Toronto snobs looked down their noses at me, just like in Texas, when they knew I was poor. To them, I was no better'n a nigger. But I'll show 'em. I'm gonna be rich one day."

"Is that your aim in life?"

"You bet your ass. I know what it's like to go hungry. I know what it's like to be treated as no account white trash. The fucking cops are always on your back and any fat cat who wants, spits in your face. No sir. If I have to steal, bribe, and kill like they do to get rich, I'll do it. I'll fuck anybody, including you, even though you're the best friend I've ever had."

It was a fair warning, and I should have refused his order that I pay our expenses. "Easier that way," he had said.

"You just keep track, and I'll settle up with you in Shanghai." But he shrewdly knew I was too casual to keep a record.

It reminded me of Ta-ko and my destiny to avoid fools but suffer scoundrels. For all the pain he had caused me as a boy, Ta-ko was exciting. He always had a plan for adventure or mischief. Yet I think I hated him as much as I loved him. When he was in one of his dark Yin moods, he would tease and taunt me, then gloat at my tearful rage. When he was happy, he could keep me laughing at his antics until I wet my pants.

The Chinese say that in the presence of a good man think all the time how you may learn to equal him. In the presence of a bad man, turn your gaze within.

Unfortunately, I was never long in the presence of my father, a good man. To equal him whenever I was, I would have had to learn all the ancient characters he was translating. In the presence of a bad man, my usual company, it would have been folly to turn my gaze within for even a moment.

In my childhood, good boys like my prissy cousins bored me, except when Ta-ko and I made them victims of some prank. Their parents, smug in the belief that God had chosen them to bring Christ to the heathen, infuriated me by their patronizing of the Chinese. Good missionaries like my father, who over the years became more and more Chinese, were too absorbed to do more than pat me absently on the head.

With the hand pressing the right phone to his ear, Tex raised a thumb in triumph. "We got her!" Gradually, I heard the faint thread of sound in the static. "Now, if the ADF ain't frozen solid," he said, "we got it made."

Anxiously, we watched the motionless radio compass needle.

"Move, you bastard. Twitch!"

I cried, "Don't curse it, for Christ's sake!"

"Nice needle. Beautiful needle. *Move*, you prick!"

We searched the horizon for signs of land, but there was only water, icebergs, and scattered clouds. An hour out, the needle was still stationary.

Tex looked mournfully at his unlit cigar. "I don't mind so much if we miss her, but three more hours without a smoke, and I'm up the wall."

"Shhh." I swore I had seen the needle tremble. "Tex!"

He yahooed. "There she goes."

Arthritically, the needle worked its way up to 350 degrees.

"How's that for navigating, Highpockets? Right on the nose. Sure I can't light up, just to celebrate?"

"Negative, you dehydrated Texas wetback."

"Hey, remember the time in Montreal?" Shouting reminders and details, we retold old adventures in dialogue and duet, and wiped away tears from laughter and fatigue. We were warmed by camaraderie and the joyful sight of distant clouds on Icelandic peaks.

ten

IN the morning we left Keflavik, a dreary jumble of runways and quonset huts on the muddy shore, and flew to Scotland. Approach Control Radar vectored us around the mountains in the overcast and brought us into Prestwick, where we dated two Scottish Airline girls to show us the points of interest—we hoped theirs. But the canny lassies only showed us the pub in the Robbie Burns Hotel.

Though we took off in good time for London, Tex discovered a half hour out that he had left his passport in operations and we had to return. The delay put us over Bovingdon at dark during a snow squall. We followed an Irish Airline DC-3 in, then followed the crew by cab to a large country mansion, forced by taxes to take in guests. We showered and shaved, shined our shoes and nails for the two Irish stewardesses, but they had dark eyes only for their captain and first officer.

"Wait until we get to Paris," I said, and told Tex about my leaves in Paris after it had been liberated. He was for going that night.

After dinner, I managed to elude him and phone Maggie. The connection was terrible, but I understood Agnes to say

Miss Margaret was out. "Where?" I demanded. "Agnes, where is she?" Her voice gurgled, "I dunno, Mister David. Are—London? She'll—to hear you—Burke—safe." I kept asking where Maggie was, but her voice became so garbled, I gave up.

I was sick with suspicion. Maggie had taken another lover. The whore!

Burke?

Why had Agnes mentioned Burke? How the hell did she know I was with Tex? And then it dawned. Tex had gone to Buffalo, not Washington. He had signed the sales contract for himself. Being so close to Toronto, he had paid Maggie a visit and told her about the ferry flight. Had she told him about us? Sure. That was why he kept asking if I had seen much of Maggie. He knew.

The rotten son of a bitch! The lying bastard! The sneak! The lousy little crook!

Was I any different?

Rather than answer, I doubted. What if Agnes, as old and as dotty as Lady Rutherford-Jones, had confused me with Maggie's husband? Lord knows I had lived the part long enough in that house. If I confronted Tex, I could blow it. If I accused him without proof, I would have to explain how I suspected him. Maggie, after all, was his wife. Who knows how he would react. He could fire me, and there would go China. But if true, it explained why Maggie was always out. She was only out to me. She was mad as hell at me for lying and joining her enemy.

I felt better.

Maggie would come around. Tex I could take care of in China. Meanwhile the game would improve, now that I knew the rules.

While we watched television, the first time for me, the Irish copilot returned from a phone with the weather report. "You chaps have had Paris for tomorrow. The progs put the ceiling right down into their metro."

I remembered Colonel Fitzgerald's invitation to knock him up in Oxford after the war and put in a person-to-person call. About an hour later he was on the line, and after he placed me, I asked if I could come up and see him the next day. "Delighted," he said. "Try and make it for lunch." He gave me the address of a pub and rang off, saying, "And do stay out of those Soho opium dens."

In the morning, our host, who owned a furniture factory in London, drove me to town in his prewar Bentley. On the way, he complained about the ruin of England by the Labour Party, and the strangling taxation. London looked grimmer than I had remembered. Perhaps it was the rain. Many of the bombed out blocks had not been touched. All that remained of one house was the different coloured wall paint and a vertical row of fireplaces on the outside wall of its neighbour.

On the train from Paddington Station, I wondered if Fitzgerald would know anything about Ta-ko. I had the feeling he could tell me where I could find my Chinese brother, Chen Yi. If not, the trip was at least a pleasant break from Tex.

Dr. Fitzgerald was now the shaggy, unkempt professor in tweeds that he had conveyed when in uniform. His eyes were busy and his lips active, as if struggling to free themselves to smile. With his pipe stem, he managed to keep discipline on one side as he watched me as one does a raconteur, who is about to tell a familiar but still amusing story.

Settled at a corner table in The Turf, with large whiskies in hand, he was curious about my years between New Delhi and the present. When I had satisfied him, I asked, "Who was Chia Pao-yu?"

His smile escaped. "Chen Yi."

"You knew all the time?"

Trying to control his smile, he shook his head. "You told us. He was right in getting rid of you."

"But I never said anything to betray him."

"You didn't have to. Certain you had been framed, we dug deeper into your background and found your long boyhood association with Chen Yi. We reactivated his dossier and then it became a simple matter of keeping our eyes open. We assumed from his skill with languages that he would be in some translating job, but even I could hardly believe the final evidence that he was Chia Pao-yu." He laughed with admiration. "The utter audacity of the man. Chiang Kaishek's personal interpreter."

"Did you betray him?"

Dr. Fitzgerald looked offended. "Certainly not. He was no affair of ours. We had nothing against him. We had no love for that little bugger Chiang and his entourage of cutthroats and bagmen. Besides, Chen Yi made those tedious meetings very amusing. It was simply delightful to know that the very man Chiang wanted for knocking off his ambassador was," he wheezed with laughter, "was sitting there right next to him."

"Do you know where he is now?"

"No. The last time I saw him was in Yalta. I was translating for Churchill, and he, of course, was telling his boss all the wrong things." He laughed. "Not really. He was too clever for that. But he was a master at subtle shading and nuances. He could bend a statement just enough to plant a seed of doubt in Chiang's mind. Not that it was difficult. Chiang was quite paranoid."

"Do you know where I can find him in China?"

"Why do you want to find him?"

"He is my friend."

"Was, would be more to the point, wouldn't you say? If you are going to fly for one of the Nationalist airlines, you and he are going to be on opposite sides of a civil war. You might find yourself re-enacting the Chungking scene. After all, if he is still Chia Pao-yu, or has infiltrated the Kuomintang under a different cover, he won't want you around any more than he did during the war. It might be safer for you not to know who he is, or where."

"But I must know at least if he is alive."

Dr. Fitzgerald puffed on his pipe with obvious enjoyment. "Suppose I do this. I still have entree with the intelligence wallahs. Suppose I ring them up and ask if they'd be good enough to glance through his dossier. They may not know anything, but I'm sure Chen Yi is important enough for someone to be keeping an eye on him." He pursed his lips to snub them into behaving a bit more seriously. "But don't be surprised if in return they ask you to have the odd chat with some bloke in China. Tit for tat, you know."

After a delicious meal and bottle of claret, he walked me to the station. Before we parted, he said, "Oh, by the way, if you get up to Peiping and happen to be near Yenching University, do me a favour and drop in to see an old friend —Dr. Wong Fo-ying. Just tell him that my work on the oracle bones is going well. Would you do that?"

"Absolutely. And many thanks."

"My pleasure. I'll ring you tonight if I have any news of Chen Yi."

On the train back to London I felt elated. My hunch that Fitzgerald would tell me about Chen Yi had been right. I was certain Ta-ko was alive and we would meet. I also suspected Fitzgerald knew more than he let on and behind his chuckly facade there lived a brilliant, serious man.

To my chagrin, I found I had forgotten to learn the name of our country inn and only knew that it was somewhere in Surrey. After a bus ride, two pub stops to confer with the locals, and a taxi, I got back. Tex was sitting hypnotized by the television, and greeted me by saying, "Boy, have you missed some great shows. You know, this TV is way the hell ahead of ours. How come? I thought America was first and best in everything."

"Did I get a phone call?"

"Yeah. Your limey friend said to tell you yes."

Ta-ko was alive! "Anything else?"

"Negative. What does yes mean?"

"Opposite of no."

"Smartass."

On our flight to Paris, the cliffs of Dover and the Channel overwhelmed me with memories. It seemed wider, but our speed was less than half my previous crossing when our Spitfires left wakes as we came in under their radar. Sinister-eyed bunkers still squatted on the beaches of France. The flak towers also stood, now probably concrete water tanks, but then they had eyes and guns only for us. I half expected a bracket of dirty bursts.

Le Bourget tower would only answer in French when we asked for landing instructions. Tex, flying copilot, swore and said, "Hell with 'em. Land."

I did, on the wrong runway. We were invited up to the control tower, where a half dozen Frenchmen confronted us in English.

"Where are you from?"

"Fort Worth, Texas."

"Ah, who is the captain?"

"I am," Tex said.

"And you? You are the first officer?"

I nodded.

"Your navigator? Where is he?"

Tex pointed to me.

"But he is the first officer."

"Also navigator."

They discussed this gravely in French, then our interrogator cleared his throat. "And your radio operator?"

I pointed to Tex.

"Impossible!" They looked at us knowingly. They had heard Texas bullshit before.

In the city, I suggested we go to a three-star restaurant, and weighed Le Tour D'argent against Le Grand Vefour, but Tex was so testy I dropped it. Everyone irritated him by speaking French. He even refused to sample a Parisian girl. I thought he would sleep it off, but he woke with the same sulks. "Let's blow this grubby town," he said. "They can't even build proper shithouses."

"Tex, you can't pass through Paris like it's a whistle stop tank town."

"Watch."

After a three day dalliance in Nice, we flew to Tunisia. North Africa had been Tex's war zone, and he laughed at the urchins still chanting, "Hey, Joe. No fadder. No mudder. You fuck my sister?"

On our flight to Cairo, the Mediterranean was a blue no artist would dare paint. The shoals were emerald. Now and then, we crossed a great maze of tracks in the desert floor, dotted with cremated tanks and trucks. Around the edges were dung heaps of petrol drums.

Headwinds cut our ground speed, and night caught us south of Benghazi. We flew north and called the RAF airfield, who finally answered, "Orient two four this is CB for Benghazi. Read you five by five."

"Orient to CB, please turn on your runway lights."

"Wilco Orient. CB out."

We circled the field for ten minutes before the lights came on. When we called CB for landing instructions, he said, "Sorry, old boy, but this is Castel Benito in Tripoli. I had to telephone Benghazi long distance to get your runway lights. Hang on, and I'll try to ring them up again."

But the line must have been busy, so we guessed the wind direction and landed. The whole RAF station had turned out to meet us. Because our navigation lights blinked, they thought we were in distress, and because we had so many they thought we were at least a B-29. Though they were disappointed we were only a "bloody Dakota," we were fed and invited to the mess.

It was like old times. Framed photos of RAF planes hung on the wall. And there was the inevitable dart board. Most familiar were the imperial quart bottles of beer that grew on each small table until ashtrays became lost in the forest, and often your pint. Then the songs, the wonderful obscene songs of English fighting men.

We were surprised to learn that the field was manned by 30 RAF men, and about 300 German prisoners of war. They were fine strapping towheads from Rommel's Afrika Corps. The Germans ran the camp, even to standing armed guard.

"But why are they still here?" I asked. "The war was over years ago."

The RAF sergeant shrugged. "Ask Whitehall. But it's a bloody shame. Most of these lads haven't been home in seven years now. Take Fritz, our bar steward. Three times now we've had word to ship him home. He packs, says cheerio, then some fucker in London changes his fucking mind."

"How come you arm them? Don't they outnumber you ten to one?"

Again he shrugged. "Where could they go? Out there is desert, over there the sea. Drink up."

In Cairo, we checked into Sheppard's Hotel. It was cool

and quiet, reserved not for tourists, but for men returning from adventure. Despite the hour—almost midnight—the kitchen was opened, waiters wakened, and the bar unlocked. They catered to us in that huge glittering dining room as if we were potentates.

On the flight from Cairo to Baghdad, we overheaded the Palestine War. Lone farm communities with shiny metal barns and silos were made islands by zig-zag trenches. A hill away were black arab tents. It seemed peaceful, but an airman's view of war is deceptive until it touches his fragile perch.

We crossed the Dead Sea, a somber, bleak moonscape, well named. We picked up the oil pipeline and road, two parallel lines across sun-blackened earth, and later sand dunes. At one point, we saw Arab horsemen riding. Ahead, the pipeline had wet fan marks on each side. It had been freshly dynamited.

The Euphrates and Tigris Rivers bore thin borders of green. Here life clung, as if with one eye on the desert, patiently waiting to cover it. The flies over a rubbish heap became vultures circling the earth-coloured minarets and walls of Baghdad.

On our next day's run south to Dhahran, Saudi Arabia, we flew over occasional saucers of grass in the desert. On these sheep grazed and Bedouins lived. Some were lush, others almost eaten bare. They were a simple, honest reason for tribal war.

The following day, twenty-nine days out of Fort Worth, we delivered the aircraft to Orient Airways in Karachi, Pakistan. They kindly deadheaded us to Calcutta, where we waited for the weekly China National Air Corporation DC-4, which took us to Rangoon, Hongkong, and Shanghai.

I was home!

eleven

SHANGHAI!

People filled the sidewalks and spilled into the streets to walk in and through traffic with disdain. Pedicabs, rickshas, cyclists, cars, trucks, and carts pulled by coolies struggled in the torrent, clanging bells, blowing horns, shouting and bellowing. A white-sleeved policeman stopped traffic, and the ragged coolies, harnessed to heavy carts on automobile tires, strained to go instead of resting. A truck loaded with cotton was attacked by a pack of urchins. The guard on top tried to beat them off with a stave, but they swarmed over the tailgate and up the sides to pull away great wads of cotton. On Nanking Road, a fat policeman snarled at a pedicab coolie for some offense, slapped him, and threw his pedicab's cushion into the gutter. Further on an amused crowd watched another policeman having a tug of war with a peddler and his tray of goods. Finally the law gave up and the peddler patted him gratefully on the back. A ragged man sat on the curb beside his empty baskets and bamboo pole, and glumly counted a few worthless bills over and over again. A Chinese gentleman in a gray silk gown, carefully tilted his head, held a forefinger to the side of his nose, and blew out a stream of snot, then daintily wiped his nose with a silk handkerchief. Two old women squatted by a store front in the thicket of legs. One puffed thoughtfully on a small pipe and listened to the gossip of the other, who gnawed a stalk of sugar cane. A boy carefully held up his gown and nonchalantly pissed into the gutter. In the mass of blue cotton gowns, beggars limped, or dragged limbs. An American voice behind me said, "Hey, buddy, can you spare a dime?"

Startled, I looked back on a Chinese beggar, and said in Shanghai dialect, "Your mother sleeps with soldiers."

He faltered for a few steps, then with a roar of laughter patted my back.

He was a cripple with one withered leg and hobbled on a stick crutch. Without thinking, perhaps from memories rushing up from the past, I asked, "Where is Chia Pao-yu?" It was a stupid question, but in the classic Chinese novel, the hero Pao-yu has two guardian Gods, one a cripple.

He stopped, and stood on one leg like a crane. A slow smile spread over his face. "Aah," he said. "You know."

While I reached into my pocket for some change, something in the traffic caught my eye, and when I turned to give him a coin he had vanished. For a moment I shivered, then shrugged it off. Most Chinese know their classics. If they can't read, they learn them from story tellers and operas.

When we arrived in Shanghai, I had expected Tex would invite me to stay in his apartment. Instead, he told me to get a room in the YMCA and went off, saying he would speak to the chief pilot about a job for me. Since he had not settled his share of the ferry expenses, I went to his apartment when I was down to twenty dollars. His servant said Captain Burke was away flying and closed the door. I spoke Chinese, and the door slowly opened. The boy listened gravely to my business, nodding with sympathy, then winked. "Telephone tomorrow morning at ten o'clock."

Though brought up in China, I was a stranger in Shanghai, having been there only once to catch a boat. Still, I looked at every Chinese officer and gentleman, hoping to find Ta-ko, or some friend from Chengtu. To my surprise, the first familiar face belonged to Frank Carlson, an American I had known in England during the war. More surprising was his uniform. He was still in the U.S. Army and now a major. "I thought you'd be the first to chuck the monkey suit when the war was over."

"It's not over," he said. "Our real war with communism is just beginning."

"Oh, yeah," I said, remembering his fetish. If all types of men had not been swept together in the war, Frank would have stood out as the most unlikely man to be in uniform. He should have been a padre and in some ways he was, only his religion cast communism as the devil. He had a deeply rooted faith in America, but it was the America of his grandfather, who had plowed virgin sod. As a hobby, this tall, gentle man built models of covered wagons, and he quoted Lincoln as if he were still President.

Frank had arrived on our airbase in one of the black, unmarked aircraft used for mysterious missions. After seeing him alone a few nights in the mess, I joined him, and we became as friendly as you can with someone who speaks little. Now and then, he would disappear for a few weeks, and on his return he looked so satiated, I asked in envy, "Where do you find your nymphomaniacs?" He would only smile.

After he left for good, I asked a British Commando officer about Frank. He drew a finger across his throat, saying, "The best."

"No, I mean the tall, blond American captain."

He nodded. "So do I. The priestly one. He has given last rites to more than one German general."

"You're full of shit," I said.

I asked Frank what he was doing in China, and he said, "I'm with the American Advisory Group." When he learned I was living in the YMCA, he insisted I move in with him and his wife. In the pedicab to his quarters, he told me about her. "Louise was the wife of my best friend. He was a surgeon and was killed while removing a live mortar round imbedded in a GI's back. It exploded."

The Carlsons had a large apartment in a military compound built by the Japanese. Louise Carlson was a beautiful woman in her late twenties, about five feet six, with long red hair, and green, green eyes full of mischief and messages. She was a relaxed hostess, and welcomed me as if I were the old family friend she had been expecting for weeks. Over cocktails, she listened with interest to my account of the ferry flight, then to her husband talking about China.

"As you probably know, last year General George Marshall almost negotiated a coalition government between the Kuomintang and the Communists. It was a farce. All during the talks, the Reds were consolidating their positions in Manchuria, while we armed Chiang with our surplus weapons, until he felt strong enough to fight. Our job is to train his armies and help them fight. It's a fiasco. It's the same snafu General Stilwell faced during the war when Chiang refused to fight the Japanese because he wanted to save his armies for the war against the Communists.

"Now he has that war, but everything is ossified, made hopeless by corruption; the power of old war lord generals and relatives of Chiang; their resistance to any change for fear of disturbing a delicate balance of power among provincial leaders, who are really only interested in their own backyard; an army poorly fed, clothed, and armed; a people brutally treated and taxed; and rampant inflation. It's a morass. The old generals are suspicious of us, and while they agree with our plans and advice, nothing is implemented. They distrust all their best field officers because they have been trained in the States. And they are repeating the mistakes made by the Japanese.

"The Kuomintang holes up in the cities and the Communists control the countryside, especially north of the Yellow River. We report all this to Washington and they react the same way they did to Stilwell, who wrote the textbook. Washington insists China is a democracy and Chiang Kai-shek is the only democratic leader. It's incredible."

Frank was called to the telephone and Louise asked if I had known her husband well during the war. "Not very," I said. "He was in the cloak and dagger business and couldn't talk much."

She laughed. "Even when he can, he doesn't. Tonight was the most I've heard him say in ages. You're a good influence on him."

Frank returned, saying, "I have to catch the nine o'clock flight."

Louise explained: "Frank works in Nanking all week, and only comes home on weekends."

My startled look amused her, then I thought with relief that she of course went with him. "I'll take good care of the place while you're gone."

She controlled her lovely face, but mirth sparkled in her green eyes. "Oh, I never go to Nanking."

I looked from one to the other, feeling I had been invited with collusion to become a cuckold, then dismissed the thought as ridiculous. But the temptation, while alone with her every night, would never let me sleep. "I'd better go back to the Y."

"Why?" Frank asked. "There's plenty of room here. Louise would like some company."

She watched me from the corner of her eyes. "You could teach me Chinese."

A car picked Frank up at eight, and Louise and I talked over coffee like old friends. We said goodnight, and from my bed I could hear her in the Japanese bath. Then she came into my room as naturally as if we had been married for years. She brushed her long hair, dropped her robe, and stood in naked splendor. "I love Frank, but he married me to be noble. The poor dear is impotent."

Not so Louise.

In the morning it took me a few minutes to place the strange room in which I was alone. The only sound was the distant clacking of a typewriter. Putting on Frank's robe, I honed in on the machine and found Louise in a sunny study pecking on a Hermes portable. Before she heard me and covered the typed page, I read, "Again I accept a love as transitory as the coins paid any whore."

The sad statement made me feel guilty, and I apologized for intruding.

"Don't go," she said and turned to the breakfast tray on her table. "Black?"

"Thanks. I'm sorry you feel that way."

She glanced at the typewriter and blushed, then smiled up at me. "I'm not so sure it's true. But then again isn't all sex a commodity to be paid for one way or the other?" She laughed gaily. "Don't think I'm complaining. I had great fun last night."

"Do you always keep a record?"

"More or less. You see I'm an aspiring writer, rather unsuccesful so far, but I did have a short story published in the *Ladies' Home Journal.*" She giggled. "It was dreadful trash."

After breakfast, I phoned Tex. His boy answered, followed by Tex, who was surprised it was me.

"Tex, what about the flying job?"

"I'm working on it."

"Well, work harder. I'm damn near broke. You owe me money from the trip."

"How much?"

"I don't know offhand."

"Show me a detailed accounting, and I'll square up."

"Okay, but in the meantime, give me a hundred in advance. I'll come by for it."

"I won't be here. I'm just about to leave for the field. I'll send it around. You still at the Y?"

"No," I said, and gave him my new address.

Louise, who had ordered a fresh pot of coffee, was curled up in her chair, eager to hear all about Tex. When I told her, she said, "A first class prick. I know the type. If I were you, Darling, I'd go right down to the Bund and apply personally. I don't think he wants you in China one little bit. I'll putter around the shops, and then we can have lunch in the penthouse on Broadway Mansions."

In a pedicab, Louise frowned with good humour. "You know, I'm really crazy. Here I push you into a job that will take you away, just when we start a delicious affair."

"I still worry about Frank."

"Don't. Frank is very apologetic about his problem, and encourages me to take a surrogate husband when I want one."

"Is he homosexual?" I asked, trying to recall any symptoms when I knew him in England.

"I don't believe so," she said brightly. "If anything, he's just asexual. I've tried every trick there is, but I can't get

97

his flag up. I was willing to try any perversion, if that's how he got his kicks. Nothing. And I swear it isn't because I'm female. Somewhere along the line, sex in any form was left out. He'd rather read a book. Honestly. It's a shame. He's such a nice, gentle man. I wanted his children."

I kept looking at her with delight. I had never met a woman so honest and open.

We passed a crowd of young men encircled by a heavy rope and escorted fore and aft by soldiers with submachine guns. Louise said, "Know who those poor bastards are? Volunteers for the Chinese army." She laughed. "I find it all very funny, but poor Frank gets terribly upset. He's too sensitive, and his job is so impossible. I feel sorry for all those AAG officers."

"What about the Chinese?"

"If it would do any good, I would weep for them all day. But it wouldn't help anymore than all our tears for someone dying of a terminal disease."

"Where are you from?"

"New York City," she said happily. "My father is a professor at Columbia, my mother an obstetrician, or tunnel toiler, as she calls herself. I grew up in a pile of books and was lulled to sleep on Bach. I married a beautiful young doctor, who was killed in Italy. After the war, Frank, who had grown up with my husband, came a'courting. On our honeymoon, I thought he was only shy because he still considered me the wife of his best friend." She threw up her hands. "Nothing. It was terribly sad for him. Me too," she said, and hugged my arm to her breast. "I hope they don't hire you."

"So do I."

She shook her head knowingly. "Just visit me when you're in Shanghai. Promise?"

"Promise." What was I doing? How could I fall in love

with Louise, when I was already in love with Maggie? Just lucky, I thought, and kissed her.

She smiled up at me. "You think you're lucky falling into board and bed with hostess, but think of me. You'd be surprised how many men go at sex determined to win the race. You are a considerate, exciting lover. Who taught you those delectable nuances?"

I laughed. "Taught?"

"Well, you never learned them from a how-to book, at least none I ever read."

"When I was fourteen, my amah arranged to have a young, experienced courtesan show me what it was all about. What a night school she ran."

Louise giggled. "You Chinese are so civilized."

You Chinese. I kissed her again.

I got off at the bund, a broad avenue of stolid Victorian buildings facing the Hwang-p'u river, filled with freighters, gunboats, destroyers, ocean junks, and a clutter of tenders and sampans. I went up to the China Air Transport office, told a Chinese receptionist my business, and in a few minutes, I sat across the desk from Captain Shiller, Chief Pilot. When I finished talking, he frowned. "That's funny. I saw Tex last night at a party and he never said anything about you." He grinned. "Hell, maybe he did, and what with the fog and the grog, I've forgotten." He leafed through my RCAF log book, and with a nod of approval, said, "What dialects do you speak?"

"Szechwan, Mandarin, and a smattering of Shanghai and Cantonese."

"Good. We can use you, Dave. When would you like to start?"

It was Monday. Frank would be back on Saturday. "How about Saturday morning?"

"Okay. If you need a place to stay, check into the CAT

Hostel on Gordon Road whenever you want." He rang for his secretary and told her to arrange the paper work. "Where would you like to be based? Peiping, Tsingtao, Shanghai, or Canton?"

Peiping had the Forbidden City, Shanghai had Louise, who should be forbidden. I was uneasy about her. She was so unexpected. I had come home to China to find myself and Ta-ko, not another woman. We were so natural together, it was unreal. I felt we shared years of intimacy and understanding, and she fascinated me as a person. But I loved Maggie!

Why was it every time I took my clothes off, somebody's wife assumed I was balls naked for her? I felt secondhand. Was I the stand-in husband of the world? Was it Tibet? As a youth, whenever I climbed into Tibet, I was enveloped in bed by my gargantuan hostess. Tibet's pleasant custom must now be universal.

I chose Peiping. I had never been to the golden city in the north. Ta-ko was there. I just knew it. Fitzgerald's Dr. Wong Fo-ying at Yenching University was a clue to Ta-ko. I could see Fitzgerald in Oxford, smiling and chortling as he anticipated my meeting with Dr. Wong. It had to be more than a message about oracle bones, which Fitzgerald could have written. Then again, perhaps Dr. Wong was the bloke in China I was to chat with from time to time.

I found the tea room, where we had arranged to meet, and joined Louise. Drawing myself up proudly, I said, "You, Madame, see before you First Officer MacCloud of China Air Transport."

Her smile was wistful. "Congratulations. When do you leave for Peiping?"

"How did you know?"

"Peiping is China, Shanghai a city of and by and for foreigners."

Holding hands, we walked along the bund to the bridge arching over Suchow creek. We stopped to watch the oceangoing junks approach and, at the last minute, ship their masts and slip under the low bridge to become part of the flotilla choking the narrow creek. In front of Broadway Mansion Hotel, a Chinese shoe shine boy informed me I needed a shine.

"No time," I said, and flipped him a coin.

He spun it back to me. "No shine, no money. Next time."

I was amazed; Louise proud of the boy. "He is an example of rare American good sense. Instead of adopting beggar kids as pets, like so many GI's have done, then throwing them back into the streets when they leave, some smart soldier bought that kid his shoe shine box and taught him the business."

We took the elevator to the penthouse restaurant and, finding the terrace warm in the sun, had our martinis outside. Leaning on a parapet, we looked out over the busy city.

"You will be back and forth to Shanghai, won't you?"

"Yes," I said.

"And you will stay with me when you're here?"

"Louise, I—"

She covered my mouth gently with her hand. "Let's not talk of love, and tangle ourselves up with promises and commitments. Let's just love each other whenever we can." She stood with her back against the parapet and studied me. "It's so strange. The moment you walked into the apartment, I knew you. It's not that you resemble my first husband in any way. And for some incredible reason, I feel I can read your mind. When I told you that Frank spent the week days in Nanking, you thought you had been invited to become a cuckold again. What's her name?"

I stared at her with disbelief. "Maggie. She's—"

"Let me guess. She has something to do with Tex. Is she his wife?"

"Jesus! You're clairvoyant."

"He won't divorce her," she said quickly. "They've been separated for years, but he won't divorce her."

I shivered. "You've got me all goose pimply. Okay, you're so damn smart, who is Ta-ko?"

Her eyes looked blank. "I don't know. I only sense something silly."

"What?"

"A shadow."

I waved my hands to erase everything. "That's all."

"No, no. Tell me about Ta-ko. Is he a shadow?"

I told her about Ta-ko and I growing up together, and when I stopped, she said, "Go on."

"That's all."

"There's more. I know there's more. What happened after your childhood?"

"I can't."

"Why? Is he a communist now, and you're afraid you'll betray him?"

"You scare me. Now stop it. Let's have another drink, then eat. And stop picking my brain."

Later that evening, as we sat up naked in bed and sipped sherry, I asked if she had always been able to read minds.

"Not until a week ago. A fortune teller told me."

"Told you what?"

"That you had arrived in China and we would meet."

"Come off it."

"I'm serious. He said a tall, lean man is now in China, and we would meet. He said, 'You will know him and know his thoughts.'"

"Who said this?"

"I don't know who he is. Just some fortune teller I met

on the street. He was a cripple. One leg was all withered."

I drew up the covers.

"Do you know him?" she asked.

I laughed at myself. "In an old Chinese novel called *Hung Lou Meng*, which means Dream of Fair Maidens, or Dream of Red Chamber, a Buddhist monk and a Taoist priest overhear a stone, which has been given the spark of life. The stone bemoans his fate and wants to live in the Red Dust, the earth, as a human. The two Immortals try to dissuade him, then agree to give him a go at it. He is transformed into Chia Pao-yu, and the novel is about his life as a boy and young man, and about the House of Chia."

"But why did the crippled fortune teller startle you?"

"In some versions of the novel, at least the one we read as boys, one of the Immortals often takes the form of a crippled beggar."

She was puzzled. "Go on."

"That's all."

"No, there's more! I know it!"

"Only if you promise not to write it down. Promise?" When she solemnly crossed her left breast, I told her the whole story. "Ta-ko's real name is Chen Yi, and his family was very wealthy. The house of Chen was very much like the House of Chia in the book, and Chen Yi reminded me of Chia Pao-yu. I have to find him," I said when I had finished.

"He sounds like your holy grail."

"Whatever he is, I feel only Ta-ko can tell me who I am."

"But do you really believe in Gods walking the earth, performing magic?"

"When you have been brought up as a Chinese, you can't help but believe it. The Chinese are affected from conception to life after death by Gods and Goddesses, Genii, deified Worthies, Ancestors, Demons, and a host of evil spirits."

Louise hugged her breasts. "What fun. You mean my fortune teller was a God, and he gave me this ability? Why?"

"To bug me." And I drew her down into bed.

Perhaps the peaking reminded her, for she uncoupled our mouths to gasp, "And do you—know what—else, he—said? He—oh!"

As I lay on her soaking, I breathed in her ear, "What did he say?"

She kept languidly stroking my back. "Who?"

I yawned. "I don't know. You said—"

"The fortune teller! He said I would bear a Chinese child. A son."

"I'm not *that* Chinese."

twelve

CAT was a casual airline. I moved into the CAT House in Shanghai on Saturday, and the next morning at 0400 hours I was in the righthand seat of a C-46, copilot of an unfamiliar aircraft. Luckily, I spoke the dialect of T.S. Wang, radio operator, who showed me how to stick the fuel tanks, operate the radios, and when the captain called for gear up, Wang's hand closed over mine struggling to raise the lever, and pushed it to release the safety catch.

The captain, Charlie Powell, reeked of whisky. He told me the cruising altitude and heading to Sian, reclined his seat and fell asleep. T.S. came to my rescue by loaning me his book on radio frequencies, and I navigated by the only three beacons on our route: Shanghai, Hankow, and Sian. But the automatic pilot was reliable, and the cockpit of the C-46 palatial compared to a DC-3. T.S. shared his large thermos of coffee and a sack of man-t'ou, steamed dough filled with a tasty meat. He gave me a cockpit check, and told me about flying procedures and conditions in China.

"Only Shanghai has air traffic control. Everywhere else we must make our own, aircraft to aircraft, when on instrument letdowns. The radio compass is the only instrument system in China. So far we have not had an air collision, but the hazard is the Chinese Air Force. They will not cooperate. They operate on different frequencies, even when we are both working our way down over the same beacon."

"But that's stupid."

He laughed. "Only one of the many stupid things you will find in China. This is not the country you left before the war. We have been at war now—what, almost fifteen years? I have known almost nothing but war."

"What about our alert captain?"

"He is not one of the best, even when sober. Be careful on our letdown over Sian. He is hard of hearing, but will not admit by turning up his volume. Shout your instructions."

Five hours out of Shanghai, we overheaded the Sian beacon, and circled at twelve thousand feet on top of a solid undercast, waiting our turn to begin the vertical zig-zag down through the clouds. I was in radio contact with the four other aircraft on the beacon, and though I shouted at Powell that it was not our turn, he dropped gear and flaps and headed for the beacon, descending at five hundred feet a minute.

I reported our position, and another aircraft screamed, "Get away! We're only a thousand feet below you."

I yelled the news to Powell, who glared at me. "Why the fuck didn't you say so before?" Grumbling, he advanced the throttles, and shuttled back and forth holding our altitude.

Finally, we were cleared by the aircraft below, and continued our instrument descent. At twenty-five hundred feet the gray ripped, and a piece of river flew by. The milk windows blued to mist, and we sped between a dirty blanket and a soaked city. On the ground, coolies unloaded our cargo and filled the fuselage with more. Instead of shuttling back up the beacon, Powell struck an instrument course and climbed out through an invisible gorge between towering mountains.

In seven days, I logged 75 hours, but the seventh day took me to Peiping. The captain was Hawkins, and the radio operator my old friend T.S. Wang. At first I liked Hawkins, a lanky American from Ohio, because he let me fly the left seat, and was the first captain to take the trouble to brief me carefully on the aircraft. But when I poured us coffee from my new thermos, he grabbed my wrist as I handed a cup to T.S.

"Don't give that damn slopey any."

"What?"

Wang's wink said never mind.

"But—"

"Negative," Hawkins said.

You son of a bitch, I thought. You stupid, arrogant son of a bitch.

"Fucking Chinese," Hawkins muttered. "God how I hate them and this fucking country."

I looked at T.S. Wang and wondered if he had heard. But he was facing aft in his radio operator's seat directly behind Hawkins in the copilot's chair, and I could not see his face.

"Then go home," I said.

"Home? You think I can make this kind of dough at home? Hell, the airlines back there start you at two fifty a month, and you might spend half your life as a lousy copilot. Flying is all I know."

Slowly, T.S. turned his head toward me. His expression reminded me of the glance that had condemned Pei to death so many years before. Like a Chinese doctor skilled in acupuncture, T.S. had found the spot to insert his long needle of revenge. It was only a matter of time and, as with all Chinese, T.S. Wang had infinite patience.

North of the Yellow River, the railway was bordered by trenches and calibrated with blockhouses. But gaps in the track and bridges lying in the rivers told of Communist raids, and control of the countryside. I felt we were going to a remote island deep inside a hostile land. The great alluvial plain became swampy. Mountains appeared on the west and north horizons, then in their elbow, a glitter: Peiping.

From the air, the three walled cities of Peiping looked like boxes of jewels, one inside the other. The fourth city, pressed against the southern wall, was junk, except for the Temple of Heaven.

The Forbidden City was the center, its Imperial Palaces proportioned for giants, and reached by broad steps, avenues, and arched bridges of white marble. The walls were faded red, and the pagoda roofs a glazed gold tile. Around the fifty foot high walls of the Forbidden City was the Imperial City of lakes and lagoons and parks, island palaces and temples with roofs of blue and green glaze. The Tartar City surrounded the walled Imperial City with a maze of compounds, veined with alleys, and through which tree-lined avenues cut wide swaths. The Chinese City looked jammed against the south Tartar wall by a tide, which had also left swamps. Rising from the grassy flats was the Temple of Heaven. The altar was a vast three-tiered wedding cake of white marble, the base over two hundred feet in diameter. The tall pagoda was crowned by three arched roofs of glazed ultramarine tile.

At Westfield, just southwest of the Summer Palace, we left the aircraft for another crew, and a CAT car drove us into the city, past ancient tombs and small brick farm houses. We entered the massive city wall through the Hsi Chih Mien gate, a semicircular enceinte topped by a high tower and galleries with loopholes.

The Grand Hotel des Wagon Lits was modern and clean, and I was given a large room with bath. After a shower, I went down to the bar and joined a table of CAT pilots. The Chinese bartenders were called Murphy and O'Reilly, and when called they came grinning as if expecting a joke on themselves.

Pilots from the three airlines in China came into the bar, straight from the airfield, the dust of Manchuria, South China, or the interior on their boots and clothes. Before even washing it from their hands and faces, they washed it from their throats with long draughts of champagne, made by a local French monastery and selling for one dollar U.S. the bottle. Their clothes wore stains of sweat and oil, their eyes the strain of long hours in the air. Then someone shouted for the dice cup, and those about to leave stayed, and tables were pushed together for liar's dice.

The hotel manager, a redhaired Swiss in shorts, was lured into the game, and it grew rowdier. The aim was to stick him for as many rounds of drinks as possible. Our noise and laughter drew frowns from the few tourists having cocktails, grins from an army pilot and navy officer, who looked as if they wished we would invite them to play.

They gave me a week off to get settled, and in proper order I rented a house, hired servants, bought furnishings, ordered lawns and gardens for the courtyards, and improved my bedroom with a part-time Chinese mistress.

thirteen

I WOKE and found Lotus asleep on her back next to me, her hair a black fan on the pillow. I gazed sleepily at her breasts and tried to name the colour of her skin. It was not yellow, more like coffee with lots of cream. Tan bamboo, but not yellow. How did the Westerners come to call the Chinese a yellow race? Their blindness must have included colour.

Not feeling horny, I got up, put on my robe, and stepped out into the little courtyard enclosed by three wings of my Chinese house and a vine-covered wall. All the red-trim windows of the slate-blue house faced in on the courtyard with an introspective stare. Flagstone paths quartered the lawn, bordered by flower beds, and lotus blossoms in broad leaves high above pots of water. Magpies scolded from the two apricot trees, and above them the flowers of a mimosa were like pink thistle. An ancient gingko tree gazed down on the tiled pagoda roof, over which came the chant of peddlers and the prolonged shrill of cicadas.

My number one boy came through the dappled sunlight with a tray of coffee. "Good morning, Captain."

I yawned. "Morning, Lu."

He put the tray on the bamboo table in the center of the courtyard, added cream and sugar to my coffee, stirred it, and handed it to me.

"Any mail?" I asked.

"No, Master."

Of course not, I smiled. No one knew where I was. I was no longer Ta-ko's Hsiung-ti, nor the son of a revered Chinese scholar and a poor missionary kid at the University of Toronto. I was not Highpockets, or Flight Lieutenant Mac-Cloud, J17383. I was not Maggie's lover, or Louise's surrogate husband. I was me, an airline captain. I was master to Lu, honey to Lotus. I was me in my own house. I was home, and I was Dave. Not David—Dave. I could scratch and fart and tell anyone to go to hell. I was on my own again, and Christ it felt good. And though I had been in Peiping for two months, I did not feel guilty for not answering the letters that came via CAT. Maggie's had lost their chill, Louise's none of their warmth. Both pleaded for replies. Tomorrow.

Tomorrow, I had to fly again. Well, then, the next day. Meio kwanshi: never mind, it makes no difference. I was one with Peiping, where if you arrived a week late for a dinner date, your host only ordered another place set.

But May had been a lost month. In the last three weeks, they flew me fifteen days for a total of 180 hours, then checked me out as captain. In June I logged 160 hours, and I was still exhausted, even after three days rest. Still, I had written to American Air Products about the sales contract, and to my parents to say I hoped to get to Chengtu soon. Today I planned to find Fitzgerald's friend, Dr. Wong Fo-ying.

I went into the bedroom to dress, and found Lotus sitting up in bed with the covers tucked under her chin. She was an eighteen-year-old refugee from the fighting around

Jehol, and spoke a dialect I could not understand. Though she could get along in Mandarin, she preferred her pidgin English. "Hello, Babee," she sang. "Come make love."

I looked severe.

"No make love?" she asked.

"You no want."

She giggled and pulled the sheet over her mouth. "Sure me want. You no want."

"You all time sleep," I said. "I can never wake you. You all time—" and I made a snoring sound.

She laughed and kicked her legs under the cover. "No, no me. You. You all the time—" and she tried to imitate my snoring.

"I think you come here to rest from sleeping with other men."

"No, no," she cried in alarm, afraid I was no longer teasing. "Me no go with other men. You say no go Alcazare, me no go Alcazare. Me stay home wait for you no fly. You believe me, Honey?"

I suspected she did go with others when I was away, but I had become fond of her. She was tall, as so many northerners were, with a full, ripe figure, and she enjoyed sex as much as she needed the money. She was pretty, very clean and, for a prostitute, very modest. To Lotus, whoring was a nice easy job, and she probably would have chosen it even if she could have found other work.

"You believe me, Honey?"

"I believe you."

She jumped out of bed and ran naked to me. After a long kiss, I picked her up, tossed her back on the bed, and stripping off my robe, got under the covers with her.

I was showered and dressed and reading the *Peiping Chronicle* in the courtyard, when Lotus came buttoning the side of her high-collared dress. By the table, she stretched voluptuously, and hugged my neck. "You t'ing hao man, Honey. You make Lotus feel very good."

"Guess I've reached the pinnacle of manhood."

She sat down and primly pulled her skirt over her knees. "What mean that?"

"Nothing. You're a nice little girl, Lotus."

"Lotus not so little."

I agreed. "Coffee?"

"No thank you. I eat home with Grandmother."

On our way out, Soo, number two boy, met us with a bow. "Morning, Master, morning, Missey."

"Morning, Soo."

"Master no go Marco Polo Street. Maybe student riot. Much trouble."

We walked between the two large twists of lava, like pieces of giant black coral, placed on the path to scrape off evil spirits, and went through the moongate into the main compound. Lotus stopped. "Babee, you give me some money, maybe?"

"What did you do with the twenty bucks I gave you a couple of days ago?"

"Yesterday Grandmother's birthday. She very old. Very homesick. I give Grandmother party. She cry, you know? She think of my mother who dead. Grandmother say, 'Lotus, I are sorry for you.' I say, 'No, Grandmother, no feel sorry for Lotus. I all right. When I have few gold bars, I marry.' She cry." Lotus laughed gaily. "We have t'ing hao party. Spend ten whole dollars. I give other ten dollars to grandmother. She say, 'No give money.' She give back five. Today I buy new shoes with t'ing hao heel. Big heel. Like so," she said, stretching her thumb and forefinger apart.

"What's wrong with the shoes you're wearing?"

"Oh, these pu hao. Me want long heel." And she giggled out of my reach when I tried to slap her bottom. "No money?"

I wondered if she were lying. But I knew that Lu and Soo and the pedicab coolie, who brought her, all demanded a share of her earnings. They would not believe I had not paid her. She told me once that Lu had threatened he would tell me that she slept with Chinese soldiers if she did not pay him. "Lu very greedy man," she had said.

I gave her five dollars. "Now save it."

She nodded solemnly, then smiled. "You want me tonight? Lotus have so much fun, no ask for more money. Okay?"

"I have to fly early in the morning. I don't get much sleep with you around."

She laughed into her hand. "Lotus only give you one quickie. You sleep better. Okay?"

"Go on, you imp. I'll let you know. Will you be home this afternoon?"

"I go girlfriend house play mah jong. I call you. What time you home?"

"Around six."

In the hutung, the pedicab coolie hopped off the passenger's seat and brushed the blue cushion. He grinned and bobbed his head, as I helped Lotus up into the seat.

"I call you six o'clock. Bye, Honey."

"So long, Lotus."

I watched the coolie push his three-wheeled vehicle, then jump on the bicycle seat and pedal up the hutung, a rutty alley flanked by high compound walls and the blank back of houses made of large Tartar bricks. Not even new white plaster with blue-black paint at the base, nor bright red lacquer and gold trim on the gates could disguise the antiquity. It was in the air, a mellow, musty smell.

114

A tinsmith, his shop hanging from a shoulder pole, strode the hutung, and let the banging of tin strips announce to all with leaky pots and broken pans that he was there with soldering iron and shears. A blindman felt his way along a wall, and flicked his wrist so a tiny hammer on a leather thong struck a small gong. The click of a stick on a disk of wood told those behind their walls that a monk was passing. The wailing chant of a fruit hawker floated over the tiled roofs bidding cooks and wives to come buy his produce. The bark of coolies at someone in their way, the howls of a dog racing from small boys—all sounds heard by Kublai Khan.

After breakfast, I went back to the hutung and got into my car, probably the only Model A Ford driven by a chauffeur. When Koo had started the engine by cranking, he hopped in behind the wheel, pointed to the gas gauge, and looked back. "Tank empty, Master."

"Go Pekin Club."

"We buy gas?"

"No gas."

"Tank empty!"

"Go. K'uai k'uai."

I had discovered that no matter how much gas I put in the tank, Koo siphoned out all but a gallon, and sold it back to the garage. I now bought one gallon at a time, and Koo was on the verge of a nervous breakdown. The loss of revenue was reason enough, but if he stranded me, he would lose face. Gas stations to Koo became like bars an alcoholic could not pass. Twice, on the short drive to Legation Street, he tried to detour to a gas station.

The terrace around the Pekin Club pool, shaded by a bamboo mat roof, was sun-flecked, the foreigners at the tables freckled with light. I joined Bill Wingate, CAT's chief pilot for North China, who was stretched out in his chair at a forty-five degree angle. His other position, except when at the controls, was squatting on his heels. I asked him once if he had piles, and he said, "Habit from saddle sores."

After I had ordered a beer, Wingate said abruptly, "Hawkins has had it."

"What happened to Hawkins?"

"Where you been?"

"Sleeping."

He smiled thinly. "I've seen Lotus. He landed wheels up yesterday."

"Anybody creamed?"

"Negative. Hardly the airplane. But the Company's going to tie the can to him."

"Tough shit." I was glad.

"It was that lousy slopey copilot."

I shrugged. "Like you always say, the second a captain assumes anything, he's in trouble. Who was the radio operator?"

"T.S. Wang."

I choked off a laugh. T.S. had done it. He must have known the gear handle was up. He always made his own cockpit check before every landing and takeoff. For making the Chinese lose face, he had let Hawkins almost lose his ass, at least his job, which was the same. Yin and Yang were in balance.

"Hawkins makes you happy?" He was watching me out of the corner of his eyes.

"Why should it?"

"You're more Chinese than not. You're the only captain who wants Chinese copilots. Hawkins made no bones how he felt."

"I was born here."

He nodded. "That's why we need you."

I liked Wingate, and not only because he had chosen me as his copilot whenever he had flown during May, then quickly checked me out as captain. He was the laconic cowboy and bronco buster Tex often tried to impersonate. From his high cheekbones, and slight Oriental caste, I had thought Wingate was part American Indian, and when I asked which tribe, he was offended. "I'm no half-breed."

During the war, he had flown the world with the Air Transport Command, but for a skilled, experienced pilot he took foolish risks. On our first flight together, he swapped our aircraft for one another crew rejected because of an excessive magneto drop. Instead of electing the long runway, despite a crosswind, he took off on the short runway toward the Western Hills, which demanded a steep climb out. If the engine had lost power or quit, we would have crashed.

On another flight from Peiping to Chinchow, he detoured to Jehol, and landed south on an airstrip blocked in the north by an 800 foot cliff. As we turned to taxi back, two mortar shells burst a few hundred feet off our wingtip. Wingate opened the throttles and we took off toward the cliff, barely clearing the awesome face. Circling up over Potala-su, a vast Lama monastery and temple carved into the sheer side of a mountain, I asked, "What was the purpose of that exercise?"

"Business. Jehol is prosperous and surrounded. I didn't know the Pa lu were that close, though. They could probably be pushed beyond mortar range, but that cliff makes the strip too hairy."

"Business? We're flying our asses off as it is. Who needs more business?"

"We have too much military and government business. The more we depend on them, the more they squeeze. Shanghai wants us to open up cities with no access other than air. The merchants will pay a premium to fly goods in and their products out."

In the Pekin Club, Wingate asked, "How would you like to fly a desk?"

"Negative."

"Half and half. Shanghai thinks you should become Goldman's assistant. In charge of new business."

"And get involved with Myra? Not on your life."

"You won't as long as you stay out of her red bed chamber."

Goldman was CAT's area manager for North China, and Myra, whom he had married in Kunming during the war, was a whore moonlighting as his wife. Her parents were emigres from the Russian revolution, and Myra had been born and raised in East China. She enjoyed telling the story about her return to China after a postwar visit with Goldman's family in Boston. The ship was full of missionaries, old adversaries of hers from before the war. "They called me a Chinese whore," she would say. "The damn fools. Anyone can see I'm not Chinese." And she would shriek with laughter.

Wingate hated her. It was common knowledge that Myra, working as her husband's secretary, was more the manager than Goldman. She would only do airline business with the Kuomintang because she knew the top officers and officials only too intimately from the wartime years in Chungking and Kunming. Also, she could not resist interfering in the chief pilot's job. Fluent in Chinese, she terrified the office people into showing her all operational messages first. Often before Wingate had read a captain's wireless query, Myra had answered it over Wingate's name. When her solution to a flying problem caused trouble for the crew, they would return white with rage, and threaten to kill him.

"No thanks," I said. "You can keep Myra. I'm very happy flying the line."

"We'll more than match your flying pay. Since you know how to wheel and deal, you should be able to pick up an extra buck or two for yourself. No hurry. Just keep it warm under your hat. The new planes won't be here for two or three months."

I sat up with interest. "What new planes?"

"The ten we just ordered from some outfit in Buffalo. Your buddy Tex. Didn't he tell you he's salesman for American Air Products? CNAC ordered ten C-forty-sixes and a hundred grand in spare parts about six weeks ago."

The son of a bitch, I thought, torn between anger and delight. Fifty thousand in commission. Tex owed me twenty-five. But could I collect? My chances were slim if he knew about Maggie and me. I had to know if Maggie had told him, and decided to try to reach her by telephone that afternoon. Fitzgerald's friend, Dr. Wong Fo-ying, would have to wait.

An angry roar rose in the distance.

"What's that?" I asked.

Wingate listened. "I saw a mob on the Glacis."

I called a waiter and asked him in Chinese. "The students," he answered. "They are petitioning the mayor for the food and housing and university training promised them."

I translated for Wingate, and said, "Must be the kids we've been hauling down from Mukden."

"I hear they're squatting at the Temple of Heaven."

Suspicious and frightened of students, the Kuomintang were evacuating them from Mukden via CAT. The government lured them south with a promise of enrollment in one of the universities, free food and quarters. From Westfield, they were trucked into the Chinese City and dumped.

They had already staged two protest demonstrations, which the police had dispersed with their usual brutality.

Why hadn't I warned the students boarding my aircraft in Mukden that the promises were lies? I knew. Was it no business of mine? Was I above and beyond the suffering in China? Aloof because it could not touch me? Let them eat cake. And Maggie. I had not written to her since Shanghai and now I wanted to phone her. Because I was anxious about her? Because I wanted to hear her voice and tell her I loved her? No. I only wanted information to help me collect twenty-five thousand dollars. I was corrupt. Was it from the all-pervading corruption in China? Or was it my new wealth, my Chinese house, servants, car, mistress? I had it made. I could afford not to bother about anybody. No wonder the world was in trouble. It was run by men who thought as I did.

"We should refuse to fly those students," I said, annoyed at my sanctimony.

"Introduce morality and China stops."

"They have their own morals, most better than ours."

My hypocrisy amused him. "Some of the missionary did rub off on you. I thought you had escaped."

"Don't you feel any compassion for the Chinese?" I cried with anger at myself.

"Does a mugger have any for the drunk he's rolling? That's what we're doing here."

I rose, anxious to phone Maggie, to begin searching for Ta-ko. In the excitement and luxury of Peiping, I had almost forgotten him. I would try to reach Dr. Wong Fo-ying by telephone. The thread began there.

"By the way," Wingate said, "you have a special cargo tomorrow on the Chinchow-Mukden shuttle."

"What?"

"Gunpowder."

To refuse meant an argument, and I was in a hurry. It was probably no worse than napalm. "If it looks hairy, I'll send you a little billydoo from Chinchow."

The one-legged beggar boy, who owned the spot outside the Pekin Club gate, was sitting in the front seat of the Ford with Koo. He hopped out as I approached, and demanded cumsha.

In Chinese, I said, "I paid you on the way in, you son of a flea."

"A door has two ways," he answered.

"But you don't, you turtle's egg."

He grabbed his crotch, then turned his arse to me. "I have two ways and know others."

I joined the pedicab coolies in laughter.

"What's going on over there?" I asked.

He opened his mouth. "I am a machine. Put in coin, pull my arm, or cock if you want, and I talk."

I gave him a rubber band wrapped bundle of $1,000 CNC notes worth about ten cents U.S. He stuffed the money in his pocket, and acted out the drama. Glancing furtively over his shoulders, he said, "This morning, one by one, we students slip through Chien Men gate, and before the police know anything, two thousand of us are in front of the mayor's house." He strutted back and forth, shaking his fist. "Give us what you promised. Give us food, shelter, books, learning." Shouldering his crutch, he hopped forward, then lay prone and aimed his stick rifle. "The gendarmes surround the mayor's house. Their packs are heavy. Sweat trickles down their backs. They cannot scratch at fleas because of their guns. Dust stops their nose, cakes their mouth. Water! Where is the water? How they hate the students. How they want to shoot them. Son of a turtle where is the water!" He jumped up, and ate with imaginary chopsticks from a hand cupped to his mouth. "The mayor eats. He has let two students come with their petition. But the mayor must eat. For two hours now he eats. The students are hungry, thirsty, angry. The soldiers are hungry, thirsty, angry. The mayor is not. He eats and eats and drinks his wine. That's where it stands," he cried and bowed.

We all laughed and clapped. I gave him another bundle of notes, and got into the car. "Home."

"Gas, Master. No gas, no get home."

"Get some on the way."

Koo drove up Marco Polo Street to the Glacis, a wide sward on two sides of the Legation Quarter that the foreigners had cleared after the Boxer Rebellion to give them an open field of fire. As we started to cross it, two students rushed from the mayor's house waving a paper. The mass swallowed them, and their cheers rose to a frightening roar. Victory! The students hugged each other, and forced the crowd to expand toward the line of gendarmes lying prone with their rifles aimed at the mob.

The car engine spluttered. Koo choked it. The car bucked and backfired. The crack of rifles echoed. A student running for the car tripped and lay still. The car rocked as they fought to get around it. A boy pressed against the door, worked his mouth, but his voice was lost in the screaming.

"Get pedicabs," I yelled at Koo, and forced the door open. The first and second student were dead, the third, a girl, lay on her back weeping silently at the sky, her blood slowly soaking the front of her dress. Kneeling, I held her head and stroked her cheek. When a pedicab came, I lifted her as gently as I could and held her in my lap to the hospital, where the nurses took her from me. But she was dead.

She was one of eleven. Eight were wounded.

Dazed, I returned to the Pekin Club. A waiter rushed over with a glass of whisky, and I felt the stickiness of my hands. They were covered with drying blood, as was my shirt and lap.

Koo roused me. "Car okay, Master. Have gas now. You come home, please."

For a lousy gallon of gas, I had precipitated a massacre.

fourteen

THE alarm at 0230 startled me, and I lay feeling hungover, then remembered the student massacre. I had been tossed by nightmares. In one, I had walked a dark arcade, along which a large black dog came running. Past me, it turned and growled.

I put on my khaki shirt and trousers and, unable to find socks, pulled my mesquite boots on over bare feet. Taking the Luger off the bedside table, I checked the clip, put it in my briefcase, and crossed the moon-bright courtyard to the dining room. Lu, who went home at night, had left a package of sandwiches and a thermos of coffee on the long table. I sleepily drank a cup, lifting my feet to the chair rung at a rustling in the bamboo matting, and watched a scorpion crawl into a corner.

Maggie had cried, "I can't believe it. You sound as if you are calling from next door." She begged me to forgive her for not accepting my phone calls, and for being so cross in her letters. Yes, she knew I had gone over with Tex. He had told her. He had called on her while I was in New York.

"Maggie, did you tell him about us?"

"Yes. I became furious when he asked why I wanted a

divorce. I told him we loved each other. Did I do wrong?"

"No, that's okay."

"Didn't he tell you, or talk about it? Haven't you talked to him about the divorce?"

"I didn't know he knew about us. But I will. Now, now, don't get so upset. I know, I know, I miss you too. I'll call you again in about a week."

Dr. Wong Fo-ying had been more difficult to reach. The university switchboard had insisted I tell them Dr. Wong's department. I guessed at linguistics, and when a voice finally came on, I thought it was a woman. Before admitting he was Dr. Wong, he wanted to know who I was.

I told him. "Dr. Fitzgerald asked—"

"You are Dr. Fitzgerald?"

"No, no. I'm MacCloud." In Mandarin, I told him of my meeting Dr. Fitzgerald in Oxford, and gave him the message about the oracle bones.

"Thank you. Are you in that line of work?"

I was about to say no, then suspected he might not mean the study of ancient Chinese. "Yes."

"Perhaps we can meet for tea one day," he said, then accepted an invitation to dinner.

I put the thermos, sandwiches, and a bottle of boiled water in the briefcase. Locking the front door behind me, I slipped the large brass key under the doormat for Lu. The outer courtyard, with its gnarled rocks and gingko tree, was eerie in the colourless moonlight.

In the hutung, I lit a cigarette and started walking. I did not like the alleys at night. They were dark and narrow, the light from the odd street lamp lost in the shadows of high walls and black gateway pits.

I turned my light toward the sound of running up ahead, and reflected a pair of eyes. A large black mongrel ran past me, turned and snarled. My tongue surged with a raw sensation. It was identical to my dream. I hit him with a rock, and walked on, poking my light into every dark recess.

"Waugh!"

The bark startled me. With my light, I searched for the source in the shadows, and found a Chinese soldier, his rifle with fixed bayonet pointing at me.

"Fei hsing chia," I said, hoping he understood my Mandarin for aviator. I turned the flashlight on myself, so he could see me, then back on him as if the beam were a foil. When he did not answer, I walked slowly past him, wondering if the big Mongol was a guard, or a deserter out looting.

Glancing back, I saw he was following me and held the briefcase against my stomach to loosen a strap. "Are you coming with me?" I asked in Chinese. He grunted.

Nearing a black niche, the entrance to a long, narrow alley through which I had to walk, I took the Luger from the briefcase, and tucked it under my belt. The thought of the bayonet somewhere behind me chilled my back, until I flattened myself against the wall, and drew the gun. The alley mouth framed the soldier in silhouette.

I hurried to the next hutung, which was wider and lit by street lamps. Pedicab and ricksha coolies, curled up in their vehicles, called out sleepily at the clomp of my boots.

On Mih Shih Ta Chieh, I sat on the curb at the corner of the empty street to wait for the airline bus. Some of the buildings were shaded by bamboo mats hanging from frames over the sidewalk. Two coolies, harnessed to a creaking cart heavy with cargo, came plodding by, and I frightened them with a greeting. The small dog following them stopped and sat in the middle of the street to stare at me.

"Hungry?"

The dog cocked his head, and I split a sandwich with him, knowing the coolies would be shocked at my feeding human food to a dog. I wondered what they would think if they saw the variety of dog foods in Canada that were advertised to feed an animal the Chinese ate.

The small airline bus came, and I climbed on. Groping my way down the aisle in the darkness, a voice shouted, "That you, Highpockets?"

"Tex?"

"Yeah. Over here."

I sat next to him. "Thought you Shanghai guys didn't like to fly north of the Yellow River."

"We don't. How's it going? I hear you have a t'ing hao house, and a hubba hao Chinese broad. When are you going to invite me over?"

"Anytime you're in Peiping." I was tempted to mention the aircraft ordered from American Air Products, but decided to wait for their answer and proof. Also, a bus full of crewmen was no place to start the hassle.

"What do you hear from Maggie?" he asked, and though I could not see his face in the darkness, I felt he was leering.

"Should I?"

He chuckled.

"What do you hear from American Air Products?" I asked.

"Should I?"

I clenched my teeth. You prick! "I'll be back here tomorrow night. What's your schedule? I want you to square up the ferry expenses."

"Sorry," he said, and I knew he was grinning. "I've got a couple of trips to Taiyuan, then back to Shanghai tonight. I was going to drop over last night, but the curfew after the student rumble locked me in the Wagon Lits."

The bus stopped at the Hsi Chih Men gate, and the

guards cleared us. One of the two huge doors was opened, and the bus drove into the semicircular enceinte. The gate behind was closed, and the giant's door in front opened.

In the clearing between the city wall and the moat, people and animals waited for the gates to open at sunrise. Men chatted in groups, others slept wrapped in their sheepskins. Donkeys and small Mongolian ponies were loaded with panniers of strawberries, coarse-skinned melons, or radishes the size of large carrots. A train of shaggy camels was being made to kneel. They had probably come from Tihwa, two thousand miles to the northwest.

"I hear you like Chinese copilots," Tex said. "You take my advice, Highpockets, and watch these fucking slopeys or the same thing's going to happen to you that happened to Hawkins. Whenever I draw one, I don't let him touch nothing. On takeoff and landings, I make him sit there with his hands on top of his pin head."

I knew the Chinese had heard him and thought, keep it up, you bastard, and they'll get you as they did Hawkins. Rather than talk to him, I made myself comfortable and dozed. The bus squealing to a stop woke me. Two soldiers and an officer, with a drawn Mauser machine pistol, stood in the headlight beam.

Pa lu?

I took my Luger from the briefcase. At night, the Communists, still called Pa lu, for Eighth Army, roamed the countryside. To delay the airlift to Mukden or Taiyuan, they had only to ambush an airline bus.

The officer came around and spoke to our Chinese bus driver. Soon they were yelling at each other.

"Let them on," I shouted to the driver.

"What's the matter?" an American asked.

"They want us to take them to Westfield," I answered.

"The driver says no. The officer says they'll shoot if we don't give them a lift."

"Let 'em on!" a pilot cried.

The driver continued to argue until someone leaned forward and slapped his shaved head. Grumbling, he opened the door, and the soldiers scrambled aboard with thanks: "To hsieh, to hsieh."

CAT operations at Westfield was in a quonset hut near the twisted steel ribs of a bomb-gutted Japanese hangar. Inside, crews crowded the counter, checking log books and weather reports. The room was loud with their talk and the chitter of wireless keys in the back.

My crew was K.S. Chu, copilot, and T.S. Wang, radio operator. Shouldering our parachutes, we walked down the taxi strip past the aircraft looming in the dark like giant lizards, sitting on their haunches, their bullet heads sniffing the weather. At T-804, I dropped my chute and briefcase by the boarding ladder and began the exterior check, while K.S. climbed out on the wing to dipstick the fuel tanks.

Two Chinese mechanics appeared, and when they recognized me, the one said in Chinese, "You have wrong aircraft, Captain."

I opened the log book. "T-804. That's what they gave me."

"No, no," the other cried, then they withdrew, and I drained a fuel sump under the wing, checking for water globules in a handful of gas.

The mechanics returned. "We already drained sumps, Captain."

I thanked them, and continued draining the other tanks. "Any bullet holes in this bucket?"

They laughed. "Not this one. Eight oh six. Yes. Pa lu bang right through elevator yesterday."

I opened the hatch to the belly hold, and searched the interior with my light.

"We already look," one of the mechanics said. "No smuggle stuff in there."

At the tailwheel, I squatted to inspect the well into which it retracted. The well was lined with canvas that zipped open for access to the wheel mechanism and control cables in the tail cone. The zipper was stuck. "Give me a pair of pliers."

"All okay, Captain. We check inside before."

"Sure?"

"Very sure."

"Okay."

The two mechanics carried my parachute and briefcase up into the cockpit. In the dim cabin lights, the five tons of bagged flour filled the fuselage like a giant sarcophagus, laced with ropes to rings in the floor. The cabin smelled of jute and flour, of the garlic odor left by the loading coolies, of gasoline from the four drums for Chinchow, and of oil and hydraulic fluid. It smelled of exhaust fumes seeping up from the auxiliary generator puttering in the belly hold. It all smelled familiar and good.

When the engines were running and the instruments had reported all in order, I asked, "Clear to taxi?"

K.S. raised a thumb as a flashlight outside said that the wheel chocks had been removed.

"Lights out."

The instruments glowed green in the ultraviolet lights. I walked the throttles forward, and the aircraft rumbled over the ruts and up on the macadam taxi strip. At the end of the runway, outlined with flare pots, we turned into wind.

I switched off the landing lights, set the parking brakes, rocked my seat to check its lock, then ran through the takeoff check: booster control on, cross-feed off, tail-wheel locked, crossover valve down, emergency brake valve down, carburetor heat cold and locked, blowers low and locked, flaps one-third down, feathering normal, circuit breakers in, fuel boosters high, prop controls fully forward, cowl flaps set for takeoff, throttle friction tight, altimeter set, gyros uncaged and set, gas selector on outer tanks, and controls free and easy.

I raised a thumb and K.S. answered with his. Slowly I pushed the throttles forward, and released the brakes. At 52 inches of manifold pressure, K.S. tapped my hand on the throttles. I put it on the wheel, and he held his behind the throttles to prevent their accidentally slipping back.

I pushed the wheel to lift the tail, and the airspeed touched 60—70—80—, rolling the elevator trim wheel back —90—95. The end of the runway came rushing. I pulled the wheel. She bumped. When the 24 ton mass lifted, I fastened my eyes on the airspeed, gyro-horizon, and direction indicator.

"Gear up."

The gear lever clicked. One wheel then the other thumped into the engine nacelles. The reference plane in the gyrohorizon jumped above its horizon bar. The airspeed fell off. I pushed the wheel to lower the nose. The yoke was springy.

The controls were jammed!

I trimmed her nose heavy and checked the booster control switch. The hydraulic power assist was on. I rocked the yoke. The controls had been free on the ground. My cheek twitched. External gust locks? But the controls were free until the gear—

"Gear down," I shouted, and beat K.S. to the lever. The nose dropped with a jerk, and I trimmed it up. The controls were free again. My kidneys ached.

We landed and returned to the parking area. On the ground, I called the two mechanics and demanded pliers.

They patted their coveralls. "No pliers, Captain."

"Then get some."

Wingate drove up in a jeep. "What's up?"

"Something jammed the controls when the gear came up."

Someone handed me pliers, and I unzipped the canvas lining in the tail-wheel well. I looked in the tail cone with a light, and stood up, swearing. "A whole goddamn case of cigarettes. When the tail-wheel came up, it jammed the case against the control cables and locked them."

I grabbed the mechanic, and yanked him toward me. In Chinese, I said, "You son of a whore. You almost killed us."

"This plane not yours last night. We would not do this to you, Captain MacCloud."

"You shouldn't do it to anyone." A stupid statement. In Mukden, everything was worth ten times what it cost in Peiping. All the mechanics were involved in the petty smuggling of cigarettes, or an extra bag of flour or rice. It was the only way they could live. Inflation was now almost six million CNC to one U.S. dollar. While the government clung to an unrealistic official rate, even the banks quoted the black market rate.

The case of cigarettes was removed and the cables inspected. The bottom of the case had been crushed by the tailwheel. They were Chinese made Lucky Boy brand, and looked exactly like Lucky Strike.

It was light enough when we took off to see the Summer Palace and marble boat in the lake. As we climbed out on a heading of 75 degrees for Chinchow, dawn lowered and washed away the soot of night. The great alluvial plain became a quilt of green and brown corduroy strips, pimpled with grave mounds. With the smoke of cooking fires rising straight, towns dotted the plain like steaming dung cakes. Into each, brown roads spoked, growing wider and deeper near the hub as if corroded by the humanity there.

The rising sun lit fires in the clouds above the mountains ahead. Inside a cloud cave, an ogre yawned over his cooking fire and raised a hairy hand to swat the olive fly. On contact, the hand dissolved into a swirl of gray, and the sun was bright in our eyes.

Cruising on autopilot, I racked my seat back, lit a cigarette, and handed K.S. my thermos. "Give T.S. the first cup. It is sad the Americans do not understand. They think the landing gear operates on hydraulics, when the real power is politeness."

T.S. quoted Confucius, " 'He who learns but does not think, is lost. He who thinks but does not learn is in great danger.' "

Below, the Great Wall of China ran like a thick seam along the back of mountain ridges, and capped needle peaks with lonely blockhouses. From horizon to horizon it rose and dipped, disappeared to snake up and over and away. Where a river had filed through a range, the stone ribbon was folded into a square city of rubble and midges.

I felt at peace ten thousand feet above the earth. The great mass of air moved to its own laws, and when it hid the earth in clouds, it did not consider our need to land. The vast storms struck without malice. The sky wished us no harm.

Nearing Chinchow, a virgin vein of iron ore ran like blood soaked sand through low green hills. And the tenacious Chinese clung and laboured food to grow in this womb of the modern world. Such stupidity, and yet how peaceful the little villages seemed.

We landed on the Japanese-built airstrip south of Chinchow, and the four drums of gasoline were rolled out the door to fall and bounce off an old aircraft tire on the ground. We took off again, and flew over the river north of Chinchow. The bombed railraod trestle lay in the shallow water and was covered, like iron filings on a magnet, with refugees picking their way across.

The villages on the Manchurian alluvion differed from those in China. From the air, they looked like wooden rake heads with a few teeth missing, the back facing north. Here, the trenches along the railroad were empty, the blockhouses deserted, and in places only road bed remained.

The once great industrial city of Mukden was dying, its ground arteries severed. The factories were shells with gaping wounds through which the Russians had taken vital machinery. The tall chimneys in the south stood like sparse timbers after a forest fire. Each day the aircraft drained more blood as they flew Mukden's people away.

We made a straight-in approach, and skimmed over the hundreds of people rebuilding the south end of the runway. They worked stone by stone, basket by basket of earth. Few looked up at our roar, fewer ducked the big wheels spinning over their heads, even though now and then a wheel killed one of them.

We parked near the ruined hangar, surrounded by the bones of Japanese fighter planes. Before our engines had stopped, a truck backed up to the cargo door. Soldiers unloaded the five tons of flour and, when the cabin was empty, one soldier swept the floor and bagged the mixture of flour, dirt, and dried vomit from previous flights. This was their food ration and, from the looks of many soldiers in Mukden, their only ration.

The truck drove off, and one with baggage took its place. When the bundles and boxes and wicker crates were aboard and tied down, the truck was replaced by a set of wooden stairs. Soldiers with submachine guns cut a group from the mass of evacuees waiting on the hangar apron and herded them to the aircraft. They were all ages: students in high-collared black uniforms, men in blue cotton gowns, girls with babies slung on a hip, and old women hobbling on bound feet. They made no sound, not even to each other, as the soldiers strapped them to the canvas stretchers. In Chinchow, they would be unloaded, their baggage thrown out into a pile. They would find their belongings in the heap, drag them off to safety, then squat and wait for the trucks to take them into the walled city. From there they would be put on board a ship, but where the ship took them no one seemed to know. Like birds, they were migrating south to escape the cold of a new winter.

fifteen

WAITING in Chinchow for our first load of gunpowder, I squatted with four other pilots in the shade of a C-46 wing. Sam Koski was telling about a Chinese pimp who had followed him in Tsingtao.

"I was sashaying back from the thieves' market when this slopey dogs my heels, singing, 'Wantchee girlee? Nice clean Chinese girlee?' Being as I was on my way to fly, I tell him to buzz off. 'What you like?' he asks. 'Nice Russian girlee?' 'Pu hao,' I says. 'German girlee?' I aim a kick at him. 'Japanese girlee?' 'Beat it,' I yell. 'Philippinee girlee?' And down the list he goes. Finally, I turn and hold up three fingers. 'Want girl with three breasts,' I say. That stops him. He falls back about five paces, thinking real hard. And I be a sonofabitch, if he don't run up, pull my sleeve, and say, 'Can do.' "

We laughed, then Dutch Maas told what had happened to him in Kiukiang: "When the flood receded, it left the airfield covered with mud, and the only way you could tell the runway and taxi strips from the rest was by those little red flags they'd planted. Anyway, I miss my turn and taxi off and down goes the right wheel until the wingtip is touching the ground. I corral a foreman, who rounds up a couple hundred coolies. They unload the cargo, and start lifting the right wing and filling in the hole under the wheel until the wingtip is up to arm's length. Then they build a platform from empty gas drums to stand on. Pretty soon that platform is two drums high and shaky as hell. I get worried and say to the foreman, 'You'd better be careful. If that platform collapses, that wing is going to kill half those men.' He laughs. 'Never mind,' he says. 'Got lots more coolies.' "

I told them about the case of cigarettes in the tail cone.

"Did you shoot the bastards?"

"It was my own fault. I should have checked."

The truck with the gunpowder arrived, and I went to inspect it. The powder was packed in long wooden boxes painted gray and stencilled: U.S. Naval Stores. Some of the corners were splintered, and the seams of the tin lining inside were split open. The expiration date was 1945.

I swore and wondered if I should take it. Old powder became sensitive. Anything—a bump—might detonate it. Or was it the other way around? Did they destroy old powder because it might not go off? Maybe that was it. Damn Wingate! I ordered the foreman to spread tarpaulins on the floor to catch the powder that spilled out.

Standing beside the truck to watch them load, I was startled to see the Chinese officer next to me smoking a cigarette. I knocked it from his hand and ground it out with my heel, swearing at him until he walked away with a sheepish grin. The soldiers loading the gunpowder laughed. Big joke.

The flight to Mukden was uncomfortable. Suppose the Pa lu put a lucky bullet into the five tons of gunpowder behind me? Would it go off? If so, there would be nothing left of me. And who would miss me? My parents, sisters,

Maggie, and perhaps Louise. The pilots would be angry and blame me. "Anybody who'd fly shit like that is asking for it. Did you see it?" I would be forgotten. Nowhere would a child remember or wonder about me.

Coming into Mukden, I concentrated on the landing and greased her on. The powder was unloaded, the canvas taken out and shaken, and the aircraft filled again with baggage and passengers for Chinchow. The second load of gunpowder was like the first, and the flight to Chinchow as tense. To my relief, the third load was packaged in sealed metal drums. While it was being loaded, I sat on my heels under a wing with another crew, until I noticed something being thrown out of my aircraft.

"Rocks?"

I went around to the loading door, and climbed up on the old truck and into the C-46. Good God! To keep the drums from rolling down the inclined floor, they had chocked them with rocks. Rocks against steel with loose gunpowder on the floor? I shouted at the foreman to unload. "Get it the hell off here. No more powder. I'll take rice."

I rejoined the crew under the wing and told them. They laughed, and one tapped his head. "They really got it."

On the flight to Mukden, I sent a wireless message to Wingate. HAVE LEFT 3 LOADS GP FOR YOU IN CKW STP SUGGEST YOU STICK SAME UTA MACCLOUD 804. A few minutes later, T.S. handed me a reply. MACCLOUD 804 YOU SOB STP WINGATE PPG. I grinned, and filed it in between the mixture controls where I kept the wireless weather reports.

In Mukden, we went into the hangar full of waiting evacuees, and bivouacked Chinese soldiers. Parts of the hangar roof had been blown off during the war, and the soldiers lived in packing crate huts around the walls. Here and there, a group in ragged uniforms and canvas shoes, huddled over a small fire cooking rice in an old oil can; rice they had probably swept off the floor of an aircraft. In a small back room, we opened the box lunches put aboard at Peiping. A soldier brought us tea in chipped cups, compliments of the Mukden Army. The tea tasted like boiled straw, the sandwiches of cold grease.

By sunset, I had flown 12 hours, and I was hungry, tired, and dirty. An old weapons carrier drove us into the city where the streets were wide with trolley tracks down the center, but there were no trams because of the power shortage. There were no automobiles, only a few Japanese three-wheeled motorcycle buses and trucks, and droshkies drawn by small Mongolian ponies. Empty pillboxes guarded intersections, and in front of the railroad station—whose tracks led nowhere—a model of a Russian tank crowned an obelisk.

The lobby of the Railway Hotel was a gloomy vault full of echoes. At the reception desk, lit by candles, I was given Room 101. Told that the water was on, I hurried up.

Room 101 was a two-room mid-Victorian bridal suite. The wallpaper, maroon brocade with gold medallions, was faded, water-stained and peeling in the corners. The dark furniture was cracked, the veneers buckling, and the canopied bed was damp and musty. The bathroom was huge, ornate with marble, tile, and chrome; complete with toilet, basin, tub, marble shower room, and a bidet. The latter intrigued me. Unlike the keyhole shaped bidets in France, which flattered the female derriere, this was square and squat. The methodical Japanese must have measured the broadest of female sterns, then added a few inches for safety. It would never do if some dignitary's wife or concubine got her arse stuck.

The water proved to be a trickle, so I had to settle for a wash. Dutch and Sam Koski picked me up, and we went to the Russian restaurant near the hotel. It had a store front with two potted palms in the window, and a low curtain behind. It lacked only a cat sleeping in it, but there were none in Mukden. Along with dogs, and probably rats, they had all been eaten. Millet was the staple, and malnutrition was rampant. The food we flew in was theoretically being stockpiled for the anticipated siege, but we knew that the Chinese Air Force was flying it south as fast as we flew it in, and selling it on the black market.

Back at the hotel, we found there was a Chinese officers' dance in the ballroom. We watched from the entrance, guarded by an ugly Mongol armed with a tommy gun. Sam spied a beautiful Eurasian girl and was about to enter, but the guard took a menacing step forward and discouraged him.

Around midnight, I was awakened by a burst of gunfire just outside the hotel. I lifted my head and listened, wondering if some poor reveler had been caught by the curfew guards, then went back to sleep.

At 0300 Mukden had a 200 foot ceiling, and the crews were allowed to sleep an extra two hours. By 0700 it had lifted to above minimums, and they began taking off, except we were delayed for an hour by a magneto drop. When we got away and climbed into the cloud layer at 500 feet, I radioed our position and altitude.

T-806 reported: "Over Mukden beacon at three thousand and starting instrument letdown."

T-820 said: "Approaching at five thousand ten minutes south of Mukden."

A voice bellowed, "So am I. Get away!"

"Eight two zero climbing to five five."

"Thanks, Buddy."

"This is the Green Hornet on top in the sunshine and Peipingava bound."

A new voice cried, "Is anybody using seven thousand

feet on the foggy, foggy road to Mukden?"

"All yours, Felix."

"To hsieh, to hsieh."

"Now that we're all squared away, anybody know what groove the Chinese Air Force is using today?"

"Yeah. Same altitude you're using and coming straight at you."

"Help."

Two transmitted at the same time and jammed the frequency.

"Knock it off."

"Who's that?"

"Green Hornet, buzz buzz."

"You through, Jack?"

"Yeah, just broke out. Visibility is getting piss poor down here."

"That'll keep the CAF on the ground, anyway."

"Hell, no. Here comes one snorting over the town. Hold your letdown eight two zero. He's climbing into it right for the beacon."

"Silly bastard. Eight two zero to all planes approaching Mukden. CAF climbing out item fox roger. Somebody walla-walla with him."

A voice spoke Chinese, and another answered. The CAT copilot said, "CAF say none of our damn business what altitude he fly."

Everybody hit their buttons and swore.

I lay back in the chair and smoked a cigarette while the autopilot gently moved the controls to keep the aircraft on course. The windshield was white, and except for engine vibration, motion existed only because the instruments said we were moving at 160 mph at 4000 feet above the ground.

Without me, I thought, we would not be moving. I close my eyes, put away the fact we are flying, and we stop. I close my eyes, stop my ears, and we are suspended. There is no time, no space, no distance. But for me, there would be no life. Had I not been born, I would not have known life, and therefore it would not have existed. Because I was born, life came into existence, and grew as I grew, and when I die, life will vanish.

Five minutes from Chinchow, I racked the seat forward, buckled on my safety belt, and released the autopilot. "Eight zero four," I radioed, "at four thousand approaching Chinchow beacon. Over."

"The air is all yours," Dutch answered. "I was the last to leave. But watch it on the ground, Dave. Lots of shooting. Tower insists it's just practice, but you know these slopeys. What's the weather at Mukden like?"

"Five hundred foot ceiling with about a mile visibility in rain. Where are you now?"

"Just crossing the river. Heard there was a CAF tooling around in the soup, so I'm going to stay under the stuff."

"Careful you don't get a bullet up your arse."

"Better that than a Charley forty-six in the face."

We made an instrument letdown, and when we broke through, the tower cleared us to land. But as we bore down on the runway, a Chinese Air Force P-51 began to taxi away from its revetment.

"Do not land," the tower said.

I grabbed the mike. "Why?"

"Fighter want to take off."

"He isn't even near the runway. We have lots of time to land and clear the runway."

"Go around!"

I swore and pushed the throttles forward. "Gear up." As we snarled over the runway, a white plume rose to mark a shell burst on a hill just south of the field. I took the angry strain off the engines. Our climbing turn buried the right wingtip in the clouds, and I slipped her down and straight in time to see the wind pull apart another plume.

"What gives with the shelling?" I asked the tower.

"Only practice."

We landed behind the fighter as it took off. Near the end of our roll, another shell hit, and I taxied quickly back to our parking area. Because of vomit on the cabin floor, I left through the cockpit window, and climbed up on the roof, then walked carefully down the top of the fuselage to the towering rudder.

The hill less than a mile away blossomed with white shell puffs. The bunkers along the southern perimeter of the field opened fire, and the air burbled over my head. Birds? Hell, bullets! I squatted on the tailplane, and looked back at my passengers standing in a truck. None fell. Either I was wrong, or they were lucky.

After four Chinchow-Mukden shuttles, we returned to Peiping with a load of students. Despite the massacre, I did not warn them, and on course above the overcast, I succumbed to sleep rather than guilt. K.S. woke me over Peiping, and I let him land at Westfield. In the car, I tried to sleep again, but was awakened when we stopped.

The road was blocked by an armed guard, and lanterns hanging from sawhorses, between which lay a corpse. The driver said that he was a CAT loading coolie, who had fallen off a truck and been run over. Since whoever touched him became responsible for his burial, he had laid there for a day, while relatives were sought. If none could be found, it became a matter of debit and credit. If there was any latter, someone would claim him along with the credit. If debit, he could rot in the center of the main highway for all the Chinese cared.

At Sui An Po Hutung, Lu met me at the door, and relieved me of my briefcase and leather flight jacket. I dropped into a wicker chair in the courtyard, and he brought me a cold beer, a bowl of Chinese radishes and saucer of coarse salt. He also brought letters addressed to me in care of CAT and sent over by the airline office on Morrison Street.

Maggie's, written before our telephone conversation, confessed she had known I lied about the ferry trip, and told of her feeling betrayed. "Tex arrived from Buffalo terribly pleased with himself. He flashed an obscene diamond ring and blew cigar smoke in my face, convinced I would be impressed by his ostentatious affluence. He had come back to 'Show me.' Well, I showed him. After a half hour, I showed him the door. We had a frightful row, I'm afraid. At least I made a frightful row. I think he was delighted when I turned him out."

The letter from Louise was sad. She missed me, and asked when I would come to Shanghai. "I'm worried about Frank. His job is too frustrating. Where once he was objective, he is now bitterly anti-Communist. Not anti-Kuomintang, mind you. Unable to criticize them, he vents his spleen on their enemy. They are the real cause of all the snafu, etc., etc."

The third was from American Air Products: "Mr. John Burke signed the sales contract on January 25, 1948. He said that you and he had a private arrangement. Since he already had two years experience in China, and since we were most anxious to have sales representation in the Orient, we signed with him. The results have proven us correct. Through Mr. Burke, CNAC has ordered a half million dollars worth of aircraft and spare parts, and CAT will shortly confirm a similar order."

You and he had a private arrangement. Goddamn them. Why couldn't they have been more explicit? That sentence could mean anything. It sure as hell would mean nothing in court. Unless I could lean on Tex, I was out twenty-five thousand dollars. And because of Maggie, I was in an untenable position. Shit!

The last was postmarked Shanghai, and bore a business firm name. It was a short typewritten note, signed by a C.J. Bart, who wrote: "My old friend Professor Fitzgerald at Oxford has written to say you are in China, and would I be kind enough to buy you lunch one day. This is to say I would be delighted. Just give me a ring whenever you are in Shanghai and have the time."

The tit for tat man.

sixteen

DR. WONG FO-YING had declined my offer to send Koo for him, and arrived for dinner promptly at seven. Wearing thick horn-rimmed glasses, he was older than I had expected, his longish hair streaked with gray, and his scraggly beard and mustache almost white. He walked slightly stooped with the aid of a cane.

Seated in the courtyard, he politely refused a drink, but accepted tea. He spoke beautiful Mandarin, and began by praising the work of my father. "The first two volumes of his dictionary are superb. We all hope he is given all the years he will need to complete his monumental work. He is in good health?"

"I believe so. At least he appears to be in his letters. I haven't had the chance to fly to Chengtu yet, but I will soon."

"Please give him my regards. And Dr. Fitzgerald? You have known him long?"

"No. I met him briefly in New Delhi during the war, and at Oxford on my way over."

"It was kind of him to remember me. We were students together at Oxford before the war." His expression was the epitome of Oriental inscrutability. "You are a Chinese scholar as well as an airline captain?"

"No. I said that because I wanted to meet you." I hesitated, wondering if I should trust him.

"Why would a busy aviator want to meet a lowly paid professor?"

"Where are your sympathies?" I asked.

"Where they are safe. Do you live here alone?"

"Most of the time. The servants go home at night. Sometimes the place is full of transient pilots, but not tonight."

Lu opened the French doors of the dining room, and his bow announced dinner. The main course was Peking duck: thin Mandarin pancakes that we spread with a dark sauce, then rolled them around scallion brushes and pieces of crisp duck skin.

"Excellent," Dr. Wong said.

"The duck must have been stolen," I said, watching him closely, but there was no change of expression.

After dinner, we returned to the courtyard and made polite conversation until Lu went home. To make certain we were alone, I saw Lu out and locked the front door.

Back in the courtyard, I asked, "Do you know Chen Yi?"

In English, he asked, "Do you know John Smith?"

"Chen Yi of Chengtu."

"Before dinner, you asked my sympathies. They are for China. Not this China, but for the new China that must come."

"Communist."

"No matter. To be more precise, anti-Kuomintang. And yours?"

"I know little about the Pa lu, or what they will do. I only know that now there is anarchy."

"Mao Tse-tung will win. It is only a matter of time. The sooner, the fewer people will suffer. You can help."

"How?"

"An organization in Peiping needs gold. It owns sufficient gold in Hongkong. The problem is delivering it to Peiping. They have an excellent courier system, but there are many hazards, and much has been seized. For a foreign pilot like yourself it would be a simple matter to smuggle gold. They will pay you well."

Expecting a clue to Ta-ko, the switch surprised me. "I don't know. Those of us based in Peiping fly mostly north of the Yellow river. We rarely go to Hongkong. That's the bailiwick of the Shanghai and Canton based crews."

"You have a weekly Peiping, Shanghai, Canton, Hongkong flight."

"You know our schedules."

"They are posted daily in the Wagon Lits Hotel."

"Let me think about it."

"In the meantime, I will try to recall where I heard the name Chen Yi."

"Then you know him? Is he alive?"

For the first time, he smiled. "When you have reached a decision, perhaps I will have remembered. It depends on you."

On my flight to Shanghai the next day, I thought about Dr. Wong Fo-ying. I was not surprised he was a Communist. Probably every intellectual in China was against the Kuomintang and had no choice but to favour the Communists. But Fitzgerald? Was he a Communist? Was smuggling their gold back into China the reason he had asked me to meet Dr. Wong? Then the letter from Mr. Bart arriving just after I had made contact with Dr. Wong. It was too coincidental.

At Hungjao Airfield, Shanghai, another pilot took the aircraft. I checked with operations and learned that Tex was scheduled to be back at noon the next day. I went to the CAT House on Gordon Road and checked into a room for my three day leave. To get it, I had had to promise Wingate I would talk to Whiting, CAT's senior vice-president, about the assistant area manager's job. I made an appointment with Whiting for the next morning, then phoned Mr. Bart. He invited me to meet him in an hour in the Shanghai Club. I called Louise, who wanted me to hurry over.

"I'll be over after lunch. Is Frank home?"

"He'll be home this evening. Please hurry."

The Shanghai Club had the longest bar in the world, shaped like a field hockey stick. A kidney shaped knot in the bar-top wood near the heel marked the territory to the toe as the private preserve of Taipans and old China hands. I found Mr. Bart "above the kidney" and well into his gin. He was a ruddy Englishman with the nose of a profound drinker. The crest on his blue blazer was Royal Navy and his tie was old school. He fussed until I had glass in hand, then became affable. "Great fellow, Fitz. Couldn't have been more pleased when he wrote to look you up. We were students together at Oxford."

"So was Dr. Wong Fo-ying. Do you remember him?"

He frowned. "Can't say I do, but then that was a long time ago, Old Boy." He burbled on, interrupting himself to exchange greetings, or the odd word with other club members. By the time we had lunch, after three drinks, he was repeating himself, and I was disappointed. He was an alcoholic old China Colonel Blimp. When we left the club, I was bored, anxious to be with Louise.

On the street, he said, "Do come by the office with me."

I looked at my watch. "Sorry, Mr. Bart, but I have a date."

"Won't take but a minute." He lowered his voice. "I do know Dr. Wong Fo-ying."

Inside his office, he became surprisingly sober. "Tell me about your meeting with Dr. Wong."

"Why should I?"

He chuckled. "Good point. You are looking for your old friend Chen Yi. I may be able to help you."

"Are you British Intelligence?"

"Let's say I was and they still call on me from time to time."

When I hesitated, he said, "Then suppose I tell you. Dr. Wong heads the Communist purchasing apparatus in Peiping. About thirty to forty percent of all American military material entering North China through Tientsin is diverted by purchase to the Communists. The Kuomintang officers, from whom they buy the material, will only accept gold in payment, putting Dr. Wong's group in constant need of gold. He asked you to smuggle gold from their banks in Hongkong."

"Is that why Fitzgerald asked me to meet Dr. Wong?"

"Yes."

"Then Fitzgerald is a Communist. And so are you."

"Quite the contrary. We are realists. Let me explain. I'm certain you understand that in every government there are groups with divergent opinions. In the Foreign Office, one group favours a weak, fragmented China. Another is convinced Mao will take over the country. They approve. A unified country of six or seven hundred million people cannot help but be a power in world politics."

"But it will be a Communist China, allied with Russia."

"They predict an eventual split between China and Russia. Mao has no love for the Soviets. He distrusts them for their betrayals in the late twenties. The threat of China on Russia's eastern borders will force her to ease her pressures on Europe. We are also certain that the Americans, with their obsessive fears of communism, will pigheadedly oppose a Red China. This will preoccupy them and draw their attention away from Europe. Not now, but in a dozen years or so, when Europe will be strong enough to want to free herself from American domination. A strong China will weaken America and distract the Soviets."

"And aid the British."

He smiled. "We need all the aid we can get. We're broke, without an empire. We have to live by our wits again. When men like Dr. Wong Fo-ying come to power, they will remember those of us who were sympathetic. No matter what their political structure, China is a tremendous market."

"Back to bucks."

"Never back, always toward. It's our only carrot, you know."

That afternoon, I lost myself in Louise, then sopor. To keep from floating away, I locked my limbs to hers, and drifted in her pungence. Her darlingdarlingdarling in my ear transported me to a Tibetan monastery morning with monks chanting, "Om mani padme hum"; their every dawn dok-dok-knocking on a hollow wooden fish, beseeching its spirit to give up the souls of the Chinese swallowed on their return voyage from Jerusalem, where they had been sent in 60 A.D. to discover if the rumoured Jesus were Buddha reincarnated. Then I fell into a troubled dream, and was rescued by her return to bed with glasses and a bottle of sherry.

When I sat up, she handed me a sherry, which I tossed down like a whisky. "Feel better?" she asked.

"Sorry. I'm not at my best during matinees."

She giggled with skepticism.

"What time will Frank be home?"

"Not for hours. The first flight from Nanking never arrives before six. But you're not worried about Frank."

"I am. I'm beginning to feel people meet to plan my life and determine my fate. I don't want anyone new on that board of directors. I have enough."

"Who's on it now?"

"Christ, everybody."

"Me?"

"Yeah, you. You, Maggie, Tex, Fitzgerald, Wingate, Bart, Dr. Wong Fo-ying, even Ta-ko, I'll bet."

"Who is Dr. Wong Fo-ying?"

"I wish I knew."

After a few sherries, I told her about Dr. Wong. She was fascinated. "Are you going to do it?"

"I don't know yet."

"But suppose you're caught? What will they do to you?"

"Pinch the gold and slap my wrist."

"For smuggling Communist gold?"

"Who is to know? Gold is gold. Hell, you should see the smuggling that goes on. Our radio operators carry the biggest briefcases built. They're so heavy with stuff, the poor buggers can hardly carry them aboard. And they're on that wireless key all the time checking prices, getting quotes, finding out who wants what where. Often you have to whack them on the head to get a weather report."

I left at five, saying, "If Frank wants, I'll have chow with you. Call me at the CAT House."

A former old residence on Gordon Road had been converted by CAT into a hostel for transient pilots. It was well staffed, and the cook could be roused at any hour to prepare a meal. The most permanent occupant was T'ing Hao, a Lama temple dog. With Oriental patience, T'ing Hao would, on anyone's command, hold a begging stance, even a lighted cigarette in her mouth, then slowly topple.

Also permanent was a bridge game. Whatever the hour, there was always someone to replace the fallen, and the game went on. As I came into the living room, South left for the airport.

"Slide in here, Davie Boy," North said, "and we trim these Yankees."

I pointed to a pilot stretched out on the couch reading a comic book. "It's Johnson's turn."

"No it ain't. That Tennessee ridge-runner don't play bridge. Leastwise, he don't play with me."

After the first rubber, Johnson drew up a chair to kibitz. I noticed him rifling the deck I was to deal, but it was only with one hand, and for no more than a few seconds. I dealt and looked at my cards. Good God! Thirteen spades. I bid them, and the others threw in their hands, shouting, "God-damn you, Johnson. Keep your cotton picking hands off the cards."

He had stacked the deck to give the other hands garbage. I laughed with admiration, then became uneasy. Was it an omen? Were the cards being stacked for or against me?

The number two boy came in. "Telephone, Captain MacCloud."

It was Frank. "How about meeting us for drinks at the officer's club. Then we can have dinner at Sunya's."

The U.S. Army Officer's Club at Suchow Creek was a collection of the barren rooms you find in Legion halls, and temples for Moose, Elk, Shriners, etc. Bare tables and hard chairs surrounded a dance floor in front of an empty band-stand. The room was stripped for boozing.

Major and Mrs. Frank Carlson were one of the forlorn couples absently stirring their drinks with swizzle sticks and sweeping the room with vacant stares. After a greeting and ordering me a drink, Frank became a mute.

Frank had envied my job with CAT because it took me to Peiping. Now when I told him about the city he most wanted to see, he did not listen. I asked about his work, and he shook his head. When he went to the men's room, I asked Louise, "What the hell's wrong with him? Is he sore at me? I mean does he know I was with you this afternoon? Is he jealous? What gives?"

Louise said, "I'm afraid he's on the verge of a nervous breakdown. He's so utterly frustrated in Nanking. It must be awful when, you know, he can't get any release through sex. It must be terrible for him. As I wrote you, he has become bitterly anti-Communist. He blames them for everything. He can't accomplish anything working through the Nationalists. They thwart him at every turn. I believe he has reached the point of wanting to strike directly at the Communists. I seriously think this is what obsesses him. He wants to find some way to deal directly with the problem. I'm really worried. You know he is capable of sacrificing himself in some silly one man attack, or something."

I recalled the British Commando officer claiming that Frank was one of their best assassins.

We had a delicious, though silent, Chinese meal at Sunya's. I wanted to go back to the CAT House, but Frank suddenly came alive, and insisted I go home with them for brandy. "I want to talk with you," he said.

But in their living room, he said nothing. When I started to leave, he said, "I forgot to tell you. There's a curfew tonight. You'll have to stay here."

I fell asleep wondering about Frank, and was awakened by someone in the room. Louise? Dammit, not with her husband in the house! But whoever sat on my bed was too heavy for Louise.

Frank!

I sat up, and he said, "Don't turn on the lights."

"What's up?"

"I want to talk to you. I want you to help me. I want you to fly me over Yenan."

"Yenan? What the hell for?"

"I want to parachute into the caves of Yenan. I'm going to assassinate Mao Tse-tung."

"You're out of your fucking head."

"No, I've done it before. Many times. I'm serious. Dead serious."

"Dead is right. You wouldn't last five minutes in the Communist inner sanctum. This isn't Europe. You're not Chinese, and you can't even speak the language, for Christ's sake. If you want to commit suicide, do it closer to home. Better yet, go see a head shrink. You're sick, Frank."

"You just don't understand me, David. In England, you never understood me."

He laid a gentle hand on my thigh.

Oh, shit!

"Goodnight, Frank."

"Why do you say that?"

"Fuck off!"

He removed his hand. "You'd rather have Louise," he said bitterly.

"Sorry, Frank, but I get my jollies the old fashioned way. I'm not very proud of myself. About Louise, I mean. You gave me hospitality, and I took your wife. But she told me you sanctioned her having a lover. Tell me you don't, and I'll never see her again."

"Why not," he said sadly. "Someone has to perform my conjugal duties."

"Why can't you? Have you been to an analyst? Can't they do something for you?"

He laughed quietly. "I have no desire to have them do that something for me."

"Oh. Well, everyone to their own kicks. Sorry, I can't oblige."

"Why not?"

"Goodnight."

He got off the bed. "If I can enlist the Chinese to do the job, will you fly them over Yenan?"

His breathing made me switch on the bedboard light. He was standing by my bed, naked. Masturbating.

"Get out!"

With a nervous giggle, he turned and walked out. I lit a cigarette with a trembling hand. Jesus H. Christ. Now I had a queer on my board of directors.

After a fitful night, I left the house at dawn, and went to the CAT House for breakfast, then caught an airline jeep to the office on the bund. I was early for my appointment, and Harry Whiting called me in to join him for coffee. He was still built like the star halfback he had been in college. Only the streaks of gray in his full head of hair and his weathered face betrayed his fifty years. Though gentle and affable, he was a restless man who hated an office and made every excuse to visit the airline outposts so he could fly.

"Wingate told you our thinking?"

"Yes, sir."

He went to the wall map of China. "Take Weishien. It's only eighty statute miles west of Tsingtao, yet cut off completely overland by the Pa lu. Some goods get through by road or the river, but the Communists demand very high levies." He returned to his chair. "I know you'd rather stay a line captain, and I can't blame you. But suppose we just try it. We'll schedule you tomorrow to Tsingtao. Take an empty airplane and check the airstrip at Weishien. If it looks okay, land, and go into the city. Talk to the merchants, and learn the military situation."

"Has anyone talked to the Tsingtao merchants? Are they interested in trading with Weishien?"

"Yes, but so few people get in and out of Weishien, no

156

one really knows what's going on. There's no telephone, or even radio contact with them. We know a local militia general holds the city, that's all. Find out what they need, how much they're willing to pay for staples, and what cargo they have to ship out. Here's the schedule of rates we worked out for a Tsingtao-Weishien shuttle."

I went to the map. "The airfield is at Erh-shih-li-pao, five miles from Weishien. Suppose the Pa lu cut the road?"

"That's the risk you're going to have to take. We'll pay you a double hazard bonus for the trip."

"That's fine, Boss, but why risk a three man crew, and a Charley forty-six? Let me take that old Piper Cub we have out at Hungjao, and go in alone. I'm not trying to be heroic, it's just that in case of trouble, I can run faster, and talk faster if alone."

Whiting was delighted. "You can't make Weishien from here in a Cub, but we'll ship it to Tsingtao. Good. I'll get right on it."

"For one favour."

He grinned. "Shoot."

"I want to get to Chengtu. My family is there and I haven't seen them since before the war. I'd like—"

He was already on the phone to operations, and when he hung up, said, "Okay, there's a flight leaving here at thirteen hundred. Canton has one coming up from Chungking three days from now. You can catch it back. You'll have to deadhead, but we'll pay you flight time. How's that?"

"Thanks."

At Hungjao, I met Tex walking in with his crew from the aircraft. He seemed surprised to see me standing in the rutty field, halfway between the operations shack and the parking line. He shouted, "Hi, old Buddy. Where you bound?"

"Nowhere. I want a few words, old Buddy."

"Here?"

"Here."

His copilot and radio operator walked on, and Tex dropped his parachute and briefcase. He looked around warily, then gave a cocky grin. "Hey, I hear by the old vine they're gonna make you an assistant area manager up there in the north. Nice going." He rubbed his thumb and fingertips together. "T'ing hao cumsha in a job like that."

"Not near as much as selling a million bucks worth of aircraft for American Air Products."

He measured me with a grin. "Been wondering when you'd wise up."

"You owe me twenty-five grand."

"How do you figure that?"

"I set the deal up."

"Maybe you did, but as I remember you weren't interested. I signed the contract, and I don't rightly recall that you and me have a piece of paper saying we're partners. Do we? Sue me if you want."

"You sneaky, lying bastard!"

He laughed. "Aren't you. Oh, I ran into Maggie once on the street." He clucked his tongue. "It's not nice to tell lies, Highpockets. The way I figure it, we're even. Twenty-five grand for all that fucking with my wife. Maggie's worth it, wouldn't you say?"

"Your wife. You don't give a shit about Maggie. Why the hell don't you give her a divorce?"

He wagged his head. "I don't understand you, Highpockets. If I divorce her, she'll marry you. This way, you get all that screwing free and clear. If you're hankering for her, bring her out. Be my guest. I don't care if she shacks up with you over here."

"You're a first class prick, Tex."

"Ain't it the truth. Oh, by the way, how much do I owe

you for the ferry expenses? I don't want you to think I'm a welcher."

I stepped forward, and he jumped back, pulling a .38 automatic from his jacket pocket. "Don't get stupid, High-pockets. You forget I'm the guy with a motive."

And that was the end of it. I was not even as furious as I wanted to be. Perhaps I knew it would turn out as it did. And perhaps I was too excited about going home to Chengtu.

seventeen

MY father now wore only Chinese gowns, a great improvement. Being a tall, gaunt man with less hips and buttocks than a monkey, the crotch of his western-style trousers had always hung half way to his knees. He was as absent-minded as ever, vague about the passing years, puzzled. "The war? Oh, yes the war. It did not reach us." I think he would have said the same if shells had fallen outside the compound. Seeing him surrounded by piles of papers and books, I was reminded of the time a fellow missionary admonished him for losing Jesus. My father had looked up distractedly and pawed through his papers, certain he had it somewhere. He lived only for his dictionary.

My mother was something else. Her energy, always boundless, seemed to have increased with her years. Though fairly short, and now stout, you felt she towered over you. Instead of cancelling some of her many activities, she made space for my homecoming by simply pushing them apart, as if expanding the day by two or three hours. I was surprised how much Maggie was like her.

Almost immediately, she wanted to know when I was going to get married and to whom. When I lied that I had no one in mind, I could see her mentally ticking off her list of eligible girls. "Well," she said, "we'll just have to have a party to celebrate your return. My, but you should see how pretty Annabelle has become. Of course, she is your cousin, but I don't think there's any danger with second cousins."

I laughed. I had been home a few hours, and she had already picked me a wife and was planning the wedding. "Listen, you Irish marriage broker, don't try to make me your client. As far as Annabelle is concerned, forget it. Unless the dentists out here are magicians, I'll bet my pretty cousin still has buck teeth and is ugly as sin." I held up a hand. "Yeah, yeah, I know. She has a beautiful soul."

My amah wept when I picked her up like a child and hugged her. This Chinese woman, more mother to me than my own, was now a fragile figurine. She keened Chinese endearments as she led me by the hand to the servant quarters to show me off to her grandchildren.

All day there was a steady parade of uncles, aunts, and cousins, and with each a fresh pot of tea. To most of them, the civil war was remote, more like some Balkan uprising. They were more worried about the rumors that Ma Hung-kwei, Governor of Ningsha, and Ma Pu-fang, Governor of Chinghai, were planning to form a Northwest Federation to resist the Communists. Torn between fears of a Moslem regime and a Godless Communist government, many still prayed for Chiang Kai-shek. The younger men were for Mao Tse-tung, confident he would let them stay and carry on their good work in education and medicine.

My father said that Ta-ko's father, Chen Tai-hua, was very ill. "He grieves for an heir. After Chen Yi's death, he took new wives, but alas, only daughters."

I sent a boy with a note asking if I might visit Uncle Chen the next day. The reply said, "Come early."

That evening the uncles and aunts and cousins came to dinner. They were warm, gentle people who made me feel I had never been away. They treated me as if we had all been together last week. Their conversation was the same as when I had left. They talked of their missions and hospitals, the schools they had built or were building, the problems of cost and financing. They were interested in Canada for news of relatives. World War II existed because it had killed "poor cousin Charley." They were not very curious about China's civil war, or about conditions in Shanghai and Peiping. To them, even the Chinese in Chengtu seemed to exist only for their missions, hospitals, and schools. They were snug and secure in their Szechwan Basin, shut off from the world by the mountains.

I asked, "What makes you think Mao will let you stay?"

"Because our school system, copied in other provinces, brought the liberal philosophies that made their movement possible."

"Chou En-lai admitted it."

"But when they are in power," I said, "will they want a school system that teaches liberalism?"

They fell back on God. "He will not forsake us."

The next morning after breakfast, I walked to the House of Chen. The city had not changed, except for the new Kuomintang headquarters, guarded by smartly dressed M.P.'s in U.S. Army uniforms. There were a few army trucks, but goods and people were still moved by coolies. The people looked well fed, and I met no beggars.

The hutungs filled me with nostalgia. Bare-bottomed children stopped their play to shout, "T'ing hao, hubba hao." Around one corner, a small boy squatting with his split pants parted, was too busy at his toilet to give me more than a thumbs up welcome.

The Chen's red gate was as faded as the others, and gave

no hint of the opulence inside the compound wall. At my knock, the small door in the gate was opened by an old Chinese, who recognized me. He gave me the Buddhist salutation, "O mih-t'o-fuh"—Blessings O Jewel.

The path lead through a bamboo grove, formal gardens, and moon gates. Pagoda-roofed houses clustered around courtyards, each complex the private home of wives, daughters, relatives, and retainers. At the main house, I was ushered into a six pillar room. Uncle Chen, whom I called Ta-yeh, my father's elder brother, sat in a rattan chair, and wore a quilted gown despite the heat. His wrinkled face looked smoked and shrunken. He beckoned me to him, and I greeted him as a Tibetan. Bowing, I showed him my tongue and palms.

"Like precious ginseng, you restore an old man, Tzu tzu."

Here, I was second son.

"If Chang tzu could stand beside you, it would not matter what mischief you two had done, I would stuff your mouths with sweets." His voice was thin.

"Ta-yeh," I said, "Ta-ko did not die in Paris."

He glared at me. "I know. The body from Paris was not his. What do you know?"

"I saw him in Chungking during the war."

"Have you seen him since?"

"No, but I think he is in Peiping."

"Why has he made me mourn him all these years?" he demanded angrily.

I hesitated. "For political reasons. He must stay underground. They must not know he is alive."

"Who?"

"The Kuomintang."

"He is still a fool."

"No, no, Ta-yeh. You do not feel the wind here, but it

blows for change. Ta-ko is right. Forgive me."

He brushed aside my need to apologize. "You young live on the wild, windy surface. Age sinks man into life that is and will be. Down here, I know the storms I do not feel will calm, then blow up again. It matters not. All that matters is to provide the spawn to rise and sink. That is the only purpose of life. It asks no more. We are an ancient people, and give this wisdom early to each generation. Now you foreigners have caught their minds. You know only the surface, which you torture and tear more than a mad Devil King."

"You said, 'you foreigners.' Am I a foreigner to you?"

"Poor Tzu tzu. You are a chiao lu."

He was right. Like a jackass, I was a hybrid.

He clapped for a servant, who was ordered to bring whisky. "I do not drink it, nor do your hymn-singing relatives, so I assume you are thirsty."

"Extremely."

When I had my drink, I toasted him, and he lifted a cupped hand in response. He waited until I had finished. "Tzu tzu, my death approaches. Your news lets me die happy. Find Ta-ko. Tell him I forgive him." He closed his eyes. "Go now."

I bowed and left, thinking he was asleep, but as I neared the door, he called me back. Without opening his eyes, he said, "Take the whisky." His chuckle rustled like a dry leaf. "And tell your father that if he had had the sense to serve wine for the blood of Christ, I might have become interested in his faith."

Walking back to the home of my youth, from a past never mine, I understood purgatory. But my gloom vanished when I arrived home and was greeted by my sister, Cathy. She had come down from a village twenty miles to the north, where she taught school. My delight delayed shock.

Though only twenty-one, she looked like a bitter spinster, and when I asked why she wore such severe, unbecoming clothes, she shrugged. "And who should I dress up for?"

When I had seen her last, she had bid me bon voyage with a Bible cradled in her arm. Now her arms were limp at her sides, as from defeat, and her eyes were evasive. At first, she was excited, interested in what had happened to me, then she grew restless and eagerly agreed when I suggested we borrow horses and ride into the hills. An uncle supplied the mounts, and outside the city we galloped madly to the low mountain range to the east, which the Chinese believed to be the bones of a dragon.

We dismounted on the first rise, and letting the horses graze, sat in a meadow. "You look unhappy," I said.

She tore out handfuls of grass. "Aren't you?"

"Not really."

"At least you've been away."

"Why did you break your engagement to Steve?"

"I came to realize it was a mistake. He's the type who would say grace before making love." She glared at me for laughing. "It's not funny. Nothing out here is funny, or fun anymore. I must get away. I don't belong here. None of us belong here. Have you ever stopped to wonder at our incredible arrogance?"

I nodded. "Where will you go? China is your home."

"It's not my home," she cried angrily. "We live here as occupiers, conquerors. The Chinese hate us. They have always hated us. Every one of them."

"Not every one."

She looked up at me with brimming eyes. "I was in love with a Chinese boy and, and I know now that even when he made love to me, he hated me."

"Ah, Cathy, that's impossible. You're—"

"I'm not! He said he wanted to marry me."

"Then how can you believe he hated you?"

"Let me finish," she snapped. "We went to his father for permission, and he reacted as if I was an old syphilitic whore. I was not surprised, really, but it was the momentary expression on Lee's face. He must have known his father would refuse. For a second Lee could not hide a little smile. At first I thought it was from relief, but the more I thought about it, the more convinced I became that he was gloating. It was a glorious put down. The whole affair had been to humiliate me because I was a foreign devil."

"Lee who?"

"It doesn't matter."

"I'm sure you're overreacting."

She shook her head sadly. "Someone spread it all over town. Perhaps it was his father, but I wouldn't be surprised if Lee had boasted how he had figuratively and literally screwed a foreigner."

"I don't believe it."

"Why not? Look how we humiliate them. Patronize them. Laugh at their religions, or superstitions as we call them. We deserve it."

"Perhaps you should leave," I said. "Hell, we're all going to be forced to leave pretty soon anyway."

"You think Mao will win?"

"He's already won. It's just a matter of moving his troops south."

"Good. Then that will be the end of us here, the end of our meddling in their lives and customs."

We returned home, where a note summoned me back to the House of Chen. Uncle Chen was dying. The T'ai Pusah ceremony was already in progress. The statue of a local deity on a portable altar chair attached to two poles was being carried by four men. Two men in the lead beat gongs to warn everyone that a God was passing. Others fired off

166

strings of firecrackers. The procession, which included a number of Taoist priests, entered the Chen compound, and I followed it to Ta-yeh's pavilion.

A servant took me to his bed chamber filled with women, who were hastily dressing the corpse with padded underwear, and trousers. I approached mournfully to pay my last respects, when the dead man startled me by opening his eyes and angrily waving aside his dressers. He beckoned me to him and croaked, "Perform the duties of eldest son."

I nodded, and he gave himself back to his wives, who rather roughly pulled him into a sitting position to put on a padded vest, and then a brilliant red and yellow silk gown.

Appalled by their manhandling him, I protested to Number One wife. "You're hurting him. Stop. What are you doing?"

"He must be ready. Not those," she shrieked to a slave girl, who was struggling to stuff his foot into a boot. She ran to the bed, and tore the boot off. "Soft soles, fool! The dead cannot wear hard heeled boots."

While the women finished dressing him with a ceremonial headdress, servants put a door on two trestles. To my horror, they picked up the dying man, and laid him out on the bare wood door. He gasped with pain, and rolled his head back and forth.

"Put him back in bed," I cried.

"No, no. He must not die in bed. It would be forever haunted."

"Then at least a pillow under his head."

"No, no! If he sees his feet, his children will suffer."

Ritual was more important than the man.

It was a hard, noisy death; his groans and struggles accompanied by a din of gongs and firecrackers outside the window. Finally, he sagged into stillness, and a Taoist priest pronounced him dead. A second priest, who had been waiting with the Imperial almanac, looked to see if the time of death was propitious. Alas, it was unlucky. A third priest quickly hung a mirror over the doorway to change evil into happiness.

The women again surrounded the bier to undress and wash the body, then put his mortuary clothes back on. While the priests gravely consulted their books for the best time to lay the corpse in his coffin, one priest took me outside, where a group of men waited with lighted lanterns. I was given one, and as we walked to the temple, the priest instructed me as to my duties. In the temple, I informed Heaven that Chen Tai-hua had departed the Red Dust and begged the Gods to show him every kindness. I lighted incense, and jumped with fright at a deafening burst of firecrackers behind me.

Early the next morning, I met with the entourage in the temple to bring back Uncle Chen's soul, if we could find it. A priest rubbed a copper coin on the stone wall of the temple, and let it fall. He repeated it over and over, until the cash, for some reason, stuck to the wall.

"Ah," he cried with delight. "His soul is here."

We marched it back to the House of Chen, where paper wallets full of food were put on a paper sedan chair. The priests invited the soul to sit in the chair for its long journey to eternity, and I was told to light the structure. We stepped back to watch the smoke lift Ta-yeh's soul to Heaven.

The priests became distressed when I told them I had to leave the next day. The eldest son was vital to the coffin closing ceremony, and the time would not be lucky for two days. However, they returned to casting yarrow stalks, and after consulting their I-Ching, found that the day was lucky after all.

The corpse was laid out in a thick-walled wood coffin. A copper coin was suspended from a string, and dunked three times into his mouth held open by tiny wedges. They gave me the coin to wear around my neck. "It will bring you good luck and ward off demons." A small ball of cooked rice was put in his mouth for a farewell meal and the wedges removed.

Each of the three nails to seal the coffin had been wrapped with a hair from his head. As the cover was fitted on, I knelt alongside and said, "Fear not, Uncle. The noise will only be our nailing on the lid. Do not raise your hands, or they might be hurt by the nails."

I hammered in the first nail, and a carpenter the other two. The coffin was carried to the mortuary room, and placed on two trestles. A table at the head of the coffin was set with a red tablet bearing his name; a bowl of rice; an uncooked cock, plucked clean except for his tail feathers; a pair of chopsticks stuck into a hardboiled egg; and an incense burner. Two large red candles burned on the table, and under the coffin a small Chinese lamp with seven wicks. At the far end of the room, a mirror reflected the coffin to deceive the Gods into thinking there had been two deaths, and thus spare the family another for a long time. The coffin might remain in the mortuary room for months, while the priests sought the proper burial site and the lucky day.

I promised to return for the burial if possible, and flew back to Shanghai awed by the religious Chinese. They were much more involved with a spiritual world than the Christians, who called them pagan.

eighteen

FROM Shanghai, I flew to Tsinan, where we took on a load of cotton for Tsingtao. The cotton was in compressed bales, each weighing five hundred pounds. Two men lifted a bale onto a coolie's back, and he trotted up a shallow-step wooden staircase to the loading door. Half way up, he lost his momentum, and his legs began to tremble violently. Each gruelling step slowed his motion, and his quivering leg muscles bulged as if to burst his skin. At the last step, his foot lifted, missed, and he tottered backward. Instead of running up to give him the needed push, the Chinese below waited, ready to laugh if the load pulled him back down. With a scream, from pain, or to flog his body, he lurched onto the platform, where two coolies in the loading door caught the bale as he collapsed forward. He earned twenty-five cents a day.

Enroute to Tsingtao, I circled Weishien to study the city I was to visit in the Piper Cub waiting at Tsingtao. Weishien was two walled cities separated by a southerly crook in the river. The deeply worn road running east and west was empty, the railroad track overgrown, and I saw only one junk on the river. The airfield at Erh-shih-li-pao, five miles south, had a single, unpaved landing strip, and looked deserted.

Tsingtao was the main airbase for the United States Navy in China. Being also a Chinese Air Force base and a terminal for the three commercial airlines, it snarled with activity.

Taxiing to CAT's area, I stopped for a truck racing toward us up the taxi strip. The driver apparently did not see us until a hundred feet away, then swerved the truck off the strip and spilled half his load of soldiers. The mass, all arms and legs, bounced on the tarmac, slid, and burst apart. One did a grotesque cartwheel. The truck circled back, and the soldiers still aboard laughed nervously at their companions strewn on the ground.

I reported the accident to the U.S. Navy tower operator. "Roger, CAT. We saw it."

A jeep arrived with a Chinese officer, who jumped out shouting at the injured. Some struggled to their feet and staggered off. Others fell, then crawled when nudged by the officer's foot. A boy with a strange twist to his head did not obey and was kicked, but he was dead. They dragged him over to the side.

With flaps down, I taxied slowly past them, pitying the Chinese soldier. The rich escaped the draft simply by paying two hundred catties of rice. The poor became soldiers and poorer. If paid, it was by the official rate made worthless by the inflation. They were half starved because their officers were forced by their own low pay to sell part of their men's food ration on the black market. Each company was understrength for the same reason. Rosters were padded to increase the ration for sale. A CAF lieutenant was paid the equivalent of about $2.00 U.S. a month. If he flew fighters, his P-51 was usually armed with cartons of cigarettes instead of bullets. If he flew C-46's for the Chinese

Air Transport Command, he sold tickets and flew passengers, while we commercial airlines transported soldiers and ammunition. The Chinese Nationalist Army was so busy fighting to survive corruption and inflation, it had little time to fight the Communists.

When not drafted, the Chinese were impressed. In Tsing-tao, I had watched an officer count the number of soldiers waiting to be flown to Tsinan and battle. Fifty-nine? He counted them again. One missing. Drawing his Mauser, he climbed over the nearby perimeter fence, walked up to a farmer and put the gun to his head. With the farmer he had his full complement.

Another time, two soldiers hopped the same fence and lit out for the hills. Their comrades tumbled out of the trucks with shouts of glee and, lining up at the fence, fired away at the deserters. The farmers in between never missed a hoe stroke. Luckily, the fifty-eight guns missed everyone.

At the parking area, I paused in the open cargo doorway to stare at a CAT C-46 as it took off and went into a steep climb, engines screaming. Sirens wailed. The C-46 shuddered, dropped a wing, and slowly cartwheeled down to explode on the runway.

"Jesus!"

Four U.S. Navy fire engines reached the billowing smoke and poked their fog booms into it. But the men dressed in asbestos suits did not bother getting off the trucks. Suddenly, the fire engines backed up and drove away, as shells rose like rockets from the smoke. A large explosion threw a fan of debris.

I joined the knot of pale pilots standing outside operation's quonset hut. "Who was it?"

"Tully."

"The poor bastard."

We held a wake for ourselves, not Tully. We were shaken, our invincibility questioned, and our confidence jarred. The ease of Tully's crash made fragile our perch in the sky, rigid the laws, and swift the retribution if we broke one. Each of us felt doomed. Then, desperate to find the mistake Tully had made, the mistake we would never make, we began a litany of possible causes.

"Some slopey soldier fired his gun accidentally and shot him. He had sixty troops aboard."

"Naw. One of the bastards dropped a grenade. Shit, they carry 'em around in a bucket. You've seen 'em."

But that could happen to any of us and we disagreed.

"Gust locks. I'll bet some stupid damn mechanic slipped gust locks on his elevators while he was being loaded. I saw a kid in the army take off with 'em on. He went up and down just like Tully."

"Tully? Christ, I never knew a guy to run his controls through like Tully. Twice. Once after start-up and again before takeoff."

"He could have been beat. He was on his third shuttle to Tsinan. He never left the cockpit while they loaded him that last time. He'd been flying the same crate all day. Why couldn't he have thought there was no need to run his controls through again?"

It sounded plausible. It was an obvious error none of us would make. We always ran the controls through before takeoff. Those who had forgotten from time to time, which was every one of us, vowed never to forget again. Freed of Tully's death, we mourned him and reminisced over lunch in the chow shack.

"To think it could happen to Tully after all these years over here. He was a Flying Tiger, then flew for CNAC during the war. Hell, he must've logged close to ten thousand hours in China alone."

173

"Hey, Dave," Sam Koski asked, "where you going in the Cub?"

"Weishien."

"What the hell for?"

"To drum up some new business."

"Watch your ass. That place is swarming with Pa lu."

After a bowl of fried rice, I went to operations and signed for the Piper Cub. Ed Lawson, the chief mechanic, met me at the little yellow aircraft. "I think she has all her rubber bands." He grinned. "Watch out for all that power she's got. We put two jerry cans of gas in the back seat. Don't think the pumps are working over there in Weishien."

He swung the prop and started the engine. The tower gave me an aldis-lamp green to taxi, and it felt strange sitting so close to the ground. The smoke from Tully's wreckage was drifting across the new active runway, and I flew through it on takeoff, holding my breath against the smell of burnt flesh. I was ham-handed on the controls, but after a few practice turns over Chiao-chou Bay I got the light feel of the toy-like craft. At Chiao-Hsien, I picked up the railroad tracks and followed them, thinking about Tully, Louise, and Maggie.

I had phoned Maggie from Shanghai after my return from Chengtu, and told her to come out to China as soon as possible.

"You mean he's going to give me a divorce?"

"Negative. The hell with it. Just come out and live with me. He said he wouldn't care, or make trouble."

"What about mother?"

"That's your problem, Honey."

She promised to work on it.

Over Weishien, I spiraled down and buzzed the city in hopes someone would send transportation when they realized I intended to land at Erh-shih-li-pao. Finally, an old

174

truck loaded with soldiers came out through the city gates, and waited at the barbed wire check point. I came over low, waggled my wings, and headed for the airstrip. Dragging it for holes, I came around, landed, and taxied to the small group of buildings. I kept the engine running, ready to rise at the first threatening sign. When the truck arrived, I cut the engine and went to meet it. The soldiers covered me with their rifles, while a captain came from the cab with his Mauser drawn but not pointing at me. In English, he asked who I was.

In Mandarin, I said, "Captain MacCloud of China Air Transport in Tsingtao. I came to talk to your general and leading merchants about opening air service between Weishien and Tsingtao."

He holstered his gun, barked at his men to relax, and with a wide grin, waved me into the truck. On the way to the city, he said, "We need much. Our last battle left us short of ammunition. We sent a man to Nanking to ask for supplies, but they said they could not spare us any. With our own money, we bought arms in Manila, which Tsingtao customs has impounded. We cannot raise the money for the squeeze they demand. We sent our man back to Nanking to demand they force customs to release our weapons, but though Nanking said yes-yes, nothing has been done. They promised the CAF Air Transport Command would open a service to us, but you are the first aircraft to land."

"How close are the Pa lu?"

"They hold Ch'ang-lo, fifteen miles west, and are about the same distance south in the hills. They were closer, but after our last ambush, they pulled back to lick their wounds."

The approaches to the city were guarded by concrete pill boxes and an intricate network of zig-zag trenches that surrounded both cities. At a barbed-wire roadblock, an officer talked with the captain, and we were passed under the pole barrier. One of the sentries was a wistful boy shorter than his rifle with fixed bayonet.

We entered the walled city through a tunnel in a stone blockhouse. The dirt streets were narrow and bordered by frontless shops framed and draped with signs displaying large Chinese characters. In front of one shop, two men were cutting a 53 gallon drum into strips of steel with hammer and chisel. Another shop made crude tools and wrought utensils from the metal. Nearby five boys sat on the floor in a stall, each turning a small lathe with a bow and holding the cutting tool with the other hand. They supported their work, short pieces of branch, in a chuck and a wood bushing fastened to one knee. Coppersmiths beat thick slabs of copper into thin sheets, which others worked into bowls; silversmiths wove fine silver wire into delicate pins and broaches; potters turned their wheels with a foot treadle and shaped vases to be decorated with many dragons; brickmakers laid raw bricks in the sun to cure—dozens of varied home industries that had met the needs of the country for centuries.

We drove into the army compound, and I followed the captain into operations, a map-walled room filled with desks and a few officers, where I was introduced to Colonel Shu, a short, plump man with scraggly whiskers. "Where you from?" he asked with a Canadian accent.

"Toronto."

"Know it well. The chow still good at twelve and a half Elizabeth Street?"

"I ate there all the time," I said.

We talked about Canada, where he had lived for many years. He had been with the Canadian Army during the war, and while visiting his family in Weishien in '47 had been caught up in the civil war. I told him my business and asked about the military situation.

"It is quiet at the moment. The city is defended by a local militia only, commanded by General Li Tso-lin, a very remarkable man. He does not believe in static defense from behind walls. Three times we have let the Pa lu come within mortar range, then attacked them from the rear. If we had more weapons, we could push them back even further, and keep the area clear. We have trained every able bodied man and woman. Everyone must spend so many days a month on active duty or building fortifications. The morale is good, but would improve if we had more food and supplies. Your airlift is most welcome. For the commercial aspects, I suggest you talk with Mr. Tung. He is our leading banker and will call together the merchants he thinks will be interested in chartering your aircraft."

He phoned Mr. Tung, who said he could see me immediately. Colonel Shu gave me a jeep and driver and said I should return for dinner with General Li. "He will want to meet you."

Mr. Tung's bank looked more like a narrow shop with a typical long counter, but with no merchandise on display. He listened intently to me, studied the rate schedule, flicked the beads on his abacus, and said, "I will speak to some merchants this evening. If you will return tomorrow at ten, they will be here to discuss details."

Back in the army compound, Colonel Shu invited me to his quarters for a drink. He told how he had gone to sea from Tsingtao, leaving a wife and young son in Weishien. "Before I could get back, the Japanese had occupied the area, and I did not see them again until last year. Now my other family in Toronto is more or less in the same fix."

"I could fly you out tomorrow."

"No. This is my home, and General Li needs me."

"But you're fighting a hopeless war. No matter how successful you are here, the Kuomintang will lose the rest of China."

"We are isolated. I see the war from here, and the Pa lu are not difficult to beat. Of course, they have only about two thousand irregulars, and they don't want to capture Weishien. They're too smart to hole up in cities. This is the mistake the Japs made and which the Nationalists are making. We don't hole up either, and our guerrilla tactics keep them fairly well off balance. Also we are defending our homes, which makes a big difference in morale. How bad is it out there?"

"The Communists took Kaifeng to capture the food stores. When they pulled out, the Chinese Air Force, which had done nothing to help defend Kaifeng, bombed the city. There wasn't a Pa lu within miles. They say about two thousand civilians were killed."

He nodded sadly. "I have discussed with General Li the possibility of making some sort of accommodation with the Communists, but he is adamant. He views the conflict as just another battle in the constant war he has had to fight against war lords. When the Japs came, he was forced to retreat into the hills, from where he harassed them as the Communists harass us. But he is provincial. The city has virtually belonged to the Li's for generations. He feels it is his duty to protect his people. He scoffs at the ambitions of Mao. He does not believe the Communists can remain a unified movement."

"You can't blame him for holding out. He would be the first one shot by the Pa lu."

"General Li Tso-lin has no fear of death. He is old, and I think almost looking forward to it. He has enough sons and grandsons to tend his soul."

We went by jeep to General Li's compound, and inside I was reminded of the House of Chen. In a similar six column room, we were greeted by the general, a slight man of indeterminate age. He wore a simple charcoal-gray gown, his only uniform, and a gray fedora. His voice was soft, his Mandarin perfect in pitch. He said he approved of my mission, and led the way into dinner. After polite conversation over the first few dishes, I spoke of conditions I had seen in China and my fears of a Communist victory.

"Mao Tse-tung may defeat Chiang Kai-shek," General Li said, "but it does not mean he will unify China. Only he who has the Mandate from Heaven can unify and rule China. A hundred years ago there was a similar uprising. The Taipings were a pseudo-Christian movement, just as Mao's is pseudo-Communist. The Taipings almost reached the gates of Peking before they began to fall apart from the inside. Yet they held Nanking until eighteen sixty-four, and pockets for another decade. Our militia was formed by my great grandfather to protect our city from the Taipings. Since the fall of the Manchu Dynasty, I have led the militia against war lords, Japanese, and now the Communists. All movements tainted with foreign faiths and thoughts will wither and in time disappear. Mao may overthrow a corrupt regime like the Kuomintang, but he can never overthrow the ancient virtues. They will survive. We will defend our homes and hold to The Way. Life will go on the same, if not for me or my sons, then for their sons and grandsons. A gap here and there means little. Our family has survived worse disasters over the last three thousand years."

The next morning I met with Mr. Tung and six merchants, all dressed in the same blue cotton gowns. After the first round of tea, Mr. Tung rose and spoke for the group. "We are in accord. The city needs much and our goods, though few, are wanted in Tsingtao and will bring a good price. Is there room in your small aircraft for a passenger?"

"Yes."

"Then if you will take Mr. Chu here to Tsingtao, he will act as our agent there."

"How much tonnage is involved?" I asked.

"Twenty-five each way to start."

"Weekly?"

"Daily."

I was delighted.

"Can you handle it?" Mr. Tung asked.

"Easily. One aircraft making five shuttles can haul that amount."

"One small point," Mr. Tung said. "Who will assign the contracts for the charters?"

"I guess I will. In the beginning anyway."

"We would prefer it continues to be you."

"Thanks, but why?"

"When other merchants, here and in Tsingtao, realize the profits that can be made, they will want to charter your aircraft. This would deprive us of space and profits. If you will only grant charters to this group, we will pay you personally one tael of gold per ton."

Good Christ!

A tael was 1.33 ounces and worth U.S. $45.55 in Hongkong. Twenty-five tons each way meant a daily take of $1138; almost eight grand a week.

nineteen

IN Shanghai, I reported to Whiting, who congratulated me on the Weishien success. "There's one rub," I said. "They're provincial people. The've been screwed so often by people on the outside, they will only deal with me. I'll have to spend at least one day a week in Weishien. I don't mind using the Cub from Tsingtao, but it will mean juggling the regular schedules to get me back and forth from Peiping. If I had something with more range and speed, I could scoot down from Peiping. I could also scout around for other cities like Weishien."

Whiting snapped his fingers. "How about an AT-Six?"

The Harvard. "Perfect."

"I think I can con one out of the CAF. General Chou owes me a favour."

"They also want me to act as courier to Hongkong at least once a month."

Whiting was not surprised. Every major city in China acted as an independent country with its own customs and currency control. With no central banking, inflation ranged from three million CNC to one U.S. dollar in Canton, six million to one in Shanghai, and nine million in

Peiping. Since money could not be transferred by mail or telegram, banking transactions were handled by couriers, or smugglers. Foreign pilots were favoured as smugglers since they were rarely, if ever, searched.

"Wingate will give you the Peiping-Hongkong run once a month. Will you personally have to carry gold?"

"It's the only way they can transfer funds to pay CAT," I lied.

"Don't tell me about it. If you get caught, it's your ass."

"Business is business, Boss."

Whiting phoned the Chinese Air Force general, and in the end had to lease the AT-6 for U.S. $400 a month cash. Off the phone, Whiting said, "They'll ferry it over to Hungjao this afternoon. I'll get maintenance to go over it. Check with them in the morning. Make it pay."

"You bet I will."

I bounced out, chanting, "Piece of cake, piece of cake!" Once a week, I would pick up my 15 pounds of gold from Mr. Tung; once a month I would smuggle 60 pounds into Hongkong, and deposit around $32,000 to my account. In my Harvard, I would find other Weishiens with the same deal. I had it made. Intoxicated, I phoned Louise to come celebrate with me.

She hesitated because Frank was home, then agreed to meet me in a small Japanese restaurant. I was flirting with the geishas when she arrived, and at first I thought the girls annoyed her. When I dismissed them, Louise asked, "Why did you leave the other morning without saying goodbye?"

"Frank made a pass at me."

She chewed her lower lip. "Damn."

"Didn't you know he's queer, or were you just trying to kid me?"

She was distraught. "I knew, of course, or had strong suspicions. Maybe I didn't want to believe it. It's not very pleasant. I guess I hoped you would not find out. I didn't want you to hate him. He's basically very nice and kind."

"He's crazy." As I told her what had happened, her eyes filled with tears.

"Poor Frank," she whispered.

"He must see a psychiatrist. Not for his faggotry, but for his one-man army bit. Maybe the two aren't connected, but if he rings in the CIA and Chinese assassins you're a widow again. Talk to him or his boss. Someone has to blow the whistle."

She became alarmed. "Do you think he's already in danger?"

"Louise, for Christ's sake, every foreigner in China is spied on by the Kuomintang secret police. People like Frank are also covered by the Communists. Hell, he can't make a move without someone knowing about it. As long as he keeps his insane plans in his head, he's all right. The second he starts talking, he's in deep trouble. If he goes so far as to hire Chinese cutthroats, they'll take his money, go to the Communists and get paid to knock Frank off."

Louise shivered. "How horrible. What should I do?"

"Will he listen to you?"

"I don't know."

"Then go to his boss."

"And destroy his career?"

"That or his life."

She pulled herself together. "I'll talk to him. Where have you been?"

I told her about Chengtu, but not Weishien.

"Do you think you'll find Ta-ko?"

"Dr. Wong said that if I helped them with their problem, he would remember what he knew about Ta-ko."

"Then you've decided to you-know-what?"

I grinned because while waiting for Louise, it had occurred to me to sell my Weishien gold to Dr. Wong for credits against their gold in Hongkong. It would save a lot of hauling, and give me a lead to Ta-ko.

"The plot becomes more bizzare than the one I'm writing," she mused absently.

It struck me like a slap in the face. We were only actors on her stage—mere characters in her novel. "You knew Frank was a homosexual before you married him!"

Startled, she denied it.

"You're lying!" I shouted. *You knew!*

With surprising nonchalance, she answered, "Suppose I did. So what?"

"So what! He's nothing to you but grist. So am I. So is China. You married him so you could come to China. He told you he was posted to the AAG."

She shrugged. "What's so terrible about that? Frank needed a wife as cover and I needed financial security so I could write. We discussed it all very openly. I was tempted when he agreed I could take lovers, but the prospect of coming to China made the deal irresistible."

Her cold ambition shook me. "You're a bitch!"

Stung, she replied with sugared fury, "And you, Darling, are hopelessly naive."

"You've written down everything I've told you!"

She saw my fright and sensed the danger I was in. "No! David, I swear I haven't. I promised I wouldn't and I haven't. You must believe me! Please, Darling."

I refused. "Has Frank seen any of your work?"

She was now frightened. "Never! I keep my papers locked and he would never pry."

"How about the servants?"

"The cabinet lock has never been touched, and I never leave papers alone on my desk. David, I even burn whatever I've thrown in the wastebasket. Besides, I haven't written a word about Ta-ko, Dr. Wong, the gold—*nothing!*"

Two Japanese girls entered with trays and after bowing, knelt beside the brazier to cook our dinner. Morosely, I watched them stir fry the thin slices of beef and vegetables, until I noticed their almond eyes shunting between their work and Louise.

She was sitting stiff-backed with eyes closed and, like a child unjustly beaten, wept silently, her tears streaming down her face onto the chopsticks, clenched in her teeth, and dripping off the end like rain drops from a gutter. Gently, I took away the sticks, drew her head onto my shoulder and dried her face with a napkin. The girls kept a concerned eye on her as the sobs subsided, then concurred with smiles and bobs when I ordered lots of saki.

What right did I have to condemn her for a marriage of convenience: common practice in China. Nor would she betray me. I was being paranoid. We ate quickly and took a taxi to the Park Hotel to heal our wounds.

A hydraulic leak and a few minor repairs kept the mechanics working on the Harvard all morning. They sprayed out the Chinese Air Force insignias and painted the CAT tiger on the tailplane. It was the same yellow of RCAF training days, and I was eager to take her up.

I was off at noon, and north of Shanghai dropped down to the deck. She was no Spitfire, but I enjoyed racing over the rooftops and looking into the farm courtyards. I startled one couple copulating in a field, and laughed at the action my sudden appearance overhead must have caused. A donkey plodded in a circle, turning a millstone. Farmers threw up wheat for the wind to winnow the chaff. Many houses were roofed with cobs of early corn. Crossing the Yangtze, I panicked a junk's crew by approaching at deck level, then lifting over the bamboo cloth sail at the last moment. I stayed low over the shallow lakes and canals of the Grand Canal system, and landed at Hsuchow to refuel. I flew the last leg at 3000 feet. North of Hsuchow the countryside belonged to the Pa lu.

In Peiping, I reported to Wingate at the CAT office on Morrison Street. Whiting's wire had outlined the Weishien success and he wanted details. "If you're going to smuggle gold for those merchants," he said with fatherly concern, "you make damn sure they pay you. I think the going rate from Tsingtao to Hongkong is about a buck an ounce."

I feigned astonishment, and he became exasperated. "Didn't you missionary kids learn anything about China?"

"Certainly. Never drink unboiled water and never eat fresh vegetables unless they have been soaked in potassium permanganate."

He shook his head, then returned to business. "Okay, now if they can use one airplane a day making five shuttles, they can use two, even three. You get that kind of business out of a crappy little town like Weishien, and we got ourselves a new area manager."

"And Myra is . . ." I drew a finger across my throat.

He allowed a thin smile. "At times you do show signs of being aware."

I grinned most of the way home. Lu met me at the door with anxiety on his round, pockmarked face. "Major Tai inside."

"What the hell does he want?" I did not like Jack Tai and trusted him less. He was chief of a special branch of the Peiping gendarmery. His men had shot the students outside the mayor's house, about which he often bragged. He spoke excellent English and spent much time being a buddy to the American pilots.

The night I had picked up Lotus in the Alcazare, Dutch Maas, another CAT captain, had been with me. As soon as we were seated at a table in the beer hall courtyard, Jack

Tai, in T-shirt and slacks, joined us. When Dutch went to pay for the first round of beers, he discovered his wallet missing. Major Tai snapped his fingers, and a Chinese, also in T-shirt and slacks, hurried to our table. Bending toward his boss, he squeezed a large revolver out of his waistband, and they both grimaced as it clattered on the floor. When the embarrassed assistant had retrieved the gun, Major Tai gave him instructions, and in a few minutes the Alcazare was surrounded by a bicycle platoon of gendarmes. Major Tai was called outside and returned with Dutch's wallet. "A pedicab coolie," Jack Tai said.

Dutch's four $20 U.S. bills were missing. "You didn't find the money on him?"

"Sorry, Dutch."

A few days later, Major Tai arrived at Sui An Po Hutung with a beautiful brass and mahogany table, a gift for Dutch. Though I said nothing, I knew it was to repay Tai's theft of the eighty dollars.

Whenever I complained to Lu about a missing bottle of whisky, he would roll his eyes. "Major Tai, Master. He come often when you not home, search house, then take bottle. Evil man."

I suspected Lu of using the major to cover his own thefts, until I returned home around midnight after three days in Manchuria. As I crossed the dark courtyard to the bedroom, something moved in front of me, and a blunt point was jabbed into my stomach. I recognized it as a gun, and stood very still. "What do you want?"

"That you, Dave?"

"Roger."

The shadow laughed. "It's me, Jack Tai."

"What the fuck are you doing here?"

The gun left my stomach. "Just waiting for you. Wanted to show you my new Beretta automatic."

I switched on the light over the bamboo table in the center of the courtyard. "How did you get in?"

"Your boy let me in."

"He leaves at eight. You've been waiting four hours to show me a lousy gun?"

"Sure, Dave."

With men like Major Tai it did not pay to argue.

Now, he was sitting in the courtyard drinking my champagne. "Where have you been?" he asked.

"Just got in from Shanghai," I said in English, because I refused to speak Chinese with him.

"I know, but what took you so long from Westfield?"

I poured myself a glass. "You got a minimum speed limit in Peiping?"

He laughed. Tai was a handsome man, who looked half his probable age of forty. "I came over because I heard you'd flown back in a new aircraft."

"News sure travels fast."

"Not with telephones."

"What do our aircraft have to do with you people?"

"Nothing, until they're different. Anything new makes us curious. What are you doing in a CAF AT-Six?"

"Who says it's Chinese Air Force?"

"My men could see the CAF insignias under the new paint. Where did you get it?"

"Ask CAT in Shanghai. They assigned it to me."

"Why?"

"Because I'm an ex-single engine pilot and twin engines make me nervous."

"Suppose I told you the CAF reported the plane stolen."

"I wouldn't believe you."

He smiled, and poured himself another drink, but the bottle of champagne was empty. He shook it to let me know, but I ignored him and wished he would leave, then changed my mind. He was a poor drinker—or pretended he was. If the former, perhaps I would learn more than he. I called for another bottle, and after Lu had filled our glasses, Jack Tai said, "You're a funny guy, Dave. All the time we've known each other, and you never told me you'd been born and raised in Chengtu."

"How do you know now?"

He smiled at my facetiousness. "And most interesting is the fact that you grew up with Chen Yi. Tell me about him."

My dossier must have reached Peiping. "Why?"

"He's famous."

"How could he be famous? He died in Paris in his early twenties."

"He is a martyr to the Communists."

"I wouldn't know."

"Also, he is not dead," Jack Tai said.

"Then you know more than I do."

"Lots more."

"Well, I guess that's what you get paid for. Jack, I'm bushed. I just spent four and a half hours hand tooling that little bird, so if you don't mind, I'm going to crap out for a couple of hours."

He finished his drink. "You'll need it if Lotus is coming over."

"Yeah." The bastard! Lotus was probably his agent. I saw him to the door, and when he was gone, I told Lu to lock it. "Wake me in a couple of hours. If Lotus calls, tell her I'm sick."

In bed I was unable to sleep. Tai worried me. In one way, I was glad he had come. With nothing to fear, I had discounted Major Tai. But soon I would be carrying gold and hiding it in the house. It was better to know his people were watching me. I had planned simply to phone Dr.

Wong and invite him to dinner, but not now. My phone was probably tapped. Tai's knowledge of Chen Yi was the most ominous. I must not lead Tai to Dr. Wong. How could I contact him?

I resolved it the next day on our first flight to Taiyuan. On course, I gave K.S. Chu the controls, and called T.S. Wang back into the cabin. "T.S., where are your sympathies?"

"I don't understand."

"Here in China."

He did not change his expression. "Why?"

"Do you know Major Tai?"

He said nothing.

"He's bugging me."

T.S. waited.

I had to trust him. "I have to meet with a Dr. Wong Fo-ying of Yenching University. I'm afraid to phone him, afraid to have him to the house. I can't trust the pedicab coolies in our hutung to carry a message, and if I go to him, I'll be followed. Can you help?"

"When do you want to see him?"

"Tonight."

"Leave it to me."

After three round trips to Taiyuan, ten and a half hours in the air, we secured the C-46 at Westfield. Walking in from the aircraft in the dark, T.S. said, "Make certain no other people come in taxi with us."

I was about to ask him why, then remembered Dr. Wong. But hell, we had only left the aircraft at Taiyuan. How could T.S. have arranged a meeting?

In the cab, I fell asleep until the rattling old Dodge stopped. Soldiers again asking for a lift. They got on the running board, and I dozed off.

T.S. nudged me. "We get out here."

I sat up and looked out. The headlights shone on a small farmhouse. "Where are we?"

"A village. Come."

Getting out, I saw that the two soldiers were still with us. "Who are they?"

"Friends," T.S. said, and led the way into the house. The room was lit by a kerosene lamp, turned low. T.S. motioned me to a chair by the table, and I sat down as a figure emerged from a dark corner. "You wanted to see me, Captain?"

Dr. Wong. I looked at T.S. "How the hell?" and then I knew. The wireless! How goddamn clever. With agents as radio operators in the air and on the ground, the airline wireless network gave the Communists a China-wide communications system. With every radio operator tapping out and receiving smuggling information in various codes, no one could detect, or even suspect a Communist code.

"You have decided to help us," Dr. Wong said in Mandarin.

"Yes, but with a source of gold inside China, if you will give me credits against your gold in Hongkong."

"Easily arranged. How much can you deliver?"

"Fifteen pounds a week. Too much?"

"Too little. We can use more."

"I may get more. How do we work it?"

"T.S. will instruct you."

"What about my credits?"

"You will receive chits, which the Nensing Bank in Hongkong will honour."

"How do I know?"

"Because we need each other. If we cross you, you could harm us. But you are now in danger. You obviously know our communications system. If there is a leak, you will be blamed and probably killed."

"Without a hearing?"

"We cannot afford liberal luxuries."

"I can leave evidence behind," I said.

"Also relatives in Chengtu."

"The deal's off."

"Too late, Captain," he said gently.

"I want to see Chen Yi."

"Chen Yi is dead."

"The hell he is. Even Major Tai knows he's alive. My finding Chen Yi was part of the deal."

"That is impossible for now. But he is well. He said to tell you the duck in Chungking was not stolen."

"I must see him. I have an important message from his father."

"I will convey it," Dr. Wong said.

"Not for free."

"Terms?"

"A fair shake if anything goes wrong," I said.

"A hearing?"

"A favour."

"It depends on the message," he said.

"His father died last week. I acted as eldest son, but before he died, I told him Chen Yi was alive. He said the news would allow him to die happy."

"Is that all?"

"He said to tell Chen Yi he is forgiven."

"I will tell Chen Yi." Dr. Wong stood. "Beware of Major Tai. He has your dossier. Though he knows nothing of importance, he is curious and watches. Work only through T.S. He will give you codes and procedures. Be careful. If there is a serious break, we may not be able to move fast enough to honour the favour."

twenty

THE Weishien operation ran smoothly all August. Once a week I flew down in the Harvard and collected my fifteen pounds of gold from Mr. Tung. The eighteen 10 tael bars, each like a thin chocolate bar, fitted easily into my briefcase. I arranged to land at Westfield after sunset and at the tie-down the mechanic, who climbed up on the wing-root to help me disembark, slipped me a half CNC bill. Under the map light, I checked it with the half T.S. Wang had given me. If they matched, I let him carry my briefcase and parachute to operations. He stored the chute and returned my briefcase fifteen pounds lighter. If bad weather made me return to Peiping in daylight, I kept the briefcase and gave the gold to T.S. the next time we flew together.

But keeping gold in the house made me nervous. Afraid to leave it, I stayed home and ruined my social life. Afraid Lotus was an agent for Major Tai, I broke with her and ruined my sex life. The rare times that the Peiping long distance radio telephone operated, I called Maggie to hurry out to China.

When forced to babysit a gold shipment, I would invite people to dinner; usually pilots with their mistresses or whores, and some foreign correspondents and wives. Lu's dinners were always delicious; the guests never dull.

One shapely Russian girl loved to dance the can-can. When encouraged, she would drop her underpants and high kick them into one of the apricot trees. In the morning, the magpies would shriek until Lu removed the indignity. After four champagnes, a sloe-eyed Eurasian beauty was ready for bed with anyone, starting with the gentleman on her right. If he had a wife across the table, words flew, sometimes rolls, once a full plate. Skull Sanders, an American copilot, arrived at the house sober; to the table drunk and naked to the waist. His hairy chest detracted from his ugly face. Unscathed by the war, he had been scarred and left with a silver plate in his head by a postwar habit of rolling cars when drunk. After one party, I went to brush my teeth and caught Skull climbing fully clothed into the empty bathtub.

"What the hell are you doing?" I asked.

"I, you damn fool," he said with dignity, "am going to bed."

At one dinner, Spencer, the AP correspondent, told about his new swimming pool, which had only cost one hundred dollars U.S. "Plus a twenty foot deep dry well to drain it."

What a perfect place to hide gold: on the bottom, in the drains, or the dry well. I ordered a pool from Spencer's builder, plus the renovation of an empty three pillar wing of my landlord's house. It was to be a separate apartment for Maggie because of my Methodist conscience.

The morning the pool was finished and filled, I said, "Now for the first swim," and disturbed the bland expression on Lu's face. I went through the foyer into the outer courtyard and started for the pool at the far end. Drawn by the sound of hammering, I took the path between the lava stones to the moongate in the wall. On the other side was the little house being remodelled for Maggie.

The Chinese were ripping dimensional timbers from logs with primitive bucksaws and hand-planing the frames for the panes to glaze in the front of the house. Inside, the moongate into the bedroom had been given its black cement border. The fireplace in the living room was almost finished. A crew was installing the fluorescent lights built into the walls and ceiling. The terrazzo floor was being ground by a large flat stone pushed and pulled by coolies at the end of a pole and rope. The whole house, rebuilt except for the columns and roof, was only going to cost U.S. $280.

The pool was 30′ x 15′ x 8′ deep. A dozen Chinese had dug the hole, built a double brick floor and walls, and plastered on three layers of cement. When a wall of Spencer's pool collapsed, I told the builder to put in steel rod reinforcement and two more inches of concrete. This cost an extra U.S. $100. Then we discovered there was only a one inch water main feeding the compound, much too small to fill the pool and supply the five houses. The city put in a larger main for U.S. $100.

"Everyone must think it's the smallest bill I have," I grumbled.

To my suprise, the pool was empty. "Lu," I shouted. "Get the builder."

He came limping on his crippled leg. When I pointed indignantly at the concrete pit, he grinned, pleased with his work. "All finished," he said in Chinese. "You can put in water."

"I did last night. Where did it go?"

"In deep hole. It works fine. You left drain open."

I gave the valve a twist. "Not open. Where did the water go?"

"I not take."

"How come the damn pool is dry?"

He grinned. "Pool leaks."

"But why does it leak?"

"Water always leak through cement. Cement not hold water."

"Did you know that before you built the pool?" I asked.

"Oh, yes."

"You mean you knew the pool would leak?"

"Oh, yes."

"And you're in the pool business?"

"No more. Start with Mr. Spencer, finish with you. Not many customers for big cement hole."

"How long have you been in the house building business?"

"Start with you."

"Great."

"Not great," he cried. "Need more money."

"You got your down payment. You don't get another damn cent until the house is half finished. That's our agreement. Right?"

"Right. But if you no pay me more money until house is half finished, I no get house half finished. You give me a little, please."

"Nothing."

"Twenty dollars?"

"No."

"Maybe ten," he said hopefully.

"Nothing."

"Need money to buy glass. Glass very dear. You give me five dollars."

"Not one cent."

He sighed and returned to Maggie's house. On my way

in, I saw a strange Chinese sitting on the little outside verandah. Inside, I asked Lu, "Who's that joker?"

"Builder owe him plenty money for building your house."

"What's he hanging around here for?"

"He wants money."

"That's between him and the builder."

"He ask me to ask you to pay builder a little money."

"Get the builder and bring 'em both in."

When all were assembled, I explained the contract that called for a third down, a third when the house was half finished, and the balance on completion. "Is that clear?"

"Oh, yes," they said.

"You both understand?"

"Oh, yes."

"Good. Now you get lost," I told the stranger, and pointing at the builder, I said, "And I don't want another word out of you about money. Okay?"

"Okay."

They walked out with Lu, but at the door they stopped and turned like a chorus. "Oh, Master," Lu said. "Just one small thing."

"Now what?"

"You pay them maybe twenty-five dollars?"

I admitted defeat with a burst of laughter and gave them ten dollars. "And paint the pool with paint, oil paint, not whitewash."

"Oh, yes."

To my surprise they used the right paint and stopped the leaking. Tying the gold into a string of bars, I dove to the bottom and pushed them into the horizontal four inch drainpipe with a straightened coat hangar. If Major Tai, who probably could not swim, opened the valve to drain the pool, the bars would be flushed safely into the dry well. I had marked the buried manhole cover by pacing and triangulation.

My hiding place was finished just in time. On the first of September, Weishien tripled their charters. Three C-46's began flying five trips each. My take rose to U.S. $3416 a day! But the gold now weighed 44 pounds a week, too much for my briefcase.

"What'll we do now, T.S.?"

He laughed. "See how much trouble money makes?"

On our next flight together, he gave me a fine canvas vest with a hundred pockets, each the exact size for a gold bar. The shoulder straps snapped apart so I could drop the vest without removing my shirt or flight jacket. At Westfield, the mechanic with the half bill took the vest and in seconds, he had it under his jacket. T.S. returned the empty vest with my chit on our next flight.

On the eve of my first monthly flight to Hongkong to cash in my chits, Myra Goldman invited me to dinner. I begged off, but she insisted. "Dave, you must come. We haven't seen you for ages. Where have you been hiding? You're not trying to avoid us, are you? John does want to talk to you about business. After all, you never come into the office."

I finally accepted because I had been avoiding them. I knew from Wingate that the increase in Weishien business worried them because they had always told Shanghai there was no money to be made servicing isolated little cities. Weishien had proved them wrong.

The Goldman's rented one of the many large Chinese houses owned by an American missionary. A houseboy escorted me through columned rooms and moongates to a small sitting room. Myra, her voluptuous body barely covered by a tight, black sheath, greeted me with a kiss meant for a lover.

"Sorry I'm too early," I said, as she led me to sit beside her on a couch.

"You're not, Darling. There's just us. It's time we two China hands had an intimate talk," she smiled, "and things."

There was nothing subtle about Myra. She exuded seduction, but her mood was business and her eyes were a fierce green. "Have you found any other Weishiens?"

"I tried Paoling-fu, but the Pa lu lobbed a mortar shell on the field. Jehol wants service, but they'll have to build a new airstrip. That cliff makes the one they have too hairy."

"You have been busy," she said sweetly.

"That's why Whiting gave me the little yellow bird."

"Why didn't he work through me? I mean John. After all, he is the area manager."

"Don't ask me, Myra. I don't make policy. The boss said try Weishien and I did. You talk to him."

"I have, and he intimated you might get John's job."

"No thanks. I don't want it."

"But Wingate does," she snapped.

I lifted a hand. "Leave me out of that. Myra, they picked me for this new business bit because I can fly and speak Chinese. I'm not out to screw you, or—"

She laughed raucously. "Why not?"

"God, you're a hussy. The more business I bring in, the better for you."

"Only if we handle it. It's ridiculous for you to fly back and forth doing the work of a station manager. It's time we put one of our men down there."

I shook my head.

She squinted with suspicion. "Why not?"

"They will only deal with me."

"How much squeeze are you getting?" she demanded.

I smiled at her. "Not enough to split, Sweetie."

"Ha! We'll see about that."

"Don't get greedy, Myra. Remember I speak Chinese better than you do. I know what's going on and can guess what your take is. I also know some Chinese gentlemen who are very unhappy. Seems they were forgotten when it came time to cut up a pie. That's very naughty of you."

"Balls!"

"And you get your share of them, too."

She laughed. "You are a bastard. I like you, Davie. We'd make good partners."

"Where?"

"Wherever you like." She kissed me and filled my mouth with her tongue. I slipped my hand in on her breast and she stroked my thigh.

"Here?" I asked.

"My passion room," and she led me upstairs to her Chinese red bedroom. With one zip she was naked and helped me undress. She dazzled me with the talents of her vaginal muscles. Yet I could not escape the feeling that my pumping actuated a meter, whose tally I would one day have to pay.

When we were dressed in robes, we had dinner served in the bedroom. After brandy, I picked up my clothes. "It was a great meeting of two old China hands."

She laughed gaily. "Stay."

"I have the Hongkong run tomorrow."

"But it leaves at a civilized hour."

"Where's your good husband?"

She shrugged. "He wouldn't dare come in here except by invitation."

I felt like the Surrogate Husband of the World.

"We proved one thing," she said. "We're good partners in bed. Now how about business?"

"Sorry, but Weishien's mine."

"We each split. Half of mine may be more than half of yours."

"What about John?"

"If Whiting gives you his job, what can I do? I don't make policy. We're a natural combination, Davie. John doesn't have a clue about China. He got the job because of me. He's rather useless in many ways."

"You'd dump him?"

She snapped her fingers. "Like that."

"My girl may be coming out from Canada."

"I won't interfere."

"Let me think about it."

twenty-one

ON September 15, the day Tsinan fell to the Communists after a five day battle, Maggie arrived in Shanghai. As she came off the Pan American DC-6, I saw I had forgotten how beautiful she was. When she saw me standing at the bottom of the ramp, she almost tripped in her haste.

In the CAT car to the suite I had reserved in the Park Hotel, she alternated between crying and hugging me. She asked questions, then talked before I could answer. In bed, we went wild, and she would not let me go tame. At last she sat up and with a long sigh, smiled with contentment. "You have no idea how much I have thought, dreamt, wanted, and needed you."

I moaned into my pillow.

"You poor dear. Did I hurt you?"

"I think you broke it for good."

The next day, I showed her Shanghai, explaining it was different, on the verge of panic. The shops were almost bare, not because the Red Armies were moving south, but because the merchants did not trust the new Gold Yuan currency. When CNC had inflated to six million to one U.S. dollar in Canton, nine million to one in Shanghai, and twelve million in Peiping, the government overnight stabilized the rate of exchange at twelve million to one, and replaced the CNC with Gold Yuan at 4 GY to U.S. $1.00. The Chinese threw up their hands and buried their goods.

Devaluing the currency nationally at the highest black market rate only proved how blatant was the deception of the official rate by which the government paid its employees. Worse, every GY note, printed in the States during the war, bore a 1945 date. "If the new money is any good," the Chinese reasoned, "how could the government afford not to use it for three years?" Then by decreeing that everyone must turn in all gold, silver, and U.S. currency for GY, or face a death penalty, the Kuomintang put a gun to their last supporters. "It's obvious," I said to Maggie, "that the boys in the back room are cleaning out the till before they run away."

China fascinated Maggie. She asked questions like a precocious child, stopping every now and then to hug me. "Watch the ribs," I cried. "Watch the ribs."

"I love you."

"Later."

"I love you now, before, later, forever."

Our Chinese audience grinned and bobbed their heads.

That night, we flew back to Peiping. On course, I called Maggie into the cockpit and K.S. gave her his copilot's chair. Holding hands, we drifted north through a starlit night. Then a glow appeared on the horizon and grew into a patch of scattered coals; still glowing.

"What's that?" Maggie asked.

"Tsinan. That pile of rubble now belongs to the People's Republic of China." I wondered how many had died below; how many more would be denied the chance to enjoy or suffer the new China.

"How awful," Maggie said.

"We can take some credit. Progress, our most important product, has helped tear apart their Yin and Yang and all the king's horses and all the king's men can't put it back together again."

In Peiping, Maggie loved her little Chinese house. She loved Lu and Soo and Koo. She loved the children in the hutung. She loved the city. And somehow, she had enough left over to love me.

The Chinese took to Maggie as quickly as she took to them. They called her Ta kuniang: tall girl, and wherever she strode, children and beggars trailed as behind a pied piper. The pockets of her flowing coat were filled with sweets for one, coins for the other. In the markets and shops, she bargained with a zest they admired. To help her, they taught her finger bidding and a smattering of Chinese.

When a rainstorm collapsed part of a house on our hutung, Maggie stood knee deep in the rubble, helping the family shovel mud and find utensils. In the yap of dogs and chant of peddlars, she could hear the wail of a sick child and find the house. And they yielded to her, though all she really had to offer was love. They understood.

I told her about having the two pedicab coolies in our hutung pick the apricots in the courtyard. When the living room verandah was filled with bushels of fruit, I sent Lu out to invite in the hutung kids. He returned saying they were too shy, but soon a pair of dark eyes peered from behind the tree. One by one, the children came timidly, and we had to convince them they could eat all they wanted. One little naked boy became streaked with juice. Afraid they would gorge themselves sick, I told them to take all they could carry and leave. They helped each other stuff pockets and shirt fronts. The naked boy left clutching as many as he could. Minutes later, he was back for deserved seconds.

"Oh, David, let's give them a party."

I gave Lu twenty dollars U.S. and said, "Make the arrangements and invite the kids, but if you take one penny squeeze, I'll break your shaved head."

He rolled his eyes indignantly.

Almost three hundred children arrived in their finest clothes. The naked little boy came naked, but scrubbed pink. Almost as many parents crowded in the open compound gate to watch the troupe of magicians and jugglers Lu had hired. There was so much ice cream and cake and cookies, I suspected Lu had contributed money.

The foreign colony never asked Maggie's last name. Though the pilots knew she was Tex Burke's wife, they said nothing. They had a strict code of honour about women. But at one party, the young wife of a pilot somehow discovered Maggie was married, but not to me. "You're living in sin!" she shrieked.

Her husband became furious. "It may be a sin in Topeka, but here it's none of your damn business. Go missionary on me, and you're back in Kansas."

Maggie was not as tolerant. I came home one night to be greeted with the announcement that she was leaving to move in with Tex. I was aghast. She watched me sideways, her head high. "After all, he is my husband."

My rush of words tumbled out as an incoherent roar.

"Why shouldn't I?" she demanded.

"You're crazy! What the hell's gotten into you?"

"It's what you get into."

"What are you talking about?"

"Lotus, Darling. Sweet little plump-assed, big breasted Lotus. Your Chinese whore."

I juggled imaginary balls and dropped every one. "Lotus?"

"Lotus."

"Just where did you run into Lotus?"

"Right here. She came this afternoon prepared to spend the night."

"I didn't invite her."

"It seems you don't have to. She comes regularly. Oh, stop squirming. We had a delightful chat over tea."

"You and Lotus."

She nodded.

I showed palms of defeat. "Okay. But I haven't touched Lotus for a month."

"And won't?"

"Maggie, for Christ's sake, why should I? How could I? Lotus was just better than nothing."

On the 24th of September, we evacuated our people from Chinchow and managed to fly most of our drums of fuel to Mukden. Wingate was the last to try landing, but on his approach, a shell burst behind a CAF P-51 taking off. He asked the tower to confirm shelling and was told, "Oh, no. Only fighter exhaust." But bursts trailed the fighter all the way down the runway. With the fall of Chinchow, the Nationalist's lost their only seaport in Manchuria.

I came home after a week, feeling I had spent all of it in the air. Maggie literally bathed and dried me, and tucked me in to sleep all day. In the evening, we sipped champagne by candlelight in the courtyard. A dented-coin moon rose behind the gingko tree into a sky of jet and diamond dust. The apricot trees were silhouettes and against the glow of Cioffanni's courtyard next door, the mimosa draped like black lace. A victrola played softly from the living room.

Lu came and said in Chinese, "There is a lady to see you."

Lotus! What game was that bastard Tai playing? But the foyer was empty. "Where is she?"

"In Missey's house." Lu was not going to repeat the

mistake he had made before with Lotus. "Her name is Missey Carlson."

I ran through the moongate and saw Louise pacing inside the house. She met me at the door. "David, there's trouble!"

"How did you get here?"

"On CAT. Mr. Whiting. I tried to phone you, but couldn't get through, and Mr. Whiting—oh, David." She was pale, trembling.

"Sit down." I made her down a stiff drink. "Now what's up?"

"Frank took my journals."

"Your what?"

"Journals. Manuscript."

I felt weak. "You broke your promise."

"Yes," she whispered.

"You wrote everything down? Ta-ko, Chen Yi, Dr. Wong Fo-ying? The Communist purchasing ring? Gold? The works?"

She nodded and I jumped up to pace angrily. "How could you be so stupid!"

"I'm sorry."

"Sorry? Shit! I thought I could trust you. You promised! This isn't *Ladies' Home Journal* suburbia. Here they take heads off for what they suspect is inside. People don't dare talk, much less write *anything* down." I gulped a straight whisky, then made us each one with water and sat next to her. "Okay, it's done. Tell me exactly what happened."

She had to take a few deep breaths before she could speak, then choked back sobs. "You—you know I—I want to write. I kept a journal and had started a novel. Frank knew, but—but he never looked. He—oh, David!" she wailed and burst into tears. "I'm so—so sorry."

"Please, Louise. It's important." My life was at stake.

"I kept them locked in a cabinet. Maybe he—he saw a page. This afternoon, after he left for Nanking, I found the cabinet broken open." She sniffed and blew her nose. "I phoned and demanded them back." Tears streamed down her cheeks. "He said he would. He said he only wanted to copy the information. He thanked me. He said he could now do something. I asked what, and he said he was going to Peiping to get Dr. Wong Fo-ying and break up his ring."

"Alone?"

"I think so."

"The damn fool. He won't last two hours. Are you sure he didn't mention the CIA?"

"I don't think so."

"He must have." If I told Wong that only Frank knew and had come alone, they would cut his throat. "Frank will be flying up on the regular army transport, which arrives noon on Wednesday. Is that today or tomorrow?"

"Tomorrow."

We had time. I rang the buzzer for Lu and told him to bring Maggie. She burst in and bristled at Louise. I introduced them and said, "I want you two to stay here and turn all the lights off. Keep the front door locked and don't let anyone in but me."

Maggie studied Louise's tear-stained face and sensing my tension, turned out the lights without a word. She locked the door behind me and in my house, I told Lu to go home.

"No dinner?"

"No dinner. Go."

I phoned T.S. "I can't raise the damn office. Do you have a copy of tomorrow's schedule?"

"Yes."

"And do you have an extra copy of the new letdown procedure charts? The cover is broken on mine."

"Okay. I'm busy right now, but I'll send someone over with them."

"Thanks, T.S."

I went to the bedroom for my briefcase, but could not find it. Goddamn tidy women. Where the hell had she put it now? I finally found it in the bathroom, hanging from the shower curtain rod, drying along with her undies and stockings. She had washed off the mud. But where were the contents? My Luger? I rifled drawers, looked under beds and pillows, and found it on the top shelf of the medicine chest, safely out of the reach of children.

Turning out all lights, I left the front door unlocked, blew out the candles in the courtyard, drew a chair into the shadow under the apricot tree, and sat down to wait. For whom? Who would come? Major Tai because a strange foreigner had come straight from the airport? Anything different interested Tai. Dr. Wong Fo-ying in need of help to escape? Or would it be his gunman with a shot in the dark, because I had broken Dr. Wong's cover?

He had promised me a favour. At least a hearing. I had not told Louise about their communication system. That apparatus was safe. All she knew, and all Frank knew, was that Dr. Wong Fo-ying headed a Communist weapon pur-chasing group. Wong had only to disappear.

My chair faced the foyer door into the courtyard. My back was to the little door connecting my landlord Ci-offanni's courtyard and mine that I never heard open.

The gun was a cold ring pressed against my neck as a hand reached over my shoulder and took my Luger. I held my head straight and swiveled my eyes to watch a shadow walk to the center of the courtyard and sit at the table. Unable to see his face, I worried. Was it Major Tai, or Dr. Wong?

"Who are you?"

"Whom did you expect?" the shadow asked in perfect English.

"Not someone with a gun in my neck."

"Remove it," he ordered, adding, "This is your hearing."

"Who listens?" I asked.

In Mandarin, he said, "Pei died for a stolen duck."

"*Ta-ko!*"

But for a dog barking in the hutung, the courtyard remained silent.

"Ta-ko?"

"I am Dr. Wong Fo-ying," he finally said in Chinese, which I did not believe because the voice was not Wong's. His reference to Pei said he was Ta-ko, but his pitch was wrong for Chen Yi. Since Dr. Wong knew about Pei, perhaps Major Tai had learned of our code, but it was not Tai speaking. Afraid I was faced by an unknown assailant, I strained to make out the vague shape in the shadows of the apricot trees. "Is it you, Ta-ko?" I pleaded.

"Speak. This is your hearing—Hsiung ti."

It was Ta-ko! But instead of being overjoyed, I became as angry as I had in Chungking during the war, when he had greeted me with a curt order to leave China. "Why do you break my bowl instead of embracing me as your brother?"

"If you prefer a brotherly chat to your hearing, prattle on—for your last few minutes."

As if his cold blood flowed through me, I told him with a tremor about Louise and her journals.

When I finished, he asked, "And you swear you told her nothing about the communications network?"

"I swear."

"If you're lying, you only postpone your death."

"I own a favour."

"The favour I owe you cannot forgive that betrayal."

Knowing there was no danger, I relaxed. "What now?"

"My cover being broken is not serious. Dr. Wong Fo-ying was destined to vanish in a few days. Colonel Chen Yi has been ordered to active duty. But now I cannot wait for my transportation. You must fly me to my command."

"Where?"

He laughed softly. "Weishien. Your days of corrupt wealth are numbered, Hsiung ti. We will go in your small aircraft."

"We can't leave until around four o'clock. There are no runway lights at Weishien."

"Might Major Tai visit?"

"He's done it before. I think it would be safer if you waited in the other house with Mrs. Carlson. If Tai drops in here, he will only find Maggie and me in a domestic scene."

"Lead."

Maggie opened the door. In the dark, Louise gasped when I introduced Colonel Chen Yi. I explained they must keep the lights off. "The alarm in the bedroom is set for three. The cab will pick us up at about three-thirty. I'll bring you a flight jacket."

On the flagstone path to the moongate into my outer courtyard, I began to gasp like a blown runner. In a way I had raced death and run into Ta-ko at the finish line. Only it was a starting line on a new track with unknown hurdles, and the starter fired bullets. All was elbowed aside by Maggie striding past me to vanish in the black hole of the moongate. Oh, Christ, I thought wearily, Louise has told her about us, and I expected to be ambushed when I entered the house. But she had swept through to the bedroom; the drapes in the living room were still swaying from her wake.

I knew then that Louise had not squealed. If so, Maggie would have been standing on the hearth like a vengeful goddess, arms akimbo. Not that Maggie needed to be told. She could detect infidelity as a male moth could a molecule of female estrogen floating on the night air. But her suspicions were deflected by the mystery and obvious crisis, and she had the sense to leave it a molehill, making her frustrated.

I poured myself a needed tumbler of Scotch and sipped it in the inner courtyard. Only this time, I sat so I could see all doors leading into the courtyard. Maggie finally called me to bed and when I lay beside her, she asked, "Who is Louise?"

"I knew her husband in England during the war, and met him again in Shanghai. He's a major with the U.S. Army Advisory Group."

"Why is she here?"

"She came up to join her husband for a holiday and when he didn't meet her at the airport and wasn't at the hotel, she came to see if I knew where he was."

"You mean the Chinese colonel is her husband?"

"No."

"Who is he? *David what happened tonight?*"

"I can't tell you now. Go to sleep. I have to get up at three."

After awhile, she said, "I could feel it."

"Feel what?"

"Her love for you."

"Oh, Maggie, please. Knock it off."

"I'm not jealous, Darling. I don't blame her. I understand. But do you love her?"

"I love you and have none to spare."

Snuggling close, her lips searched for mine. When I made no move, she whispered, "Aren't you interested?"

"We may have another visitor."

She drew away and pulled her nightie down. "Who?"

"Just go to sleep."

I lay still, listening to the dog barking in the hutung on the other side of the bedroom wall. Every rustle and creak in the courtyard held my attention. I worried for Ta-ko and wondered about him. Was my dream of his power nostalgic nonsense? Would he hold up some terrible mirror to me?

The alarm jarred me awake. Maggie whimpered and covered her head. I left without waking her and took the jacket and lunch to Maggie's house. When they did not answer my knocking, I called, "It's me, Dave. It's okay. You can turn on the lights."

The door was opened by Louise wearing Maggie's bathrobe. Ta-ko, in mine, sat like an actor in his dressing room, and I was struck by his magical transformation from a frail old scholar to a vibrant young man. He looked as he had in Chungking: handsome with high cheekbones and aquiline nose.

For the first time, he greeted me warmly and I responded, then noticed the bed beyond the bedroom moongate. They had slept together! Before I could check my jealousy, I glared "whore!" at her.

While I glumly munched a sandwich, Ta-ko regaled Louise with tales of our adventures and pranks as boys in Szchewan. Now and then he would interject, "Did you write that down?" She replied with happy laughter.

I swore at the knock on the door. "Your man pinched my gun."

"You won't need it. It's only your taxi driver."

"How do you know?"

"My men are outside."

On the step, he shook hands with Louise and said goodbye. When I did the same, she drew me inside and closed the door. "Don't be angry, Darling. After all it's your fault, you know, leaving us alone in a house with only one bed.

When he told me how his work had forced him to live like a monk, and considering all the trouble I've caused him—well, it was the least I could do."

"Have you forgotten the fortune teller?"

She looked puzzled, then clapped a hand over her mouth. "That I would bear a Chinese child," she whispered, and her eyes rolled as she mentally searched for her diaphragm. "Oh, my God!" It was obviously not in the right place. Then she gave a chirp of laughter. "Won't everyone be surprised."

I turned the doorknob. "I'll see you in Shanghai."

"I doubt it," she said sadly. "All army dependents have been ordered home immediately. Will I ever see you again?"

"One day." And I kissed her fondly as if she were my sister-in-law.

Not certain of the taxi driver, a shaved head protruding from a greasy sheepskin coat, we rode in silence. At Westfield, Ta-ko waited outside operations, while I went in to sign the log book and pick up the parachutes. I gave Ta-ko his and we walked quickly to the Harvard, where I helped him buckle on his chute. When airborne, he asked over the intercom about his father's death.

I told him, then asked about Chungking during the war. "Did Colonel Fitzgerald ever let on he knew you were Chen Yi?"

"At Yalta. We had a long talk about the future of China."

"Then he is a Communist."

Ta-Ko chuckled. "You still see it as original sin, don't you? No, Fitzgerald is an opportunist."

"Like you," I said.

"You are the fisherman without net or pole, content to take whatever flops at your feet. I bend or dam the river for mine."

"Or steal your neighbour's cormorants."

"If necessary," he said. "Why do you persist in defending this evil we are trying to erase?"

"Because I doubt you will erase it."

"We will by eliminating corruption and the foreigners who drain our wealth."

"At what cost to the people?"

"Cost? You talk nonsense. Look what life costs them now. When we wipe away the old habits of greed, the old superstitions—"

"You sound like the missionaries you hate," I shouted. "Those superstitions are your religions. You know that the essence of Chinese culture is obeisence to ritual, family, prince, and emperor. Give them new rituals, new families, new princes; give them your Mao Tse-tung as a new emperor to love and follow, but don't destroy a balance that has enabled China to survive as a civilization while all others have risen and fallen. Where is Egypt, Greece, Rome today?"

"Where is China, my pompous brother?"

"Burning, but if you scatter the ashes, your phoenix will never rise again. Civilizations fall when one extreme tries to surpress all others, and they lose Yin and Yang."

"You should have been a lecturer in some liberal university."

"You should have been a better student."

Approaching Weishien at dawn, he told me to land someplace behind their lines. Circling over the fields west of Ch'ang Lo, I chose the east-west highway where it was on the surface and smooth. After landing, we left our chutes in the cockpit and got out. Ta-ko strode around, flexing his arms and breathing deeply.

I watched him. "I've seen you so often in memory and shadows, or with different faces, it's strange to see you as

215

you are, or were. But who are you, Ta-ko? Chen Yi, Chia Pao-yu? Wong Fo-ying? Colonel Chen? Which one are you?"

"All and none," he said, smiling.

"No, you are Colonel Chen itching for a battle."

"True. I have been behind desks and masks too long. I want the instant results that only war can provide. I want to shout, 'Fire!' and see walls crumble."

"And men die."

"There is poetry in finality."

"But why Weishien? It has no value. Why not bypass it?"

"Your loyalties are tearing."

"I had dinner with General Li Tso-lin. He's a remarkable old man. Much like your father in many ways."

He laughed. "You are a sentimental ass. As for General Li, he is no longer in command. It is now General Ching, who retreated with his regiment from Tsinan and elbowed his way into Weishien. That old war lord loves walls as much as gold. Before we start the battle, we must buy the excellent American artillery Ching managed to take with him. For this we need your gold here."

"There's not much in Weishien right now."

"The take of a week or two is all I need. Ching will accept the balance in chits, as he did to pull out of Tsinan. Just buzz the town and land here. I will send a jeep."

A truck arrived bristling with guns. It took Colonel Chen a few minutes to prove his identification. He then returned to the aircraft and shook my hand. "Goodbye, David. Thank you for comforting my father. Last night, Louise told me you thought I could help you find yourself. You have worn as many masks as I. Which yourself do you want to find?"

"Am I only the bastard of two diverse cultures?"

"You are either a man, who knowing death, desires life;

or a man, who knowing life, desires death."

"Don't Yin and Yang me."

"You are the one who thinks Yin and Yang are so important."

"Then which one am I?"

He patted my arm. "You must choose," he said, and walked away.

After takeoff, I flew back over the truck and pulled up into a victory roll, without right. I felt defeated. If I warned General Li Tso-lin, I betrayed Chen Yi. Silent, I helped doom Weishien. Impaled, I squirmed and clutched a coward's straw: do nothing; neither talk, nor supply gold. At first the plight of Mukden intervened and drew all aircraft north. When service to Weishien was resumed after two weeks, Tex Burke appeared.

twenty-two

THE night being warm, we were making love in the dark on top of Maggie's bed, when the room lights triggered her scream in my ear. I broke her scissor grip, rolled off her and sat up. Tex was leaning against the moongate border, an automatic dangling in his hand.

"Well, well," he drawled. "Now ain't that a pretty sight. Sorry to interrupt. Go ahead, I'll wait 'til you're finished."

Maggie, clutching at bed clothes to cover us, kept shrieking, "Get out! Get out of here!"

"Why so modest?" Tex asked. "I've seen your hairy snatch often enough, though never occupied."

"You filthy beast!" she cried.

"Filthy beast. Oh, how veddy, veddy British of you m'dear. And how veddy whorish of you, love."

"What do you want?" I demanded.

"What do I want? I want vengeance, that's what I want. I'm a cuckolded husband. That woman sir, is my wife. Unhand her." He laughed. "Isn't that the way it goes?"

"You agreed to the arrangement."

"Did I? Have you got it in writing?"

"Okay, Burke. What do you want?"

"Maybe I want to shoot you both."

"Bullshit," I said.

"You sure?"

"I'm sure, because there's no dime in it for you."

"You think I need dimes?"

"You'd take pennies off dead eyes."

He waved the automatic. "Fuck off, Maggie."

"No!"

"Go on, Maggie," I said. "He won't do anything."

"Hell I won't. Open that front door my darling wife, and you'll see how fast I'll do something. You just wait out there and keep your big mouth shut."

Wrapping herself in a blanket, she swished past him with head-high dignity and spat, "Pig!"

"Bitch!" Tex wiped his cheek and glowered after her, then at me. "There's wildcat in that broad. You watch yourself with her, Highpockets. I swear she liked to kill me one night."

I reached for the bedside table and the automatic came up. "Don't get stupid," he said.

"A cigarette. Okay?"

"Just ask, Buddy. Just ask. But don't reach nowhere. You wouldn't be the first head I've blown off, though you'd be the first white one."

"You're full of shit, Burke."

"You think any court would convict me? This would be, you know, a crime of passion. I caught you fucking my wife. Hell, everybody knows you're shacked up together. Temporary insanity. I should do it just for kicks."

"Kicks don't pay off."

"In some ways you're smart, Highpockets. In other ways, stupid. You should know better than to get yourself in what they call a compromising situation. You know why I let you have Maggie like this? Something told me you might get smart here on home ground. If I let you have her, I figured it might be like money in the bank. I'd be into you. Maybe you'd pay off, maybe you wouldn't. But the way to make money is to have people hooked. Sooner or later you find a need for them and they have to contribute for a pay off. That's the way the mob works. That's the way the Chinese work. And that's why you worry me, Highpockets. You know all this. How come you let me get into you? For a piece of ass?" He shook his head. "I always felt sorry for you."

"Spare me the sympathy. What do you want?"

"You still want that cigarette?"

I nodded and he tossed me a pack and lighter.

"Now, the purpose of this whole exercise," he said jauntily, "is the Weishien deal."

When I said nothing, he waggled the automatic at me. "No games, Highpockets. I'll put one through Maggie first and still make you pay off. So act as smart as you can be at times. I know all about the Weishien deal."

"If there was one, how the hell would you find out?"

He grinned broadly. "Little old Myra, that's who."

"So it's your turn in the red chamber."

"You bet your sweet ass."

"That's a dream chamber," I said. "Don't believe anything you see or hear in it."

"I believe this."

"Myra's no proof."

He aimed the gun. "But this is. We want in. Half. Myra got it from a little Chinaman in Tsingtao. You've been getting one tael per ton. We're now going to put five crates a day on that run, each making five shuttles. That, Buddy, adds up to one hundred pounds of gold a week."

If they took over, I was off the hook. I could not deliver

the gold Chen Yi needed to buy General Ching's artillery. I would be absolved from helping destroy Weishien. Nor would the city last long. Tex was not getting such a big deal.

"Okay. I'll cut you in for half on two conditions. One, you divorce Maggie. Two, you smuggle the gold to Hongkong. I think they're on to me."

He smiled slyly. "Now that little divorce, Highpockets old buddy, is going to cost you the whole deal. Starting now. Know why? Because when Maggie's old lady kicks off, there's plenty bucks coming her way. So I want all the Weishien deal, just to even things up."

"No divorce, no key to the vault."

"Okay. One divorce for the whole Weishien deal."

I smiled. "As soon as you're divorced, the Weishien operation is yours."

"I can't wait until then," he screamed. "Who the hell knows how long it'll take to get a divorce, for Christ's sake. I don't even know where I have to do it. Here, Texas, or Canada. And you know as well as I do that Weishien ain't long for this world."

"Then I want a bond."

"I promise to divorce her. Give me the key."

I laughed. "That's not the bond I had in mind. You post a twenty-five thousand dollar bond in a Hongkong bank, then get a lawyer to draw up an agreement saying that Maggie gets the dough if you haven't divorced her in, say, six months."

"I get it back when we're unhooked? And I get the key when you get the paper?"

"Roger."

"You're on. Don't you move any loot in the meantime. It's all ours from now on. But you got to tell us how we get it past Hongkong customs. You sure as hell don't carry it through in a briefcase anymore. Not the way they're searching bags."

"That's your problem. You want the whole deal, you figure the gimmick."

"We'll pay."

"My share of the commissions from American Air. Twenty-five grand."

"You're crazy! I did all the work. Five thou."

"Twenty."

"Negatega. Ten. Final."

"In advance."

"Sure, sure. I got it right here in my pocket."

"Just give me a certified cheque with the lawyer's paper and I'll give you the key and the rig."

He looked at me with admiration. "You're tougher than I thought, Highpockets. Okay, back to fucking. Hey, Maggie, haul your big Canadian ass in here and finish this poor guy off." He left chuckling.

Maggie came in trembling with rage. "Unspeakable wretch!"

"Now, now, we both know he's—"

"Not him. You!"

"What?"

"Gold smuggler! I heard every word. You, of all people, exploiting the Chinese. How could you?"

I drew a deep breath to explain and defeat deflated me. What could I say? She was right. "One day," I said lamely, "you'll appreciate that little nest egg."

"Blood money!" Her harangue rose to a sermon and in her zeal, she lost her blanket. Visualizing what her naked effect would have been on congregations I had known, I started to laugh, but her accusations sobered me. I was more bastard than the unwanted child of two cultures, and for reasons Maggie did not know. Feeling no guilt, I helped a government I despised by flying their troops and ammunition, while I supplied gold so the Communists could buy their arms. I drank Colonel Shu's whisky, but did not warn him of General Ching's planned betrayal. I lived in a no man's land between Yin and Yang, yet slept like an innocent. Ta-ko had said, "You are either a man, who knowing death, desires life; or a man, who knowing life, desires death." Straddling both, I took what anyone offered and repaid by wearing the mask they wanted to see.

Mukden, long besieged, came under attack and we began to evacuate our supplies, equipment, and ground personnel. We landed in rain, over the heads of people still working on the south end of the runway. In the hangar, Chinese huddled in groups, separated by streams of water from the shattered roof. It was a desolate terminal of stranded travellers who would never leave.

One by one, the fat aircraft waddled in through mud and puddles, disgorged sacks of rice and swallowed crates of equipment. The cargo maw closed and one after the other they left without the people. The realization that they were being abandoned flashed through the crowd and they poured from the hangar, sweeping along the tommy gun armed guards. Our engines were turning as the flood rushed toward us.

"The props!

The loading truck was still backed up to our fuselage.

"Clear the truck," I shouted. "Clear the truck!"

The CAT ground personnel in the cabin took up the cry. T.S. came running forward. "Clear. Go. Go."

I gunned the port engine and, turning our tail to the advancing mob, raced for the runway. We had hit no one, but our prop blast must have felled some in the front ranks, and I hoped they were not trampled. Swinging onto the runway, we saw a truck drive in front of the last CAT C-46, forcing it to stop. Its cargo door was still open and people were falling out.

I radioed. "You okay, Dutch?"

"Not really. We're overloaded and got to toss out a couple dozen nonpaying passengers, and now I got me a real pair of wheel chocks. Let's see how good he is at playing chicken."

Dutch edged the huge propellor disk closer and closer to the truck cab. Suddenly, the truck jerked away backwards. He radioed, "Go, Davie, go."

Above the overcast, Dutch slid toward us and we flew home in loose formation, talking over the radio.

"There goes another page from our route book," he said.

"Do you think we got all our people?"

"Don't know, but I got a couple of extra in case we're short."

The surf of the white sea broke in slow, slow motion on island peaks, then the undulant cover curdled into herds of sheep we scattered off the mountain ridges—stage flats stacked one behind the other in haze; the last seamed by the Great Wall. On the horizon, the sun experimented with extravagant new shorelines of orange lagoons and purple cliffs calving bergs into a bay of blood. As a final gesture, the sun ignited the golden roofs of the Forbidden City and smelted Peiping's lakes and ponds into silver.

The next day, Whiting wired me to return the Harvard and I flew it to Shanghai. At Hungjao Airfield, I was told Whiting wanted to see me at the office on the bund. Driving in along Hungjao Road, I was amazed by the construction of a ten foot high wall of sharpened logs. They were surrounding Shanghai with a palisade to protect it from a modern army.

My driver was glum. "Everything bad. Prices go up

every day. In newspaper, Mayor Wu beg merchants to have a conscience." He laughed bitterly. "The government admits GY is no good. They take away price ceilings. Everything go up. Already we have food riots. Everyone wants Pa lu now."

A few blocks from the office, we were stopped by a traffic jam. Finally, I got out and pushed my way through the mob toward the mounted gendarmes in front of the CAT office next to the Shanghai Bank. "What's happening?" I asked, and a Chinese said, "Gold riot. Every day government sells a few gold bars at official rate to prove GY is good." He found this very funny. "People wait in line all night for bank to open. Now there is big fight between them and people who try to push into line."

I reached the edge of people around a clearing that the gendarmes on big horses kept open by walking the perimeter and trampling any feet that failed to retreat. On the sidewalk, a line of people were pressed against the buildings. Suddenly, it buckled and people popped out. The horses were backed into them and hoofs hammered the line straight. They left a woman hunched on the curb, clutching her pelvis and screaming soundlessly. A boy stared at the strange crook of his leg.

I dodged between the horses and reached the line blocking the entrance to the CAT office. When I said I had to get through, they laughed with good nature, shouted, "One, two, three," and pushed backwards. I leapt through the momentary opening with thanks.

In his office, Whiting said, "We're evacuating all nonessential people from Peiping. You'll have three days to pack your household goods and get your families out."

"It's that quick?"

"What's the situation in Weishien?"

"I didn't land on my way down."

"Go back in the morning and check."

But on my way out, the chief pilot called me. "Get out to the field. We have to put every plane on the Hsuchow run. It's shaping up into a major battle. If they can keep the Reds from crossing the Grand Canal, they might save Hanking and Shanghai."

At Hungjao, my aircraft was already loaded with five tons of ammunition and a passenger: an American-trained Chinese doctor, who had volunteered to go to the front. Hsuchow was 150 miles northwest of Nanking and as we approached the Chinese Air Force base, we could see fighting to the north.

When we were unloaded, trucks with wounded arrived. Some were half naked, their clothes blown or torn off, their wounds stuffed with clotted rags. The dripping stumps and rag wrapped swollen heads made me nauseous. To escape, I went to inspect the long lines of parked CAF aircraft: B-24's, P-47's, P-51's, Mosquitoes, C-46's and 47's.

My God! They had been strafed! Every one was riddled with holes. But the Communists had no air force. I looked under tailplanes and wings. Intact. None of the bullets and shells had gone through. The holes had been made with ballpean hammers. But why? Then I remembered reading in the newspaper that Generalissimo Chiang Kai-shek had recently inspected Hsuchow. Embarrassed to have him see so many aircraft grounded because of maintenance, the air force had saved face by destroying them and blaming enemy action.

The Hsuchow-Nanking shuttle became a nightmare. On our third landing at Huschow at three in the morning, the Chinese doctor came aboard, weeping. "There is nothing here. Nothing. They knew this would be a major battle. They knew. And yet they shipped all medical equipment south. There are no operating facilities, no X rays, no drugs. Nothing. Just a few crates of bandages." He stood behind me, crying all the way to Nanking.

I flew 27 hours out of 36. In Shanghai, my first mouthful of proper food made me violently ill. Before I crawled into bed, I tried to phone Maggie, but long distance to Peiping was dead. Finally operations reached Wingate, who wired back that Maggie was being looked after. "Stop worrying."

Tex came to the CAT House and woke me. His papers contained proof that the bond had been posted, which the agreement said would be forfeited to Maggie if he had not divorced her in six months.

"Give me the key," he demanded.

I tore a Gold Yuan note in two and gave him half.

"This is a key?"

"Roger. In Weishien go to the Tung Bank," and I told him directions, "show Mr. Tung that half. I'll give him this half, with instructions to pay the gold to whomever has the matching half."

"It better work, Highpockets. Where's the rig?"

"Cheque first."

He handed me a certified cheque for ten thousand U.S., and I gave him the vest. "Load it with the bars and wear it under your shirt."

He tried it on. "Very neat. When are you going to Weishien?"

I looked at my watch. "In about three hours."

"I'm stuck on this lousy Hsuchow shuttle. Don't know when I can get up to Tsingtao and Weishien. Don't you touch one bar, Highpockets."

"It's all yours. I just want to get Maggie and our gear out of Peiping."

twenty-three

LANDING at Tsingtao after dark, I went to the Opium Den: a Bauhaus design of cubes with corner casement windows and flat roofs. Built by a German in the twenties, it was now owned by five CAT pilots, who had converted it into one of the most disreputable hotels in the Orient.

After dinner, the Russian *whore de jour* was sent to bed and the pilots gathered in the living room with the Den's 27 dogs of all sizes, shapes, and breeds. The favourite was Irene, an alcoholic terrier the size of a fifth, which she would drink if given. To dry her out, she was rationed to a nightly saucer of beer.

Captain Maximillian Muldoon, a bearded behemoth with eyes the blue of watered milk, had gathered seven dogs on his lap, when Skull Sanders entered indignantly. "Know what I just discovered? This concrete barn was only a summer house. It ain't got a heating system. What'll we do come winter?"

"Just pull on another dog," Muldoon growled, and waggled a finger at Irene, who, woofled to her eyebrows, was staggering over to bite a hound ten times her size. Though she missed and fell on her snout, the hound ran yelping. Muldoon clucked his tongue at her. "Mercy, what a temper." Four letter words had become too common for Muldoon and he swore with "goodness, gracious, darn, or shucks." Delivered with the resonance of a kettle drum, they shocked.

"Want some bubbly water?" Skull asked Muldoon. "We just got a new shipment in from Peipingava."

Muldoon lifted a hand to caution Skull. "That cham-pag-knee ain't fighting whisky. Gives you big ideas but nothing to do it with. Why gracious, the other night in the Wagon Lits I take umbrage at some foolishment Ole Doc said, and jump up to remove his ears. Darn, if he don't have to hold me up while I talked severely to him."

After bellowing at the boy to bring him another drink, Muldoon said, "Speaking of fighting, I just got a letter from a ole buddy, who is over flying in the Palestine War. He says it ain't so bad flying for the Ayrabs, because when the Jews catch you, they just shoot you. But he's flying for the Jews and he's a mite worried about getting caught by them Wogs. He say they have a real mean habit of cutting off your very own personal genitals, sewing 'em to your lips, and sending you back home to die of boredom."

"What about the Pa lu?"

"Oh, they just club your head dead."

"Did you hear that Kaffen picked up two bullet holes coming out of Weishien today?" Skull said. "Missed his inner gas tank by yea much."

"What's the word on Weishien?" I asked.

"Trouble," Muldoon said. "Something's up. Leastwise according to our mechanic, Charlie Chan. This afternoon, he says to me, 'Weishien is out of harmony.' I ask for a translation, and he says, 'Today brings little changes.' Someone passing a small village called Ping Yuan saw everyone working the fields as if it were planting, or harvest time. He asked a farmer the reason. The farmer said soldiers came and told them to leave the village until dark. Then one car came from Weishien and another from the direction of Ch'ang Lo, which is Pa lu owned. This afternoon the black market price of rice drops. Charlie Chan says, 'When today not same as yesterday and day before and day before, wise man pack his cart.' "

I grimaced with worry. Had Colonel Chen Yi and General Ching met in Ping Yuan? Had Ta-ko bought the American artillery? I rose to leave for bed and Skull asked what time I wanted the Russian broad. "Not tonight," I said.

"A piece of ass goes with the price of the room," Skull said. "If you don't like a wet deck, you can have first crack."

"Next time."

"Wish you would sample her. We're trying her out and need customer reaction. The last one bit. Shit like that could ruin our reputation."

At dawn, I rode with Muldoon to the airport. The road climbed up from the harbour and over the mountain. Descending, we passed lines of coolies pushing large cargo wheelbarrows uphill, each with a square-rigged sail to harness the wind.

Deadheading to Weishien with Muldoon, I lay on one of the stretcher seats and dozed until we landed. The airline jeep drove me to the city. Halfway, we had to pull over to the side to allow an army convoy to pass. A dozen Dodge trucks, each pulling a 155 mm howitzer, headed for Erh-shih-li-pao. If they were Chen Yi's guns, he would take the airfield to get them. I told the driver to hurry.

I went first to the army compound and found Colonel Shu, whom I asked about the howitzers. "General Ching has sent them to reinforce the Erh-shih-li-pao garrison," he said.

"But aren't they vulnerable as hell way out there?"

He nodded gravely. "They can better protect Erh-shih-li-pao firing from here. There they are practically on the front line. General Li was furious, but Ching would not listen."

I ran back to the jeep. "Tung Bank. K'uai, k'uai."

Mr. Tung was not in.

"Where is he?" I asked.

"Mr. Tung," the clerk said in Chinese, "does not inform me of his whereabouts."

"Where does he live?"

"I cannot tell you."

I offered a bribe, then threatened, but the clerk would not talk. In the jeep, we raced back to the army compound. The people we passed looked calm; too calm. Colonel Shu had gone on an inspection tour and the captain could not tell me the sector. Nor did he know where Mr. Tung lived.

We returned to the bank, but he still had not arrived. I was frantic. I had to instruct him personally. He would not accept the change of procedures through his clerk. Rather than wait at the bank, I went to the CAT office and radioed Erh-shih-li-pao about conditions.

"All is calm, Captain."

"The new howitzers. Where are they?"

"I do not know."

Shit!

I returned to the bank. All I could do was wait. A clerk kept bringing me pots of tea. If the fix was in, Chen Yi would cut the road to the airfield. The garrison would put up a token resistance, then surrender. When Chen Yi had his artillery, the battle for Weishien would begin and I would be trapped.

Mr. Tung arrived at noon. I gave him the half GY note and instructed him to pay the man who presented the matching half. With a nod, he slipped the bill up his sleeve. "You will not come again?"

"Depends on the situation. What happens to you?"

"My family is away and safe."

"What about your gold and yourself?"

"My gold has flown away. As for me, meio kwanshi."

Though anxious to leave, I asked, "Are you sad your China is dying?"

"As for a loved one. But a dynasty, like people, grows old and must die. Death struggles are never nice. A new China, like a son, will take over business. Maybe son good. Maybe bad. Never mind. He will die, and his son take over. What happens in one or two generations not important. Only what happens over hundreds of years."

We said goodbye and in the jeep, I told the driver to step on it. I hung on, closing my eyes at every near miss, certain some pedestrian would fail to leap clear in time and come crashing through the windshield. The guards at the checkpoint recognized us and waved us through.

About three miles from the city, an armored car came at us around a bend in the deep road. It skidded sideways to block our path and swung its turret gun at us. I stood up and waved my arms. An officer rose from a hatch and yelled, "Go back! Pa lu attacking airfield. Go back!"

"Go to the Lahdia Yuan Mission," I told the driver. Being east of the city, it gave me a chance to escape on foot if the airfield fell.

The walled mission, surrounded by a small village, was a pleasant blend of Gothic and Chinese architecture. The short, redhaired priest was delighted to have a guest. When I told him of the attack, he said with a German accent, "Ja, I know. I hear they have already captured Erh-shih-li-pao."

He showed me a small whitewashed room opening onto the long arcade and I tossed my briefcase on the plank bed. "Do you have a telephone?"

"Ja, ja. In my office. Come."

As we walked along, he introduced himself as Father Schmitt. "You would care for some beer, maybe? This year the beer is good."

While I tried to get through to army headquarters, he brought me a stein of his home brew and waited expectantly for my opinion. "Very good," I said.

He bobbed his head. "Ja, ja, this year—"

"Hello, hello. Colonel Shu? MacCloud. What? I can't hear you. Yeah. No, I'm at the Lahdia Yuan Mission. How's the airfield?"

"The garrison has surrendered. We are going to counterattack."

"If you don't recapture it, what's it like east of here? For making it on foot to Tsingtao?"

"Very poor. They have us completely surrounded."

"Shall I come back to the city?"

"Stay where you are," Colonel Shu said. "The area between the mission and the city is mined. I'll send a guide as soon as I can spare someone."

Sitting in Father Schmitt's office all afternoon, I listened to the distant sound of battle and kept phoning the CAT office in Weishien. Their reports were optimistic until one of our aircraft flew over the battle and radioed that the airstrip was pitted with shell holes. As it grew dark, I called Colonel Shu about the guide.

"In the morning," he said. "Our attack failed. Erh-shih-li-pao is lost."

During dinner, Father Schmitt said, "It was a sad day when General Ching came to Weishien. General Li was born here. His men have reason to fight. This is their home.

We mean nothing to the Nationalist soldiers, less to Ching."

I felt strangely disinterested. Now that I was trapped, I no longer worried. Was it my ambivalence? Did I feel I had friends on both sides? Did I think I could cross the Communist lines and Colonel Chen Yi would give me a safe conduct pass to Tsingtao? Or was the war remote because it was not my war? Why should anyone want to harm me? I had felt the same over Europe. Though I saw the Germans shooting at my Spitfire, I never believed they were seriously trying to kill me.

Colonel Shu phoned. "There may be fighting near the mission tonight. Stay under cover."

Father Schmitt took two large steins and led me down to a cellar room lined with barrels of beer. He filled the steins and we clinked them.

"Better than a trench," he said. "You were in the last war?"

"Air Force."

"Russian front. Not nice."

"You were a priest then?"

"Nein. It came later."

"Because of the war?"

"I think so."

The thick walls muffled the thumps and chatter of battle, while we talked over our beers as if sitting in a rathskellar. When the guns stopped, the silence reminded us and we wondered who had won. We waited for the door to be burst open by soldiers. None came and the beer forced us outside to piss. The night breeze brought the faint cries of the wounded.

"That chorus," he said. "It plays always in my head."

The whimpering aftermath of battle. I had never heard it before. I used to hit and run. Twice we strafed the field full of German soldiers we surprised at their calesthenics. While they wept, we were on our way home to a second breakfast.

"Is there nothing we can do?" I asked.

"Nein. In the morning, I do what I can." He shrugged. "I am no doctor, but by then most need Last Rites and graves."

Dreams I could not recall disturbed my sleep. I was awake when Father Schmitt came past at dawn with his Bible and robe. He declined my offer of help. "The village people will bury them. Wait for your guide."

"Wouldn't you be safer in the city?"

"That is not my job. *Aufwiedersehn.*"

My guide, dressed as a farmer, came at mid-morning and said we must hurry. The Communist attack on the village had failed, but there were enemy patrols everywhere. Outside the mission, we heard the wail of women and the dirge followed us across fields fertilized with human manure. The farmers we passed ignored us as they did the war until it struck them. We came on a water buffalo lying across a path, his front legs gone. He waved a bloody stump as if pleading for help.

"We are now in the mine field," my guide said. "Stay behind me."

"Can we put it out of its misery?"

But neither of us had a gun or knife. The guide kept taking sightings on objects behind us and the walled city about a mile ahead. Now and then he stopped to search the ground. Once he made an abrupt turn and waved me to one side. We had just missed stepping on a mine. In sight of sand-bagged trenches, he called me to him; his face streaked with sweat. "We okay now," he said, grinning.

He shouted a pass word, but the rifles kept us covered until we were in the trench. We walked along on duckboards and through mud, past dugouts and soldiers with whom I traded nods and smiles. A tunnel took us under the city wall and at army headquarters, I was served a pot of tea, then taken to an underground operations room. Three officers were lined up by Colonel Shu's desk and I stood on the end of the line, waiting my turn at the lost and found wicket. I've lost my wings. Too bad, he would say. You must now suffer like the rest of us mortals.

"What now, Dave?" Colonel Shu asked.

"No chance of retaking the airfield?" I asked, amazed by my request. Send dozens, hundreds of men to their death so that I can escape. Instead of telling me to go fuck myself, he said, "I'm afraid not. Sorry."

"We have a Piper Cub at Tsingtao. It only needs a small field."

Colonel Shu wearily pushed himself up from his chair and went to the wall map. "They are too close to try a field outside the trenches. There's no space between the trenches and the city walls."

I pointed to a soccer field just outside the south wall of West Weishien, but Colonel Shu shook his head. "They hold the railroad station only two hundred yards away. I suggest you try some place inside the walls."

We selected a school yard in West Weishien. Colonel Shu ordered a work detail to the school and a jeep for me. "If you're still here by dark," he said, "come back for a drink. I have a case of Scotch left and there's no sense hoarding it."

"They got the howitzers, didn't they?"

He nodded. "If we still had them, we could hold out."

"Was it a sell out?"

"I think so. Ching is a treacherous bastard, and Chen Yi, the new Communist commander, is a slick one."

"But why do they want to take Weishien?"

"Why not? We're the only garrison between them and Tsingtao. If they bypass us, we could be reinforced by air drop and threaten their rear."

I thanked him and left. Outside, I saw a C-46 circling the city and hurried to the CAT office, where I called them on the radio: "Weishien to CAT. Over."

"Whiting to MacCloud. You okay?"

"Roger. They're going to clear a landing area in the southeast corner of West Weishien. When it's finished, I'll mark it with a white T. Send the Cub."

"Okay, Dave. We'll keep someone overhead to radio for the Cub when your field is finished. We'll also try to get another one for standby."

twenty-four

THE school principal was horrified. "Why are you going to destroy my school?"

I did not dare say, "So I can escape."

The teachers were herding the children from the building.

"Why must you destroy my school?" he shrieked.

"So an aircraft can land on your playing field," I said, watching soldiers cut down trees at the far end.

"But why my building?"

"It is in the way," I said. It is in my way.

"Do not argue," the officer said. "Clear everyone out. Quickly!"

The principal began to cry and I walked away.

Why should these people destroy a school so I could escape, while they remained in a doomed city? Who was I? "Which yourself do you want to find?" Chen Yi had asked. Not this person. I should stop them. I should try to escape on foot. If captured, they might take me to Chen Yi. He still owed me a favour.

It was too late. The CAT transport circled overhead like a buzzard; the Cub was waiting, a pilot standing by. But it was not too late. I simply wanted to fly away rather than walk. That was me: one who flew from trouble. Why not? Only a fool would risk his arse on the ground. Also, I had to get Maggie out of Peiping, knowing the airline would look after her. I was afraid of war on the ground.

The squad emerged from planting dynamite charges in the school building. At a signal, the walls bulged into a ball of smoke. The children covered their ears and cheered; the principal sobbed.

A duck pond was filled and the basketball backboards removed. Twenty trees were felled, telephone wires removed and the rubble cleared away. The finished field was shaped like a meat cleaver, boxed in by walls and buildings. By landing diagonally, the Cub had about 400 feet, plus the almost 100 foot long handle, not much wider than a Cub's wingspan. The end was blocked by a wall and a roof, which we had to clear on takeoff, then fly between a tall building and a smokestack. It was a lousy airstrip.

I went to the CAT office and radioed my doubts about the field. Dutch relayed them to Tsingtao and called back: "Cub driver says sheet no sweat."

"Who is it?"

"Tex Burke. Claims he can land these rubber band models on a stamp. Mark it."

Tex was coming for his gold, not me and I wished I had bought another gun. Back at the school yard, I laid out the T with strips of white cloth.

The Cub came over high and, like a yellow butterfly, circled slowly down to buzz the strip and fly away. "He can't believe this is it," I said. He returned, dragged the yard, and when I waved, he waggled his wings. His first approach was too fast and she kept floating until he gunned her to go around again. On his second try, he came in slow, nose high, so low I was afraid his tail would hit the wall.

He chopped power, dropped, bounced; her tail lifting as he braked.

I ran after him, yelling, "The dogleg! Use the dogleg!"

He saw the alley just in time and slewed the Cub up it. I was apprehensive until I turned the corner and saw he had made it, but barely.

Tex had climbed out and was staring at the prop hub only a few feet from the wall. "Jesus H. Christ, Highpockets. Four to five hundred feet, no sweat, but you didn't say one goddamn word about these walls."

"I told Dutch."

"He sure didn't relay it. Let's get the bullion. The way I figure, there should be about one hundred pounds."

"Go ahead. You know where it is."

He smiled grimly. "And leave you to fly away in my little bird? Negatega, ole Buddy."

"You know damn well this crate can't fly out of here with the two of us plus a hundred pounds of gold."

"Roger. That's why they're sending another. They figured they'd need two."

"What are you talking about? What other? This is the only lightplane we have. Risk two aircraft to rescue me? You're full of shit."

"I'm not. Come on let's get my loot. They're sending another, I'm telling you. They're going to get an L-Five from the navy in Tsingtao. How do we get to Tung's bank from here?"

"You get your gold," I said, "and I'll take the Cub. You can wait for the L-Five."

"No!" he shouted. "Use your head, Highpockets. Two and the loot will be too heavy for even an L-Five. I've got to take the Cub. It'll carry me and the extra hundred. Don't try to fuck up the deal. I came across with my part of the bargain."

"But you're not leaving without me until the other one lands."

"Okay, okay, let's go to the bank."

I knew he was lying. Once he had the gold and the Cub was in position for takeoff, he would hold me off with his automatic, maybe even shoot me. I had to find a gun. In the jeep, I told the driver in Chinese that I would pay a ten tael gold bar for a handgun. "Can you get one while we're in the bank?"

The soldier shook his head. "Take many hours."

Mr. Jung, standing behind the counter of his narrow bank, bowed to us. In Chinese I said, "This man comes for the gold. It belongs to him, but he has a gun I need. Not to steal his gold, but to protect myself. Will you help?"

Tex became nervous. "Hey, what're you talking about?"

"He introduces you to me," Mr. Tung said in English, and asked for the half note. Satisfied it matched his, he excused himself. "It will take a few minutes to count out the bars."

When he left, the gun in Tex's pocket rose like an erection. "No tricks, Highpockets."

"Relax."

We waited in silence, each plotting. Finally, a clerk appeared in the doorway and bowed us into Mr. Tung's office.

"You first," Tex said. "It's aimed right at your back."

Inside, Tex gasped. Part of the floor was carpeted with a dazzling layer of gold bars. I stepped aside for him. As he stared with disbelief, two Chinese stepped up behind him and pinioned his arms. I reached into his pocket and took his .38 automatic. Tex recoiled in terror.

Mr. Tung looked him over as blandly as if he were a live hen chosen for dinner. He said to me in Chinese, "I had planned a feast for you, but time vanished. If you wish, he will do the same. It is the least I can do to repay you."

241

The offer startled me. I had only wanted his gun, but how tempting. Chinese bankers were skilled in the disposal of errant couriers. There would be no risk. It solved the problem of my escape and it returned my gold. One nod would condemn him.

Just like Pei.

"Release him." To Tex, I said, "Load your vest."

He was stupified.

I hefted the gun. "This is all I wanted. The loot's yours. Pack up."

"What are you pulling?" He tried to watch everyone at once.

"It's yours," I said. "I'm not welching on the deal. Just the gun, so you wouldn't be tempted to strand me. Let's go."

Suspicious, he removed his jacket and the vest, sank to his knees, and still watching us, slipped the bars into the pockets. Then the feel and fact of the gold aroused him into raking armsful toward him, loading faster, scurrying about on his knees to retrieve bars. The eyes of the Chinese were solemn with contempt. Still kneeling, he put on the loaded vest and was unable to rise. A hand reached to help him but he shrank from it, hugging his chest like a frightened mother her baby.

In the jeep on our way to the school yard, he pleaded, "Let me go back alone in the Cub. I'll split with you. I swear I'll split with you. We both can't go. I can't leave it. I won't! Half, Highpockets. I'll give you half. Let me haul it to Tsingtao. I'll come back for you. I promise. I'll give you half. Honest."

"Half, shit. Shut up! I could have had it all. You lying prick! There is no other aircraft is there?"

"Sure there is. There is! The admiral said no, but Muldoon said he was gonna steal it. He will." He sagged from the weight. "Maybe not today. They found an L-Five in Okinawa and sent a forty-six for it. I'll come back for you tomorrow."

"No other crate, no vest."

"Leave a hundred pounds of gold?" he asked hoarsely. "Are you crazy?"

"Stay with it then and buy your way out."

"I'll give you enough to buy your way out," he cried eagerly. "You speak the lingo. How about it?"

"On the road that gold is worth one lead bullet."

"You know the two of us will never get over that wall and roof in a Cub."

"I'll chance it."

"The hell you will," he shouted. "You're gonna kill me! That's why you took my gun. You're—"

"Don't tempt me."

In the school yard, I said, "Let's pull her back to takeoff position. You lift the tail and I'll push."

Tex staggered under the weight of the tail and vest. When we had the Cub in the corner, he gasped for breath. I checked my watch. We had an hour of daylight. "Five minutes and we go minus your boodle."

Tex searched the sky and suddenly screamed, "There it is!"

"Where?"

He pointed a trembling finger at a high-winged speck: an L-5, the U.S. Army's aerial jeep in World War II, spiralled down and flew over rocking her wing as if in horror at the size of the field. The approach was good and touchdown was smooth, but too fast, too fast. The tail rose higher each time he braked. The dogleg. Turn! Turn! Just before hitting the wall, the L-5 flipped up on her nose.

When I reached it, Dutch Maas was inspecting the smashed propellor. "Sorry, Dave, but I didn't think my wings would fit in your extension. What's wrong with the Cub?"

"Nothing."

"When you didn't take off, we figured it was kaput, so I went back to Tao to get this bucket."

"Where did CAT get it?"

Dutch laughed. "Muldoon swiped it from the United States Navy. Let's go radio for the spare prop."

twenty-five

WE sat with Colonel Shu in his quarters drinking Scotch. Dutch Maas, an ex-marine fighter pilot, eyed Tex and his grin exposed buckteeth. "You got some fever, Son."

Colonel Shu smiled wearily, as if grateful for the respite. Earlier, he had said, "They attack tonight."

Tex, sweating in his leather flight jacket, had been sullen ever since I had refused to let him take off alone in the Cub. "You'll have your new prop in the morning," he had screamed. "Why should I have to wait for you two? Dutch, let me go!"

"Why you?"

Colonel Shu glanced at his watch and with a sigh, rose. "It's time we went underground. Take the bottle. You may need it."

The colonel bothered me. Why had he stayed? I knew he had sent his family to Tsingtao, but why had he remained behind? He had a second family in Toronto. As an experienced soldier, he knew Weishien was doomed. General Li was deluded by the past, but not Colonel Shu. Why did he stay to fight a hopeless battle? On our way to operations, I asked him.

He covered a number of steps in silence. "If I desert Weishien to save myself, I am one with General Ching, who betrays for money."

"But Canada is as much your home as China. Why not run to fight another day? You know Weishien doesn't stand a chance in hell."

"War grows a bond between men to replace their fear of death. Without it, they cannot fight. I feel I must defend General Li as I would my father." He smiled with embarrassment. "Old virtues; the scourge or salvation of man. Who can say?"

Love in hate. Life in death. Yin and Yang.

In the command post, officers held their telephones and stared at the wall map—musicians poised for the baton. Two explosions tapped for their attention and the battle began.

Each roar showering dirt made us flinch and talk louder, until Dutch was shouting, "Whiting asked to borrow," we ducked, "their L-Five. The admiral *wow* said it would be an act of U.S. intervention. In the chow shack," he covered his drink and shook sand off his head, "let's finish bottle before the bastards hit it. Muldoon looked *shit* looked out and says—" The lights went out for a moment. "Muldoon says, says—anyway, he spots—Christ, they got our number. Anyway, Muldoon spots the L-Five sitting all alone out on the boondocks. He and Irwin—"

The lights came on and we picked ourselves off the floor. Dutch continued, "I think we're under ground zero. Anyway, pass the bottle, they jeep out, thanks, and lo and behold the crate is parked next to a bucket of paint with brush." He cocked his head at a pause. "They paint out the U.S. insignias and Irwin drives her back. And here I am. Christ, if I'd only known."

The blows overhead moved away, but the room still

trembled from explosions stomping back and forth. We watched lines being shifted on the map and realized trenches were being overrun. The CAT office radio, which we had transferred earlier, squawked and Muldoon's voice said, "Greetings to the mole people. Unstop thy ears and mouths and speak to us in the wild blue yonder."

"You fuck!" Dutch yelled into the mike. "Do something you fat bastard!"

"Mercy, such language. Would you like a little light on the subject?"

"Light?"

"It appears we have somehow acquired *beaucoup* large candles that drift gently to earth."

Flares!

"Hey, Colonel Shu. Muldoon's upstairs with a load of parachute flares. Where do you want them?"

"Manna. Light beyond the north wall of West Weishien. The trenches there are under heavy attack."

Dutch relayed the instructions.

After a moment, Muldoon said, "And now sport fans, we bring you a blow by blow account of Bantam Joey Irwin wrestling a genuine canister. If he gets it out the open loading door and stays with us up here, he gets two points. If not, he gets lost. There he goes, folks. Oh, it's tip and nuck. He's got it to the door. He's—he's—it's gone. They're gone? Joey? Joey Irwin? Hurray! He's still here, folks. Two points for Bantam Joe Irwin. And now for the flare. Yep, she's lit. Oh, pretty, pretty. Mercy, what a mess down there. Oh, dear, those poor fellows. For some reason, sport fans, some people downstairs don't like the light."

For almost two hours, Muldoon circled dropping flares over sorely pressed sectors and the lines on the map held. "All out of candles," he said, "but don't go away. Be back with more goodies."

Colonel Shu, who had been elated by the flares, now looked disturbed. "A patrol reports the enemy has gathered a large crowd of country folk to use as a shield. If they attack behind them, we must kill our own people."

"Can't you pick out the soldiers with searchlights?" I asked.

"We have none," he said.

"The landing light from the L-Five," Dutch cried. "Go get it, Tex. Some fresh air will do you good. You look a little green."

"Bullshit," he muttered. Tex was all wrapped up in his gold.

"I'll get it," I said.

"I'll go with you," Dutch said, and taking the half bottle of Scotch, waggled a finger at Tex. "No workee, no drinkee."

Colonel Shu ordered a truck and squad of soldiers to take us. "Bring the light to the East wall post. They will attack along the river between the two cities."

Collapsed buildings had turned the streets and hutungs into a maze of dead ends. By trial and error, we finally reached the school yard. Both aircraft were intact. We removed the retractable landing light from under the wing and pulled out the wiring. Taking the battery as well, we climbed back on the truck, which like a mouse, worked its way back and forth, in and out before we reached the East wall. On top, the battle was a steady roar. Pinpricks of light danced between the flash of shells and streams of tracers. Star-shells lit patches of churned earth and debris. Soldiers manned the crenelles, waiting for the light to spot their targets. When it did, Communist soldiers joined the bodies strewn like logs along the river banks. Ricochets sang off the battlements and the landing light went out to reappear a few crenelles away. The Reds lobbed mortar shells to snuff the light, but most fell between the walls, helping the defenders but not the civilians trapped below. At last the enemy retreated.

We left the light and in the truck driving back to the command post, Dutch swigged the bottle and passed it to me. "And to think, I used to like to strafe and rocket towns."

Around midnight, Muldoon came back on the air. "Hi ho, all you sport lovers down there, this is your very own Uncle Don with a new bag of tricks. This time, just for fun, we have something different. Now Uncle Don wants all you little bastards, sorry Mom, I mean boys to think real hard. What's long and round and has a pointed end. Naughty, naughty. If it was and weighed a hundred pounds like the ones we have, wowee."

"Bombs! That crazy Muldoon's making like the Eighth Air Force. Hey, Colonel, we got us a CAT bomber upstairs. Where do you want the eggs?"

Colonel Shu smiled. "Tell him to stand by. All sectors are quiet for the moment."

We told Muldoon and he said, "Roger. Now all you kiddies be quiet so Uncle Don can take five."

Irwin came on the radio. "Listen, you apeshit ground huggers, don't expect me to drop these fuckers into no barrel. I gotta roll 'em to the door, pull the arming pins, and get it the hell away before madman Muldoon gets playful. Know what he did on the first flare? To see it light, that sonofabitch racks her into a steep left turn, and if I hadn't grabbed the door frame, I'd gone out with it. Then he remembers me, whacks her into a steep turn to the right that slides me down the floor and almost through the fuse-lage. I tried to kill him, but the harder I punched that bone head of his, the more he laughed. He's crazy."

Colonel Shu called us to the wall map to show us some

low hills near Ch'ang Lo. "Their howitzers are in there, beyond the range of our guns. Tell your bomber to drop on those hills. If nothing else, it will surprise and worry them."

We woke Muldoon and told him. Over the target area, he reported after each bomb hit: "Got two pine trees. Large boulder. Empty ground. But somebody in those hills is trying to hose us down with tracers." Silence, then, "Bingo! That was either an overstuffed bomb, or we lit a stack of ammo. Lookit it go."

Finally, he said, "Got nothing left but Irwin. If you want, I'll give him my hogleg and he can make like a paratrooper. What's that? Hold on. Mercy, such language."

"You coming back?"

"Back? Do you realize it is two A.M. in the morning? What kind of hours you people keep?"

"The colonel says they'll be back."

"An army what fights at night, don't play right," Muldoon said. "I'll be back if the boys down at McSorley's have been guzzling like horned toads in a vat."

Dutch looked at us with surprise. "He *is* crazy."

Exhausted, I leaned back against a wall that felt alive. It trembled and thumped, as if it had a heart with an erratic beat. I closed my eyes and the crippled beggar stood before me, saying, "I frightened you in Shanghai."

"No you startled me. Your accent was so American."

The cripple laughed. "And I looked so Chinese."

"Are you?"

"For five thousand years."

"It is hard to judge the age of you Chinese."

"You were so proud of your new mesquite boots. You wondered if people recognized you as a pilot by your new boots."

"But that was later."

250

"Time does not matter in dreams. I was sitting outside on the curb when you signed the contract in the CAT office and made your mother beneficiary."

"Do you know what she answered after I had written her that I was ferrying an aircraft from Fort Worth to Karachi?"

"She said, 'I wish I were there and could fly back with you.' An adventurous lady."

"You have seen her?"

"Only in your dreams," he said.

"One time, you offered to tell me my fortune, but I hurried on. What was it? Tell me now."

"You will die."

"What?"

The cripple laughed. "Isn't that a lovely prediction? I can't miss."

"When?"

He tapped his crutch with glee. "At the end of your life."

"No, no, I mean the date."

"Perhaps in a moment."

"So soon. I mean, I'm so young."

"Are you sure? Perhaps you are old and dreaming you are young. Perhaps you are dead and only live in my dreams."

I thought carefully. "No, I am alive and trapped in Weishien."

He hopped with delight. "Prove it. You are awake and Weishien is but a dream. Look around."

I was in a red chamber.

"Isn't it beautiful," he cried. "A chamber of dreams. Back and forth. Where else can you go to the beginnings of time and forward to the eve of doom? Where else can you fly without your clumsy metal machines? Where else can you talk to me?"

"But I see you all the time. More and more I see you, and I know it's you. Even in a crowd, when I can't see you, I hear you laughing, and I know you are there. You are one of Chia Pao-yu's immortal guardians."

He held a finger to his lips. "Our secret."

"He is Chen Yi again. No, he is Colonel Chen. He is different."

"Every day you differ. Man is a vessel of death and birth. Only memory remains the same. Can you tell memory from a dream? What survives? Man? No, only his dreams. Flesh is transient; dreams are substance."

"Then I can fly from here without the Cub or L-Five."

"Where would you like to go? London? Paris? Toronto? Maggie's arms? How often have you slept with Maggie while she was half a world away?"

"It's not the same. Well, yes, sometimes. But tell me about Chen Yi. Chia Pao-yu. Dr. Wong. Colonel Chen. Ta-ko. Does he only visit the Red Dust?"

He laughed. "Every mortal only visits the Red Dust."

"I know, I know," I cried impatiently, "but is he immortal?"

"Life is immortal."

"But only the Gods are immortal."

"Only because they live in the minds of mortals."

"Stand still," I said. "You bounce from side to side."

"I am Yin and Yang," he said, and disappeared whistling.

I sat up. "What the hell is that?"

No one knew. We stared at the ceiling. From somewhere outside there came an eerie, unending whistle that penetrated the concrete and earth above us.

Dutch grabbed the microphone. "Muldoon?"

The speaker said, "Hello, Earthlings. This is Yamma Yamma Yamma from Outer Space. We come to invade your planet with a new drink that fills your ears, not your rears."

"What the hell is it?"

"Empty beer bottles. How do they sound?"

"Christ awful."

"If they work, we got it made. Think of a war fought with beer-bottle-bombs. Everybody will stay so sloshed making ammo, who's to fight? Pax Pilsiner."

Muldoon's rain of empty beer bottles stopped the attack.

twenty-six

AT 0600 we left for the school yard with a squad of soldiers. The streets were choked with rubble and bodies gray with dust and death. The soldiers cleared a path for the truck by tossing the corpses aside. One screamed as it landed. Startled, they looked at the dying man they had thrown on a bed of bricks, then at each other with nervous laughter.

Before we reached the field, a C-46 came circling low and paradropped the new propellor. Though it landed only a few streets away, it took us almost an hour to reach the chute hanging from a Gingko tree near a temple. The Chinese said it was a good omen, especially since the prop and tools were wrapped in red silk.

In the school yard, we bolted on the new propellor and pulled the L-5 back to alongside the Cub. Tex began to fret when I said we should wait for the wind to rise.

"Wait, hell. I'm going," he cried.

"Then go," Dutch snapped. He was still angry over losing the argument about Tex flying the Cub. He had insisted I take it since I was the heaviest. "Go ahead. Fly into the wall, you shithead."

Tex grumbled and tested the wind with a licked finger. He started to pace, but the weight of his vest drew sweat and he sat heavily on a box. A shell hit near the smokestack and Tex was on his feet. "Fuck this. I'm going."

I swung the prop and his engine started. Without checking his mags, he opened the throttle and released the brakes.

I ran across the width of the field in order to see down the alley. He was airborne before the entrance and made a flat turn into the dogleg. At first I thought he was holding her down to gain speed. Start climbing! My God, he was going to crash! The Cub skidded sideways and hit the wall wing first.

Running toward the black cloud at the end of the alley, I was afraid he was on fire. But it was dust, still floating when I reached the wreckage. Tex was slumped over the instrument panel, unconscious. I unsnapped the shoulders of his vest and slid it off from under his flight jacket. On the buckled floor it looked like a piece of torn canvas. When Dutch ran up, we pulled Tex out; alive, but he had a nasty gash on his forehead.

"You better take him to Tao fast," I said.

Dutch growled, "We should leave the stupid prick."

We carried him to the L-5 and strapped him in. The C-46 circled like a distressed hen. Without the battery, we were unable to call them on the L-5's radio. Dutch climbed into the front seat, saying, "I'll be back in a couple of hours."

By now there was a strong northeast wind. Dutch held her down on his run, popped full flap, and seemed to rise almost vertically out of the yard. I went back to the Cub for the vest of gold bars. But what was I going to do with it? I couldn't take it out. It would overload the L-5 just as it overloaded the Cub. Distribute the gold amongst the Chinese? No, the poor would fare best when the Communists came. I lifted the vest, hefted it, and dropping it back into the wreckage, laughed at my nonchalance and the uselessness of the gold.

Shells now fell with monotonous regularity. After a close one, I sat in what had been a cellar of the school, wondering about Maggie. I had forgotten to ask about her over the radio, or send a message to her.

By my watch, I estimated the L-5's position and visualized its progress. Fifty minutes from takeoff, I had it on the Tsingtao runway, but I was wrong. The C-46, with gear and flaps down, flew over and dropped a fire extinguisher. The note taped to it read:

"Pa lu nicked small bird. Ditched off Tao. Dutch broke arm. Tex groggy. Maggie sends love. Get on blower. Muldoon."

I felt very tired as I walked to the command post. Climbing over a pile of bricks, I stepped on something soft, but did not stop to look. The people I passed were dazed. A woman sat on the ruins of a house and wailed over a dead child in her arms. One man's teeth hung from his bleeding mouth. A little boy hugged a twisted arm and sobbing, called again and again for his mother. And the shells exploded like the slow beat of a huge drum. In the distance, guns chattered hysterically. Suddenly, I hated Chen Yi.

In the command post, Colonel Shu was asleep with his head on the desk. The officers who had been there all night were still on duty. I radioed Muldoon, who said, "Tough titty on the transportation. We got another L-Five being flown in from Okinawa, but doubt if they'll get her glued back together in time to get you out today. Unless we can steal one from our CAF buddies, you're in for the night again."

"What happened to Dutch?"

"A bullet must have cracked his oil line. He kept report-

ing a slow leak. Thought he had it made. He had the runway in sight, when the engine seized. A navy crash boat
picked them up."

"Tex is okay?"

"As okay as you can get after two glimpses of the Pearly
Gates in one day. They put a bandaid on his head and now
he's all gungho to come back for you."

I snorted. "Tell him if he's coming back for his goodies,
to forget it."

"Okay, but he's it. He's the only pint-sized driver we got.
If I were you, I'd take off as many pounds as you can."

"I have. Last night scared the shit out of me. If tonight's
a repeat, I'll be very light. Where's Maggie?"

Muldoon chuckled. "At Tao, raising hell with everyone
to get you out. Whiting is afraid to come out of his office.
She even cornered the admiral and demanded he send the
United States Marines to rescue you. If she could figure out
how to run a tank, I swear she'd steal one and come cross-
country for you. Where did you get that tiger?"

"Some day I'll tell you. Goddamn it, Muldoon, can't
somebody get the Chinese Air Force to knock out those
howitzers? Are they in those hills?"

"Roger. I took a look at 'em this morning. We tried.
Whiting even flew to Nanking to see General Chou. No
dice. Chou says they need 'em all north of Nanking. Did
you know that Hsuchow fell? The army retreated, but half
way to Nanking, the Pa lu caught 'em in a pincer movement. It looks like a wild west scene. The Nationalist army
is inside a circle of trucks and tanks maybe two miles in
diameter. The CAF B-twenty-fours are bombing the
villages outside the circle from ten thou. Their fighters
are pulling out of their strafing runs at five thousand
feet. Pulling out, mind you. And we're paradropping
ammo from three thousand feet. This should go down in

history as the Hogan's Goat War."

When Colonel Shu woke, he was surprised to see me back. In his quarters over a drink, I started to tell him what had happened, but he was not listening. "It's that bad?" I asked.

He nodded. "This morning, General Ching realigned the troops. All the Nationalists are now in East Weishien, our militia are here in West Weishien. Each has its own command post. There is little cooperation, no coordination."

"You mean Ching could pull out without you knowing about it?"

"It's what he did at Tsinan."

"If it's hopeless, why don't you surrender?"

"General Li will never surrender. He has spent his whole life fighting and resisting. He could never change that pattern near the end of his life."

"Habit."

"I suppose so."

"And because of it thousands will die."

"Habits are always the cause of wars."

He left and I fell asleep in my chair; dreamt I was sleeping in a cockpit, where I dreamt I was trapped in Weishien. In my dream, I knew Weishien was a dream and had nothing to fear. I woke with a start, recognized my surroundings, and closed my eyes to reenter the dream, but the drumming guns demanded I stay.

In the command post, I helped myself to a bowl of noodles from a cauldron on a charcoal brazier. The door opened and the officers leapt to attention. General Li entered, waving them to be seated. He wore his gray gown and gray fedora, a benign looking merchant, but his product was death. He was as uncompromising as Chen Yi. Each was an extreme, neither typical of most Chinese, who were too pragmatic to be fanatics. Greeting me with a nod,

General Li conferred with Colonel Shu, then seated himself in front of the map.

At the hour of sunset, the attack began and shook the ground. Wearily, I listened to the grim officers relay reports that moved symbols on the map. I knew them now and read defeat. The trenches north of West Weishien were overrun. The city wall became the defense line. Then a report startled everyone to their feet.

General Ching and his Nationalist troops were abandoning East Weishien and retreating toward Tsingtao. The Communists had breached the north wall and were pouring into West Weishien. Calmly, General Li ordered a retreat into East Weishien. Our only hope was to enter it before the Communists replaced the Nationalists.

I followed them up into a Dantean world. A fog had moved in, but the heat of fires had lifted it to form a vast incandescent bubble over the city. It was a glowing canopy of reds and orange, supported by columns of flames and a geodetic web of tracers. Through this fluorescent cavern, long lines of soldiers marched with weary indifference. Some were silhouettes, others fire-bright, chased by long shadows sweeping over walls as if in haste to race ahead.

The giant's door in the city wall was opened on a wall of flesh that screamed and clawed and fought to enter the city. Rifle butts hacked a path through the refugees to the bridge over the river between the two cities. The soldiers started across the stone span between the looming walls, but it led only to death. In the blinding burst of a flare, machine guns on the wall of East Weishien reaped the bridge. As the light flickered, I saw Colonel Shu stagger and join the stubble of corpses.

Someone behind me took my arm and shouted Chinese into my ear. "Stay with me. We must fight our way back into west city."

Turning to follow, I tripped over the body of the officer who had just spoken to me. I took a rifle and bandolier from a dead soldier and followed the crowd back through the mass of refugees, screaming as bullets flogged them.

Trailing behind four soldiers, I imitated them like a child; crouching when they crouched, firing when they did, though I never saw anything to shoot at. They crept so slowly along a wall, I tapped the shoulder of the man in front to ask what was happening. To my astonishment, he pitched forward. I thought I had pushed him, until a bullet smacked the wall and stung my face with chips.

I caught up with the others as they ducked into a doorway and a blast knocked me down. I lay staring at the negative of two ballet dancers poised over a ball of light. I tried to get up, then lay still. Who had killed whom, and if my friends had won, how would they know who I was moving around in the dark?

A flashlight came on and I watched the spot sweep along the floor to a bundle of greenish cotton with white tennis shoes, which moved. The shot startled me and a white sneaker kicked once.

The spot of light came toward me, touched my leg and ran up to blind me. I identified myself in Chinese. One voice was suspicious, the other said he had heard of me.

"Okay?"

"Okay," I said, and a hand helped me up. The weakness of my legs puzzled me.

A building began to burn across the street and from its light, I saw we were in a shop, half shuttered across the front. I had two companions, who lay behind a light machine gun covering the intersection, empty but for rubble and a few bodies. I could not see what else was in the shop.

I guessed they had taken the machine gun nest. The fighting sounded as if it were moving on and I wondered if they were holding the position, or just hiding. I found a half pack of cigarettes and offered them. They each took one, but refused the matches. I also stored the cigarette behind an ear and stretched out to stare at the street. I saw nothing, but they seemed intent on something. The shifting light became hypnotic and I could not tell when I was alert, or dozing.

I thought it was a shadow thrown by the flames, but as their machine gun burped, it became, for an instant, a man running, then shadow again. My companions grinned and one raised a thumb in victory. They must have known he was there and I marvelled at their patience to kill one enemy. Yet that enemy had been a direct threat. Most of the men I had killed in the war had been remote threats.

One of the soldiers put his unlighted cigarette in his mouth and made motions of lighting it. Sitting up behind the shutters, I took their cigarettes and crouching, lit a match in the cup of my hand. As I held it up, something caught my eye and I unshielded the burning match. Less than three feet away, a Chinese boy lay on his side, staring at me. He looked no more than fifteen, a young handsome boy. Thinking he had been there asleep all the while, I reached out a hand to say hello, then the light gleamed in the dark pool by his chest. He was dead. I shifted the match. He was the one who had kicked a white sneaker at death.

The match burned my fingers and I lit another, then the cigarettes. One soldier, a man of middle age, nodded at the boy. "He was wounded," he said in Chinese. "Pa lu. I had to shoot him. But I did not know he was a boy. I have a son his age."

I thought I saw something fly in—a bird—but it hit the floor and rolled when a great shock of light smashed me.

My sight returned slowly. At first I thought it was a distant tree trunk, a sapling, then I recognized it as a leg, a single leg rising by my side. A man stood beside me on one leg like a crane.

My crippled beggar.

"You are well," he said, smiling.

To my surprise, I sat up quickly.

"Come with me," he said.

As we left, I looked around for my previous companions, but it was too dark. The fire across the street had died. I followed my beggar more from the sound of his crutch, then by sight. When he stopped, we were in front of a red door in a compound wall.

"You asked me where is Chia Pao-yu," he said.

"In Shanghai. It is you. It has always been you."

He tapped three times on the door with his crutch. "He is in there."

The door opened, but I could see nothing inside. I looked at him. "Are you coming?"

"I wait here."

I entered cautiously, feeling my way along a flagstone path, but as I passed through a moongate, it became light, and I found myself in a beautiful courtyard. For a second, the apricot trees and lotus flowers swaying above their pots of water reminded me of Sui An Po Hutung, but the courtyard was too large, and the red columned buildings around it too grand and palatial. Yet it was strangely familiar; much like Ta-ko's home, the House of Chen in Chengtu.

He appeared across the court and came toward me with a quizzical smile, as if he was not expecting a visitor, yet pleased one had arrived. It was Ta-ko as he had looked when seventeen years old.

"Hello, Ta-ko."

His smile became amused. "I have no younger brother. Why do you call me Ta-ko."

"You look like my elder brother when he was young. Are you Pao-yu?"

He seemed delighted I knew him. "Yes. And you? Have we met?"

"I don't know," I said, suddenly aware of silence. There was no sound of gunfire. I looked slowly around. There was no damage; no torn roofs, broken walls, or shell holes. "Where are we?"

"In my father's house."

"The House of Chen?"

"No. Chia."

"Where is the House of Chia?"

He laughed, certain I was posing riddles. "If you do not know where, then how did you find your way?"

"I don't know," I whispered, shivering from a chill. "I came from the war."

"War?"

"There is a battle. Your city is under attack."

Knowing I joked, he clapped his hands with glee. "Go on."

"You do not know about the fighting?"

He grew serious, a trifle sad. "The only fight here is between father and son. We do not agree."

"It is the same outside."

"Then you have come from the outside?"

"Yes."

"Tell me about it," he cried eagerly. "I have never been beyond these walls."

"There is only sadness."

"There is sadness here."

"There is death."

"Death? Some here leave the Red Dust to become immortals again. One day I will also leave. Is that what you mean?"

263

I shook my head in disbelief. "No, no, out there is death, pain, blood, suffering. Your country is torn apart."

"It will be better tomorrow," he said blithely.

"You do not understand."

He smiled with ancient wisdom. "No, my friend. It is you who do not understand. It is only an adjustment to put Yin and Yang back into balance." With a slight bow, he turned to leave.

"Ta-ko, don't go."

"I must. Tai tai is having a peach festival. Next time you visit, perhaps I will have more time."

"Next time?" I asked hopefully.

"You will find the red door again one day."

The light faded and the scene changed into a dimly lit room. The room in Chungking? But there was a table between us and Chia Pao-yu now wore a uniform. Through a ringing, he asked in English if I could hear him. Confused, I clutched at my only hope. "Ta-ko?"

"Can you hear me?"

"Ta-ko?"

"I am not your elder brother."

"You were."

"In another life. Why are you here?"

"Chungking?"

"Weishien."

"Then this is no longer a dream. A moment ago I talked with you in the House of Chia. You were Chia Pao-yu and there was no war. Now you are Chen Yi again."

"Colonel Chen."

"The same."

"No. Ta-ko, Chen Yi, Chia Pao-yu, Wong Fo-ying are dead, just as Hsiung ti and Tzu tzu are dead. I am Colonel Chen, who has half a city to mop up and you are a foreigner, my prisoner and a nuisance."

"General Li?"

"The stubborn old fool fights on. General Ching sold us East Weishien and we hold half of West Weishien."

A wave of weakness blurred his dark image and hands pulled me back into the chair. A glass was pressed into my hand, which I drank greedily, gasping at the straight whisky. The tears cleared my eyes and I saw him as a grim-faced fanatic. But he was wrong. All the people we were could not be dead. "You can't wipe out the past," I said.

"As easily as wiping out a life."

"Then you must kill everyone, including yourself."

"We want nothing from the past."

"Only God can start again."

He laughed softly. "So you found God in a foxhole. War is a little different on the ground, isn't it? Not as neat and clean as in the air."

"I have never liked any part of war."

"Nor hated it. Have you ever hated anything, David?"

"You, for your senseless shelling of the city."

"Good. Perhaps now you can love."

"That's bullshit! You're full of hate. What have you ever loved?"

His nod awarded me the point. "Perhaps my hate. But one day, I hope to have the time for the luxuries of love and family."

"Why?" I demanded. "If you reject the past, why do you want continuity? Will your dynasty let sons tend their father's grave?"

He sighed wearily. "Enough of this chatter. I have a battle to finish. Besides, I have no son."

"You will," I said. "Louise."

"Don't tell me American women can feel conception," he said with scorn, "and predict the sex of a fetus not a month old?"

"A Chinese fortune teller, a cripple like one of the eight Taoist Immortals, said she would bear a Chinese son."

He smiled faintly. "No matter. But your reminding me of that pleasant night has saved your life. I was going to have you shot."

I was aghast. *"Shot!"*

"Why not?"

"I'm your brother."

"This is a war of brothers," he said bitterly.

"You owe me a favour."

"I said you were free."

"You'll give me a safe conduct pass?"

"No, we will return you to your little airfield. It will be amusing to see who reaches you first: my men, or your friends."

"Let me walk out."

"Have you lost faith in your magic carpets?"

I patted my jacket. "Then give me my gun back."

"To use against my people?"

"Against my rescuer, in case he's not my friend."

He looked surprised and said with sarcasm, "Preserve that way of life by all means. Pick one up. The streets are littered with weapons."

"Give me a pass."

"It would do you no good. As always, David, you must fly away. If you fail, you will share a common grave with many Chinese, and in time you will become Chinese as you have always wanted to be." He ordered a guard to take me to the school yard.

As I crossed the threshold, he said in Chinese, "Goodbye, Hsiung ti."

266

I stopped, but the soldier pushed me out and the door closed like the past behind me.

When we were a block away, I heard the drone and looked up. Bombers. A formation of B-24's. Now, when it was too late, the Chinese Air Force was coming to further destroy the city. The sticks of bombs started down the street we had just left and stomped buildings apart, including Ta-ko's headquarters. I tried to return, but the soldier barred my path with his bayonet.

twenty-seven

 TA-KO was dead!

It had been a direct hit, which no one could have survived. But suppose he was only wounded? "We must go back and help," I shouted at the soldier. "Your colonel is in there."

He shook his head. It was no concern of his. He had been ordered to return me to the school yard. "Pu hsing." He was nervous, so I did not argue. He did not know the city, nor did he trust me or my directions. Twice, we had to detour streets rattling with house to house fighting. We hugged walls, peered around corners, and ran across streets littered with debris and bodies. Two blocks from the school yard, I told him I could go it alone. He seemed relieved to be rid of me, but kept me covered as I ran for a corner. Around it, I searched for a gun.

I found him sitting wide-eyed in a doorway, leaning against the frame as if resting. He was a lieutenant in General Li's militia, no older than twenty. I spoke, half expecting him to answer, but he was dead, still clutching his Mauser pistol. When I took it from his hand, he fell over on the sidewalk. Half his back had been blown away by a grenade. The gun was empty, so I had to roll him over to get at his ammunition pouch. As I removed the two clips he had left, I felt he was staring at me with hatred.

The buildings along the south side of the school yard were burning and the yard was full of smoke. If not for the gold, Tex would never try to land. It had some value after all.

I dragged the vest from the Cub wreckage to leave a trail and salted it twice with bars to improve the scent. In the cellar of the razed school building, I found a doorless closet, and positioned the vest so his back would face my hiding place as he bent to pick it up. I then sat to wait for my rescuer.

Guns and grenades sounded a few blocks away. Who would reach me first? Tex, or the Pa lu? Neither would comfort me. Worse was my choice. There was no wind. The heat from the fires made a takeoff with two impossible. I either had to kill Tex or leave him to be killed.

I tried to hate him, but whatever I accused him of, another part of me excused. He would kill me if he had the chance. What are you planning? He's a bastard. So are you. "Shut up!" It was a hopeless argument. Ta-ko had been right. I lived in a twilight zone. I needed convictions: hate, anger, bias, bigotry, righteousness, faith, religion, God, patriotism, fear. I need justification to kill. All I had was Yin and Yang, who contradicted, cancelled, and balanced each other.

In the racket of gunfire, I did not hear the engine. The L-5 floated over the hazy field and vanished, so ghostlike, I wondered if I had seen it. Then in a few minutes, it dropped from the smoke over the wall, rolled past with a fluid ticketing and disappeared up the dogleg.

I peered out through an empty cellar window, waiting, watching as he came slowly, scanning with his automatic, pouncing to pick up a gold bar. He yelled, "Highpockets? Where are you? Hey, Highpockets, it's me, Tex."

I ran to the closet.

"Highpockets?"

He was close.

"High—hot spit."

He had seen the vest.

Bricks clattered as he climbed down into the cellar. His footsteps came closer. Suspicious, he would look around warily, but the gold would lure him.

"All there," he said.

Peeking out, I saw him bending over the vest. "Drop your gun."

He straightened up.

"Don't move and drop it," I ordered.

He did, screaming, "What the fuck you doing, Highpockets? Are you crazy? I came to rescue you!"

"And I appreciate it. Now walk straight ahead. Slowly."

"What's got into you?" he yelled. "I risk my ass to save you and you pull a gun."

With his .38 automatic in my pocket, I said, "Okay, you can turn around."

His mouth was slack, trembling. "Why?"

"You know why. You came for the vest, not me. We're in the same box as before. You knew the two of us and the vest could never fly out of here. If you had the drop, you'd have killed me."

"No," he said hoarsely. "I came to save you. I swear. Honest. So help me, God."

"Then we'll do it that way."

He was horrified. "You mean leave the gold?"

"And you, if necessary."

"What?"

270

"With these fires and no wind, only one of us can make it."

He licked his lips. "You wouldn't murder me."

"If I had to."

"You won't get away with it."

"Why not? I'll tell them at Tao what you planned to tell them. The commies got him. There's no Grave's Registration squad in this war."

"Highpockets, I swear I'd written off the boodle. I came to save you. I knew the three of us couldn't make it. I came—"

"Save your breath."

"For what?"

"Prayers."

The cliché frightened him. "What?"

"Pray the fires will die and the wind comes up."

And his shrewd eyes reflected his insight: I was incapable of shooting him in cold blood. It returned his colour and cockiness. "Look, Highpockets, old buddy, the L-Five's got twice the horses of that crappy Cub. We can go now. No sweat. Now, I'll tell you what we'll do." Like the first time I had met him in the RCAF barracks, Tex tried to take over. I was forced to admire his arrogance. "Let's go," he cried.

"And hit the wall like you did?"

"Let's at least haul her back into takeoff position. Let's have her ready in case they come over the wall."

I was annoyed at myself for having forgotten. The L-5, useless where she was, would have been difficult to pull back alone. "You first," I said.

"Knock it off, Highpockets."

"You first."

"You still don't believe me?"

"Negative."

With a shrug, he walked ahead, but soon slowed up. "I saw Maggie in Tao. She's all upset about you and very grateful I came back for you. She's a nice woman, and I'm glad you got her. You know, you're the only friend I really have. I—"

"Up front, Tex."

"Come on, Buddy, relax."

I stopped. "Keep moving."

With Tex lifting the tail and steering, while I pushed on a wing strut, we moved her backwards to the corner of the field.

"Okay, let's go," Tex said.

"Not yet." A light breeze had sprung up, but more buildings were now on fire. "We'd never make it."

"We can't wait!"

A mortar round burst on the bleachers and sent a plank flying end over end.

"They're coming! For Christ's sake, get in."

"You pull the prop," I said.

"She's got a starter. Let's go, Goddammit."

"You fly the front seat." I had to keep him covered.

He started the engine, reved it up, started to check the mags, and changed his mind. Holding the brakes, he pushed the throttle to the panel, then hesitated, as if he had forgotten something.

"Go," I shouted.

He released the brakes and we leapt on our way. Half way across the field, he pulled the throttle back and I slammed it forward, screaming, "What the hell are you doing?" Our loss of speed horrified me.

He yanked her off the ground and we mushed into the dogleg. Certain we would hit the wall, I cursed him. Somehow the top of the wall slid under the nose, but I braced myself for the wheels to catch and flip us over. She cleared.

The slope of the factory roof directly ahead made me throw up an arm to protect my face. The wheels hit and we ballooned over the peak.

The chimney!

Tex slammed the controls over to lift the wingtip. A jolt slewed us around. A brick floated slowly past. The wall of the city came tilting up and, for a moment, I was lost in space. Strange spurts on the water puzzled me until I saw people floating, others lying on the sand. We're over a beach, I thought, then realized we were flying over the river between the two city walls. The spurts were from bullets and the sunbathers were the dead. The alley disappeared and trenches came with soldiers so close I could see surprise on their upturned faces. One after the other, they raised their rifles and my anus closed. Like a dreamer unable to escape, we skimmed the battlefield.

Slowly, we climbed clear to a thousand feet. Even though we had lost almost a foot off our right wingtip, I regained my normal breath. "What the hell did you close the throttle for?" I yelled.

"One gas tank leaks," he said over his shoulder. "We only got the one eighteen gallon tank and I was supposed to refuel from the two jerry cans behind you. No sweat. We'll land on one of those sandbars in the river to refuel."

"Pick a field. The sand may be too soft."

"Safer on the river. Too many Pa lu around."

As the gauge neared empty, Tex picked out a sandbar and made a perfect landing. Though our roll was short, I stopped worrying about the firmness of the sand. We hopped out and pulled her back for takeoff. With gun in hand, I told him to fill the tank.

While he unloaded the two jerry cans, I watched four farmers on the south shore of the river. Tex stood in the crotch of the strut and began pouring gasoline into the wing tank. The farmers ran to the shore opposite us. Farmers? "Soldiers."

"What?" Looking up, Tex missed the intake and poured gas over the wing.

"They're setting up a machine gun," I cried.

"Jesus."

"Watch the gas," I shouted.

"Shit." The can was empty and he threw it away. I handed him the other one, but the cap was stuck. "Oh, Jesus."

They had the gun on the tripod.

"I can't get this fucking cap off."

I put the Mauser in my pocket and took the can.

They were fumbling with the breech cover.

Straining, I unscrewed the cap and handed him back the can. "Watch what you're doing. They can't get the belt started."

He concentrated on filling the tank. "What are they doing?"

"Never mind. Keep pouring."

"Done." He dropped the can, then swore. "Oh, Christ. The tank cap threads are stripped. Can't—"

"Hell with it."

We climbed into the L-5 and Tex started the engine. He shoved the throttle forward and the aircraft shook, but would not move.

"She's bogged in the sand," Tex yelled. "Get out and push."

I opened the horizontally split door and snapped the top half to its catch under the wing. Jumping out, I pushed on the wing strut and the back of Tex's seat. She waddled free, but before I could pull myself in, I had to run to keep up. "Throttle back," I screamed, stumbling. She dragged me until I managed to get my feet up under me and running again.

"Slow down!"

I thought just an extra sprint would do it, but her acceleration absorbed each one.

"Tex!"

With my last effort, I got my right foot into the strut crotch, then hooked my left heel over the hinge panel of the lower door. As I pulled myself up and forced my shoulders into the cockpit, something struck me in the face.

I fell off and tumbled through a shower of sand. I lifted my face as he broke ground and banked steeply to get away from the machine gun. Lying prone, I held the Mauser with both hands and stitched the top of the cockpit. I knew from her slew that I had hit him. She half rolled, and on her back, dove into the water.

Crabbing around on my stomach, I fired Tex's automatic at the soldiers. At the spurts of sand around them, they picked up their machine gun and disappeared over a bluff.

The L-5 sank, bubbled once, and before I swam to the north shore, I threw his gun after it. With the gold bar he had hit me with, I bought passage on a junk to Tsingtao.

Sitting alone in the bow, I suffered remorse. I had killed Tex in anger. It had served no purpose. Shooting him down had not rescued me. It freed Maggie, but he had agreed to a divorce.

And suddenly, I began to cry, gasping for breath in a torrent of tears. I wept for Tex; for the Chinese boy whose white sneaker had kicked at death instead of a ball; for Pei, beheaded for our childish thefts; for Colonel Shu, an honourable man; for Ta-ko, who now wore his final mask; for China, no longer my home. As I wept with the ecstasy of intense sorrow, I found myself whispering, "Maggie. Oh, Maggie, my love."

In Tsingtao, I disembarked and hurried up the street from the wharves, looking for a ricksha. Rounding a corner, I almost ran into a crippled beggar, his withered leg supported by a stick crutch. He opened his hand almost in my face and hefted the expected coins.

"I have nothing," I said, turning out my pockets, then remembered the cash hanging around my neck on a string; the lucky coin, because it had been dunked three times in dead Uncle Chen's open mouth. I took it off and dropped it into his cracked palm. He examined the talisman slowly, then hung it around his own neck, as if it had always been his.

"You have much," he said, in Mandarin far too perfect for a beggar. "Your brother waits beyond the red door."

Overwhelmed by a sense of peace, I watched him hobble away.